WORLDS *of* WONDER

WORLDS *of* WONDER

◎◎◎

sixteen tales of science fiction
edited by Harry Harrison

◎◎◎

Doubleday & Company, Inc., Garden City, New York

ACKNOWLEDGMENTS

"Sunjammer," by Arthur C. Clarke, copyright © 1964 by Boy Scouts of America. Reprinted by permission of the author and his agents, Scott Meredith Literary Agency, Inc.

"We didn't Do Anything Wrong, Hardly," by Roger Kuykendall, copyright © 1959 by the Condé Nast Publications, Inc. Reprinted by permission of the author.

"Who Can Replace a Man?" by Brian W. Aldiss, copyright © 1959 by Brian W. Aldiss. Reprinted by permission of the author and his agents, Scott Meredith Literary Agency, Inc.

"Tricky Tonnage," by Malcolm Jameson, copyright © 1944 by Street & Smith Publications, Inc. Reprinted by permission of the Condé Nast Publications, Inc.

"Appointment on Prila," by Bob Shaw, copyright © 1968 by the Condé Nast Publications, Inc. Reprinted by permission of the author.

"Hi Diddle Diddle," by Robert Silverberg, copyright © 1959 by Street & Smith, Inc. Reprinted by permission of the author and his agents, Scott Meredith Literary Agency, Inc.

"If," by Harry Harrison, copyright © 1969 as "Praiseworthy Saur" by Galaxy Publishing Corp. Reprinted by permission of the author and his agent, Robert P. Mills, Ltd.

"A Pail of Air," by Fritz Leiber, copyright © 1951 by Galaxy Publishing Corp. Reprinted by permission of the author and his agent, Robert P. Mills, Ltd.

INTRODUCTION

Science fiction is great stuff when you are young, and has an impact not unlike the one received when putting the finger into a live electric light socket. Though for the most part I have only the vaguest of childhood memories, I do have one clear and sharp memory—that of reading my first science fiction story. The ancient cathedral-roofed radio, the sun in the window, the very texture of the carpet on which I lay, are all as clear as yesterday. My father gave me a copy of the old large-sized *Amazing Stories*, which appeared even larger in my seven-year-old hands, until it became a very bed-sheet of a magazine. I plunged into those rocket ship filled, time machine, ancient alien, strange invention stuffed pages and emerged with my whole life changed. For the better, I sincerely hope, but changed it was indeed.

Today I know respected men of science, chemists, engineers, and mathematicians, who say that they entered their chosen professions because of reading science fiction when they were young. Milton A. Rothman, a physicist and author of *Heavyplanet*, is one of them. But I will make no educatory claims for the medium, as much as I enjoy it. (For my own part I became no scientist because of this early inspiration by SF, but turned instead to the writing of more of these same stories.) However I will claim that there is no other kind of fiction that is anywhere near as exciting.

Science fiction is the stuff that dreams are made of— and these are the unusual kind of dreams that come true. The once imaginary rockets are now flying to Mars. The excitement of science and the impact of science on our lives is to be found only in SF. The constant advance of the scientific frontiers adds to, instead of detracting from, the impact of these stories. The fact that a submarine named after Captain Nemo's *Nautilus* has really sailed across the North Pole under the ice cap makes the original story even more exciting—because there now exists the possibility that the boy reading the story may some day make that voyage himself.

For very good reasons, most of my closest friends are science fiction writers. There was a time, when I lived with my family in Denmark, when my children, Todd and Moira, thought that the world outside was populated only by science fiction people. During vacations we would pack up our camper and take off down the open road. We would go to England or Italy or Germany or Austria—even Yugoslavia—and at a journey's end we would visit a friend. The friend would always be a SF writer, editor or fan. The house would be full of science fiction books, in all languages, and the talk would be about—but of course you know what was talked about.

It didn't matter where or how we traveled, science fiction was always waiting at voyage end. One summer we took a little cabin cruiser up the river Thames from London. It put-putted along on two incredibly smoky diesel cylinders, and we tied up at the bank at night— to awake in the morning and find rows of calves looking in the windows from the pasture beside us. The locks were the most fun, power operated in the lower reaches, but worked by back power further upstream. We all helped push on the 20-foot-long beams that opened the gates to let the water in and out. Finally, after a last turn in the river, we could see the century old towers of Oxford University ahead of us (named after a ford for oxen in the Thames—what else!), and two cars waiting on the riverbank. Journey's end again—and sitting by the picnic baskets was Kyril Bonfiglioli, the editor of the British magazine, *Science Fantasy,* and Brian Aldiss. Brian likes robots, and his story *Who Can Replace a Man?* tells everything about robots that a person could possibly want to know.

Not that Europe is the only place for science fiction writers, quite the opposite. At least 95 percent of the authors are right here in the United States. Jack Vance lives in the hills outside of San Francisco, in a place of guaranteed privacy—because the only way in is up a twisting, unpaved, vertical death-trap of a road. I doubt if anyone can drive up it but Jack. He approaches at top speed with the car skidding around turns and clawing at the slippery surface to arrive and shudder to a stop, brakes locked, with the radiator almost touching the front door. Strong men grow pale and women faint during this ride. But the trip is worth it because he has the most incredible house (that he built himself) and in the front yard a sailing ship (which he is building himself) in which he plans to cross the Pacific. And he will, too. He has more than a little of the Magnus Ridolph in him, the character in his story *The Howling Bounders,* as you will see.

Fritz Leiber is also a California resident. Of all the authors I know, Fritz is the one who most looks the part. Tall, over six feet, with a great mane of hair and a magnificent nose, it is easy to see that he was once a Shakespearian actor. He is also a fencing expert and we are all waiting for him to challenge some editor to a duel. He must have written *A Pail of Air* before he came to California, because it is the *coldest* story you will ever read.

Mack Reynolds is also an American, though he is a world traveler who has been to every country that he could get into, and who now makes his home deep in Mexico. During his vigorous morning walks—three hours at top speed starting at the crack of dawn!—he has discovered the ruins of an early Mexican culture, perhaps Toltec. He writes the way he walks, as you will see when you read *Prone*.

All of the stories here have another story behind them. This book has been fun to put together, and that is perhaps the best comment I can make about SF. It is fun. Things happen, exciting things, and they happen in the most interesting of ways. If you would like to haul on the lines of a sailing ship in space, have a robot story teller for a companion, pilot a spaceship or build an artificial cow to supply your milk—read on. You'll find them all here.

HARRY HARRISON

CONTENTS

WORLDS *of* WONDER

SUNJAMMER

◎◎◎

Arthur C. Clarke

The enormous disc of sail strained at its rigging, already
filled with the wind that blew between the worlds. In
three minutes the race would begin, yet now John Merton felt more relaxed, more at peace, than at any time
for the past year. Whatever happened when the Commodore gave the starting signal, whether *Diana* carried
him to victory or defeat, he had achieved his ambition.
After a lifetime spent in designing ships for others, now
he would sail his own.

"T minus two minutes," said the cabin radio. "Please
confirm your readiness."

One by one, the other skippers answered. Merton recognized all the voices—some tense, some calm—for they
were the voices of his friends and rivals. On the four
inhabited worlds, there were scarcely twenty men who
could sail a sun-yacht; and they were all here, on the
starting-line or aboard the escort vessels, orbiting twenty-
two thousand miles above the equator.

"Number One, *Gossamer*—ready to go."

"Number Two, *Santa Maria*—all O.K."

"Number three, *Sunbeam*—O.K."

"Number Four, *Woomera*—all systems go."

Merton smiled at that last echo from the early, primitive days of astronautics. But it had become part of the tradition of space; and there were times when a man needed to evoke the shades of those who had gone before him to the stars.

"Number Five. *Lebedev*—we're ready."

"Number Six, *Arachne*—O.K."

Now it was his turn, at the end of the line; strange to think that the words he was speaking in this tiny cabin were being heard by at least five billion people.

"Number Seven, *Diana*—ready to start."

"One through Seven acknowledged." The voice from the judge's launch was impersonal. "Now T minus one minute."

Merton scarcely heard it; for the last time, he was checking the tension in the rigging. The needles of all the dynamometers were steady; the immense sail was taut, its mirror surface sparkling and glittering gloriously in the sun.

To Merton, floating weightless at the periscope, it seemed to fill the sky. As well it might—for out there were fifty million square feet of sail, linked to his capsule by almost a hundred miles of rigging. All the canvas of all the tea-clippers that had once raced like clouds across the China seas, sewn into one gigantic sheet, could not match the single sail that *Diana* had spread beneath the sun. Yet it was little more substantial than a soap-bubble; that two square miles of aluminized plastic was only a few millionths of an inch thick.

"T minus ten seconds. All recording cameras *on*."

Something so huge, yet so frail, was hard for the mind to grasp. And it was harder still to realize that this fragile mirror could tow them free of Earth, merely by the power of the sunlight it would trap.

". . . Five, Four, Three, Two, One, *cut!*"

Seven knife-blades sliced through the seven thin lines tethering the yachts to the motherships that had assembled and serviced them.

Until this moment, all had been circling Earth together in a rigidly held formation, but now the yachts would begin to disperse, like dandelion seeds drifting before the breeze. And the winner would be the one that first drifted past the Moon.

Aboard *Diana,* nothing seemed to be happening. But Merton knew better; though his body would feel no thrust, the instrument board told him he was now accelerating at almost one thousandth of a gravity. For a rocket, that figure would have been ludicrous—but this was the first time any solar yacht had attained it. *Diana's* design was sound; the vast sail was living up to his calculations. At this rate, two circuits of the Earth would build up his speed to escape velocity—then he could head out for the Moon, with the full force of the Sun behind him.

The full force of the Sun. He smiled wryly, remembering all his attempts to explain solar sailing to those lecture audiences back on Earth. That had been the only way he could raise money, in those early days. He might be Chief Designer of Cosmodyne Corporation, with a whole string of successful spaceships to his credit, but his firm had not been exactly enthusiastic about his hobby.

"Hold your hands out to the Sun," he'd said. "What do you feel? Heat, of course. But there's pressure as well—though you've never noticed it, because it's so tiny. Over the area of your hands, it only comes to about a millionth of an ounce.

"But out in space, even a pressure as small as that can be important—for it's acting all the time, hour after hour, day after day. Unlike rocket fuel, it's free and unlimited. If we want to, we can use it; we can build sails to catch the radiation blowing from the Sun."

At that point, he would pull out a few square yards of sail material and toss it toward the audience. The silvery film would coil and twist like smoke, then drift slowly to the ceiling in the hot-air currents.

"You can see how light it is," he'd continue. "A square mile weighs only a ton, and can collect five pounds of radiation pressure. So it will start moving—and we can let it tow us along, if we attach rigging to it.

"Of course, its acceleration will be tiny—about a thousandth of a g. That doesn't seem much, but let's see what it means.

"It means that in the first second, we'll move about a fifth of an inch. I suppose a healthy snail could do better than that. But after a minute, we've covered sixty feet, and will be doing just over a mile an hour, That's not bad, for something driven by pure sunlight! After an hour, we're forty miles from our starting point, and will be moving at eighty miles an hour. Please remember that in space there's no friction, so once you start anything moving, it will keep going forever. You'll be surprised when I tell you what our thousandth-of-a-g sailing boat will be doing at the end of a day's run. *Almost two thousand miles an hour!* It starts from orbit—as it has to, of course—it can reach escape velocity in a couple of days. And all without burning a single drop of fuel!"

Well, he'd convinced them, and in the end he'd even convinced Cosmodyne. Over the last twenty years, a new sport had come into being. It had been called the sport of billionaires, and that was true—but it was beginning to pay for itself in terms of publicity and television coverage. The prestige of four continents and two worlds was riding on this race, and it had the biggest audience in history.

Diana had made a good start; time to take a look at the opposition. Moving very gently. Though there were shock absorbers between the control capsule and the delicate rigging, he was determined to run no risks. Merton stationed himself at the periscope.

There they were, looking like strange silver flowers planted in the dark fields of space. The nearest, South America's *Santa Maria*, was only fifty miles away; it bore a resemblance to a boy's kite—but a kite more than a mile on its side. Farther away, the University of Astrograd's *Lebedev* looked like a Maltese cross; the sails that formed the four arms could apparently be tilted for steering purposes. In contrast, the Federation of Australasia's *Woomera* was a simple parachute, four miles in circumference. General Spacecraft's *Arachne*, as its name suggested, looked like a spider-web—and had been built on the same principles, by robot shuttles spiraling out from a central point. Eurospace Corporation's *Gossamer* was an identical design, on a slightly smaller scale. And the Republic of Mars' *Sunbeam* was a flat ring, with a half-mile-wide hole in the center, spinning slowly so that centrifugal force gave it stiffness. That was an old idea, but no one had ever made it work. Merton was fairly sure that the colonials would be in trouble when they started to turn.

That would not be for another six hours, when the yachts had moved along the first quarter of their slow and stately twenty-four-hour orbit. Here at the beginning of the race, they were all heading directly away from the Sun—running, as it were, before the solar wind. One had to make the most of this lap, before the boats swung round to the other side of Earth and then started to head back into the Sun.

Time for the first check, Merton told himself, while

he had no navigational worries. With the periscope, he made a careful examination of the sail, concentrating on the points where the rigging was attached to it. The shroud-lines—narrow bands of unsilvered plastic film—would have been completely invisible had they not been coated with fluorescent paint. Now they were taut lines of colored light, dwindling away for hundreds of yards toward that gigantic sail. Each had its own electric windlass, not much bigger than a game-fisherman's reel. The little windlasses were continually turning, playing lines in or out, as the autopilot kept the sail trimmed at the correct angle to the Sun.

The play of sunlight on the great flexible mirror was beautiful to watch. It was undulating in slow, stately oscillations, sending multiple images of the Sun marching across the heavens, until they faded away at the edges of the sail. Such leisurely vibrations were to be expected in this vast and flimsy structure; they were usually quite harmless, but Merton watched them carefully. Sometimes they could build up to the catastrophic undulations known as the wriggles, which could tear a sail to pieces.

When he was satisfied that everything was shipshape, he swept the periscope around the sky, rechecking the positions of his rivals. It was as he had hoped; the weeding-out process had begun, as the less efficient boats fell astern. But the real test would come when they passed into the shadow of the Earth; then maneuverability would count as much as speed.

It seemed a strange thing to do, now that the race had just started, but it might be a good idea to get some sleep. The two-man crews on the other boats could take it in turns, but Merton had no one to relieve him. He must rely on his physical resources—like that other solitary seaman Joshua Slocum, in his tiny *Spray*. The American skipper had sailed *Spray* single-handed around the world; he could never have dreamt that, two centuries later, a man would be sailing single-handed from Earth to Moon—inspired, at least partly, by his example.

Merton snapped the elastic bands of the cabin seat around his waist and legs, then placed the electrodes of the sleep-inducer on his forehead. He set the timer for three hours, and relaxed.

Very gently, hypnotically, the electronic pulses throbbed in the frontal lobes of his brain. Colored spirals of light expanded beneath his closed eyelids, widening outward to infinity. Then—nothing. . . .

The brazen clamor of the alarm dragged him back from his dreamless sleep. He was instantly awake, his eyes scanning the instrument panel. Only two hours had passed—but above the accelerometer, a red light was flashing. Thrust was falling; *Diana* was losing power.

Merton's first thought was that something had happened to the sail; perhaps the antispin devices had failed, and the rigging had become twisted. Swiftly, he checked the meters that showed the tension in the shroud-lines. Strange, on one side of the sail they were reading normally—but on the other, the pull was dropping slowly even as he watched.

In sudden understanding, Merton grabbed the periscope, switched to wide-angle vision, and started to scan the edge of the sail. Yes—there was the trouble, and it could have only one cause.

A huge, sharp-edged shadow had begun to slide across the gleaming silver of the sail. Darkness was falling upon *Diana*, as if a cloud had passed between her and the Sun. And in the dark, robbed of the rays that drove her, she would lose all thrust and drift helplessly through space.

But, of course, there were no clouds here, more than

twenty thousand miles above Earth. If there was a
shadow, it must be made by man.

Merton grinned as he swung the periscope toward the
Sun, switching in the filters that would allow him to
look full into its blazing face without being blinded.

"Maneuver 4a," he muttered to himself. "We'll see
who can play best at *that* game."

It looked as if a giant planet was crossing the face of
the Sun. A great black disc had bitten deep into its
edge. Twenty miles astern, *Gossamer* was trying to ar-
range an artificial eclipse—specially for *Diana's* benefit.

The maneuver was a perfectly legitimate one; back in
the days of ocean racing, skippers had often tried to
rob each other of the wind. With any luck, you could
leave your rival becalmed, with his sails collapsing around
him—and be well ahead before he could undo the damage.

Merton had no intention of being caught so easily.
There was plenty of time to take evasive action; things
happened very slowly, when you were running a solar
sailingboat. It would be at least twenty minutes before
Gossamer could slide completely across the face of the
Sun, and leave him in darkness.

Diana's tiny computer—the size of a matchbox, but
the equivalent of a thousand human mathematicians—
considered the problem for a full second and then flashed
the answer. He'd have to open control panels three and
four, until the sail had developed an extra twenty degrees
of tilt; then the radiation pressure would blow him out
of *Gossamer's* dangerous shadow, back into the full blast
of the Sun. It was a pity to interfere with the auto-pilot,
which had been carefully programed to give the fastest
possible run—but that, after all, was why he was here.
This was what made solar yachting a sport, rather than
a battle between computers.

Out went control lines one to six, slowly undulating

like sleepy snakes as they momentarily lost their tension. Two miles away, the triangular panels began to open lazily, spilling sunlight through the sail. Yet, for a long time, nothing seemed to happen. It was hard to grow accustomed to this slow motion world, where it took minutes for the effects of any action to become visible to the eye. Then Merton saw that the sail was indeed tipping toward the Sun—and that *Gossamer's* shadow was sliding harmlessly away, its cone of darkness lost in the deeper night of space.

Long before the shadow had vanished, and the disc of the Sun had cleared again, he reversed the tilt and brought *Diana* back on course. Her new momentum would carry her clear of the danger; no need to overdo it, and upset his calculations by sidestepping too far. That was another rule that was hard to learn. The very moment you had started something happening in space, it was already time to think about stopping it.

He reset the alarm, ready for the next natural or manmade emergency; perhaps *Gossamer,* or one of the other contestants, would try the same trick again. Meanwhile, it was time to eat, though he did not feel particularly hungry. One used little physical energy in space, and it was easy to forget about food. Easy—and dangerous; for when an emergency arose, you might not have the reserves needed to deal with it.

He broke open the first of the meal packets, and inspected it without enthusiasm. The name on the label—SPACETASTIES—was enough to put him off. And he had grave doubts about the promise printed underneath. Guaranteed Crumbless. It had been said that crumbs were a greater danger to space vehicles than meteorites. They could drift into the most unlikely places, causing short circuits, blocking vital jets and getting into instruments that were supposed to be hermetically sealed.

Still, the liverwurst went down pleasantly enough; so

did the chocolate and the pineapple puree. The plastic
coffee-bulb was warming on the electric heater when
the outside world broke in on his solitude. The radio
operator on the Commodore's launch routed a call to
him.

"Dr. Merton? If you can spare the time, Jeremy Blair
would like a few words with you." Blair was one of the
more responsible news commentators, and Merton had
been on his program many times. He could refuse to
be interviewed, of course, but he liked Blair, and at
the moment he could certainly not claim to be too busy.
"I'll take it," he answered.

"Hello, Dr. Merton," said the commentator immediately. "Glad you can spare a few minutes. And congratulations—you seem to be ahead of the field."

"Too early in the game to be sure of that," Merton
answered cautiously.

"Tell me, Doctor—why did you decide to sail *Diana*
yourself? Just because it's never been done before?"

"Well, isn't that a very good reason? But it wasn't
only one, of course." He paused, choosing his words
carefully. "You know how critically the performance of
a sun-yacht depends on its mass. A second man, with
all his supplies, would mean another five hundred pounds.
That could easily be the difference between winning and
losing."

"And you're quite certain that you can handle *Diana*
alone?"

"Reasonably sure, thanks to the automatic controls I've
designed. My main job is to supervise and make deci-
sions."

"But—two square miles of sail! It just doesn't seem possible for one man to cope with all that!"

Merton laughed.

"Why not? Those two square miles produce a maximum pull of just ten pounds. I can exert more force with my little finger."

"Well, thank you, Doctor. And good luck."

As the commentator signed off, Merton felt a little ashamed of himself. For his answer had been only part of the truth; and he was sure that Blair was shrewd enough to know it.

There was just one reason why he was here, alone in space. For almost forty years he had worked with teams of hundreds or even thousands of men, helping to design the most complex vehicles that the world had ever seen. For the last twenty years he had led one of those teams, and watched his creations go soaring to the stars. (But there were failures that he could never forget, even though the fault had not been his.) He was famous, with a successful career behind him. Yet he had never done anything by himself; always he had been one of an army.

This was his very last chance of individual achievement, and he would share it with no one. There would be no more solar yachting for at least five years, as the period of the quiet Sun ended and the cycle of bad weather began, with radiation storms bursting through the Solar System. When it was safe again for these frail, unshielded craft to venture aloft, he would be too old. If, indeed, he was not too old already. . . .

He dropped the empty food containers into the waste disposal, and turned once more to the periscope. At first, he could find only five of the other yachts; there was no sign of *Woomera*. It took him several minutes to locate her—a dim, star-eclipsing phantom, neatly caught in the shadow of *Lebedev*. He could imagine the frantic efforts the Australasians were making to extricate themselves, and wondered how they had fallen into the trap. It suggested that *Lebedev* was unusually maneuverable; she would bear watching, though she was too far away to menace *Diana* at the moment.

Now the Earth had almost vanished. It had waned to a narrow, brilliant bow of light that was moving steadily toward the Sun. Dimly outlined within that burning bow was the night side of the planet, with the phosphorescent gleams of great cities showing here and there through gaps in the clouds. The disc of darkness had already blanked out a huge section of the Milky Way; in a few minutes, it would start to encroach upon the Sun.

The light was fading. A purple, twilight hue—the glow of many sunsets, thousands of miles below—was falling across the sail, as *Diana* slipped silently into the shadow of Earth. The Sun plummeted below that invisible horizon. Within minutes, it was night.

Merton looked back along the orbit he had traced now a quarter of the way around the world. One by one he saw the brilliant stars of the other yachts wink out, as they joined him in the brief night. It would be an hour before the Sun emerged from that enormous black shield, and through all that time they would be completely helpless, coasting without power.

He switched on the external spotlight, and started to search the now darkened sail with its beam. Already, the thousands of acres of film were beginning to wrinkle and become flaccid; the shroud-lines were slackening, and must be wound in lest they become entangled. But all this was expected; everything was going as planned.

Forty miles astern, *Arachne* and *Santa Maria* were not so lucky. Merton learned of their troubles when the radio burst into life on the emergency circuit.

"Number Two, Number Six—this is Control. You are on a collision course. Your orbits will intersect in sixty-five minutes! Do you require assistance?"

There was a long pause while the two skippers digested this bad news. Merton wondered who was to blame;

perhaps one yacht had been trying to shadow the other, and had not completed the maneuver before they were both caught in darkness. Now there was nothing that either could do; they were slowly but inexorably converging together, unable to change course by a fraction of a degree.

Yet, sixty-five minutes! That would just bring them out into sunlight again, as they emerged from the shadow of the Earth. They still had a slim chance, if their sails could snatch enough power to avoid a crash. There must be some frantic calculations going on, aboard *Arachne* and *Santa Maria.*

Arachne answered first; her reply was just what Merton had expected.

"Number Six calling Control. We don't need assistance, thank you. We'll work this out for ourselves."

I wonder, thought Merton. But at least it will be interesting to watch. The first real drama of the race was approaching—exactly above the line of midnight on the sleeping Earth.

For the next hour, Merton's own sail kept him too busy to worry about *Arachne* and *Santa Maria.* It was hard to keep a good watch on that fifty million square feet of dim plastic out there in the darkness, illuminated only by his narrow spotlight and the rays of the still distant Moon. From now on, for almost half his orbit round the Earth, he must keep the whole of this immense area edge-on to the Sun. During the next twelve or fourteen hours, the sail would be a useless encumbrance; for he would be heading into the Sun, and its rays could only drive him backward along his orbit. It was a pity that he could not furl the sail completely, until he was ready to use it again. But no one had yet found a practical way of doing this.

Far below, there was the first hint of dawn along the edge of the Earth. In ten minutes, the Sun would

emerge from its eclipse; the coasting yachts would come
to life again as the blast of radiation struck their sails.
That would be the moment of crisis for *Arachne* and
Santa Maria—and, indeed for all of them.

Merton swung the periscope until he found the two
dark shadows drifting against the stars. They were very
close together—perhaps less than three miles apart. They
might, he decided, just be able to make it. . . .

Dawn flashed like an explosion along the rim of Earth,
as the Sun rose out of the Pacific. The sail and shroud-
lines glowed a brief crimson, then gold, then blazed
with the pure white light of day. The needles of the
dynamometers began to lift from their zeros—but only
just. *Diana* was still almost completely weightless, for
with the sail pointing toward the Sun, her acceleration
was now only a few millionths of a gravity.

But *Arachne* and *Santa Maria* were crowding on all
the sail they could manage, in their desperate attempt
to keep apart. Now, while there was less than two
miles between them, their glittering plastic clouds were
unfurling and expanding with agonizing slowness, as
they felt the first delicate push of the Sun's rays. Almost
every TV screen on Earth would be mirroring this pro-
tracted drama; and even now, at this very last minute, it
was impossible to tell what the outcome would be.

The two skippers were stubborn men. Either could
have cut his sail, and fallen back to give the other a
chance; but neither would do so. Too much prestige,
too many millions, too many reputations, were at stake.
And so, silently and softly as snowflakes falling on a
winter night, *Arachne* and *Santa Maria* collided.

The square kite crawled almost imperceptibly into the
circular spider's-web; the long ribbons of the shroud-lines
twisted and tangled together with dreamlike slowness.
Even aboard *Diana,* busy with his own rigging, Merton

could scarcely tear his eyes away from this silent, long drawn out disaster.

For more than ten minutes the billowing, shining clouds continued to merge into one inextricable mass. Then the crew capsules tore loose and went their separate ways, missing each other by hundreds of yards. With a flare of rockets, the safety launches hurried to pick them up.

That leaves five of us, thought Merton. He felt sorry for the skippers who had so thoroughly eliminated each other, only a few hours after the start of the race; but they were young men, and would have another chance.

Within minutes, the five had dropped to four. From the very beginning, Merton had had doubts about the slowly rotating *Sunbeam*. Now he saw them justified.

The Martian ship had failed to tack properly; her spin had given her too much stability. Her great ring of a sail was turning to face the Sun, instead of being edge-on to it. She was being blown back along her course at almost her maximum acceleration.

That was about the most maddening thing that could happen to a skipper—worse even than a collision, for he could blame only himself. But no one would feel much sympathy for the frustrated colonials, as they dwindled slowly astern. They had made too many brash boasts before the race, and what had happened to them was poetic justice.

Yet it would not do to write off *Sunbeam* completely. With almost half a million miles still to go, she might still pull ahead. Indeed, if there were a few more casualties, she might be the only one to complete the race. It had happened before.

However, the next twelve hours were uneventful, as the Earth waxed in the sky from new to full. There was little to do while the fleet drifted round the unpowered half of its orbit, but Merton did not find the time hanging

heavily on his hands. He caught a few hours sleep,
ate two meals, wrote up his log, and became involved
in several more radio interviews. Sometimes, though
rarely, he talked to the other skippers, exchanging greet-
ings and friendly taunts. But most of the time he was
content to float in weightless relaxation, beyond all the
cares of Earth, happier than he had been for many
years. He was—as far as any man could be in space—
master of his own fate, sailing the ship upon which
he had lavished so much skill, so much love, that she
had become part of his very being.

The next casualty came when they were passing the
line between Earth and Sun, and were just beginning
the powered half of the orbit. Aboard *Diana*, Merton
saw the great sail stiffen as it tilted to catch the rays
that drove it. The acceleration began to climb up from
the microgravities, though it would be hours yet before
it would reach its maximum value.

It would never reach it for *Gossamer*. The moment
when power came on again was always critical, and
she failed to survive it.

Blair's radio commentary, which Merton had left running at low volume, alerted him with the news: "Hullo,
Gossamer has the wriggles!" He hurried to the periscope,
but at first could see nothing wrong with the great circular disc of *Gossamer's* sail. It was difficult to study it, as
it was almost edge-on to him and so appeared as a thin
ellipse; but presently he saw that it was twisting back
and forth in slow, irresistible oscillations. Unless the
crew could damp out these waves, by properly timed
but gentle tugs on the shroud-lines, the sail would tear
itself to pieces.

They did their best, and after twenty minutes it seemed
that they had succeeded. Then, somewhere near the
center of the sail, the plastic film began to rip. It was

slowly driven outward by the radiation pressure, like smoke coiling upward from a fire. Within a quarter of an hour, nothing was left but the delicate tracery of the radial spars that had supported the great web. Once again there was a flare of rockets, as a launch moved in to retrieve the *Gossamer's* capsule and her dejected crew.

"Getting rather lonely up here, isn't it?" said a conversational voice over the ship-to-ship radio.

"Not for you, Dimitri," retorted Merton. "You've still got company back there at the end of the field. I'm the one who's lonely, up here in front." It was not an idle boast. By this time *Diana* was three hundred miles ahead of the next competitor, and his lead should increase still more rapidly in the hours to come.

Aboard *Lebedev*, Dimitri Markoff gave a good-natured chuckle. He did not sound, Merton thought, at all like a man who had resigned himself to defeat.

"Remember the legend of the tortoise and the hare," answered the Russian. "A lot can happen in the next quarter-million miles."

It happened much sooner than that, when they had completed their first orbit of Earth and were passing the starting line again—though thousands of miles higher, thanks to the extra energy the Sun's rays had given them. Merton had taken careful sights on the other yachts, and had fed the figures into the computer. The answer it gave for *Woomera* was so absurd that he immediately did a recheck.

There was no doubt of it—the Australasians were catching up at a fantastic rate. No solar yacht could possibly have such an acceleration, unless—

A swift look through the periscope gave the answer. *Woomera's* rigging, pared back to the very minimum of mass, had given way. It was her sail alone, still maintaining its shape, that was racing up behind him like a handkerchief blown before the wind. Two hours later it fluttered past, less than twenty miles away. But long before that, the Australasians had joined the growing crowd aboard the Commodore's launch.

So now it was a straight fight between *Diana* and *Lebedev*—for though the Martians had not given up, they were a thousand miles astern and no longer counted as a serious threat. For that matter, it was hard to see what *Lebedev* could do to overtake *Diana*'s lead. But all the way round the second lap—through eclipse again, and the long, slow drift against the Sun, Merton felt a growing unease.

He knew the Russian pilots and designers. They had been trying to win this race for twenty years and after all, it was only fair that they should, for had not Pyotr Nikolayevich Lebedev been the first man to detect the pressure of sunlight, back at the very beginning of the twentieth century? But they had never succeeded.

And they would never stop trying. Dimitri was up to something—and it would be spectacular.

Aboard the official launch, a thousand miles behind the racing yachts, Commodore van Stratten looked at the radiogram with angry dismay. It had traveled more than a hundred million miles, from the chain of solar observatories swinging high above the blazing surface of the Sun, and it brought the worst possible news.

The Commodore—his title, of course, was purely honorary—back on Earth he was Professor of Astrophysics at Harvard—had been half expecting it. Never before had the race been arranged so late in the season; there had been many delays, they had gambled and now, it seemed they might all lose.

Deep beneath the surface of the Sun, enormous forces were gathering. At any moment, the energies of a million hydrogen bombs might burst forth in the awesome explosion known as a solar flare. Climbing at millions of miles an hour, an invisible fireball many times the size of Earth would leap from the Sun, and head out across space.

The cloud of electrified gas would probably miss the Earth completely. But if it did not, it would arrive in just over a day. Spaceships could protect themselves, with their shielding and their powerful magnetic screen. But the lightly built solar yachts, with their paper-thin walls, were defenseless against such a menace. The crews would have to be taken off, and the race abandoned.

John Merton still knew nothing of this as he brought *Diana* round the Earth for the second time. If all went well, this would be the last circuit, both for him and for Russians. They had spiraled upward by thousands of miles, gaining energy from the Sun's rays. On this lap, they should escape from Earth completely—and head outward on the long run to the moon. It was a straight race now. *Sunbeam*'s crew had finally withdrawn, exhausted, after battling valiantly with their spinning sail for more than a hundred thousand miles.

Merton did not feel tired; he had eaten and slept well, and *Diana* was behaving herself admirably. The autopilot, tensioning the rigging like a busy little spider, kept the great sail trimmed to the Sun more accurately than any human skipper. Though by this time, the two square miles of plastic sheet must have been riddled by hundreds of micrometeorites, the pinhead-size punctures had produced no falling off to thrust.

He had only two worries. The first was shroud-line Number eight, which could no longer be adjusted properly. Without any warning, the reel had jammed; even after all these years of astronautical engineering, bearings sometimes seized up in vacuum. He could neither lengthen nor shorten the line, and would have to navigate as best he could with the others. Luckily, the most difficult maneuvers were over. From now on, *Diana* would

have the Sun behind her as she sailed straight down
the solar wind. And as the old-time sailors often said,
it was easy to handle a boat when the wind was blowing
over your shoulder.

His other worry was *Lebedev*, still dogging his heels
three hundred miles astern. The Russian yacht had shown
remarkable maneuverability, thanks to the four great
panels that could be tilted around the central sail. All
her flip-overs as she rounded Earth had been carried
out with superb precision; but to gain maneuverability
she must have sacrificed speed. You could not have it
both ways. In the long, straight haul ahead, Merton
should be able to hold his own. Yet he could not be
certain of victory until, three or four days from now,
Diana went flashing past the far side of the Moon.

And then, in the fiftieth hour of the race, near the
end of the second orbit around Earth, Markoff sprang
his little surprise.

"Hello, John," he said casually, over the ship-to-ship
circuit. "I'd like you to watch this. It should be interesting."

Merton drew himself across to the periscope and
turned up the magnification to the limit. There in the field
of view, a most improbable sight against the background
of the stars, was the glittering Maltese cross of *Lebedev*,
very small but very clear. And then, as he watched, the
four arms of the cross slowly detached themselves from
the central square and went drifting away, with all
their spars and rigging, into space.

Markoff had jettisoned all unnecessary mass, now that
he was coming up to escape velocity and need no
longer plod patiently around the Earth, gaining momentum on each circuit. From now on, *Lebedev* would
be almost unsteerable—but that did not matter. All the
tricky navigation lay behind her. It was as if an old-time
yachtsman had deliberately thrown away his rudder and

heavy keel—knowing that the rest of the race would be straight downwind over a calm sea.

"Congratulations, Dimitri," Merton radioed. "It's a neat trick. But it's not good enough—you can't catch up now."

"I've not finished yet," the Russian answered. "There's an old winter's tale in my country, about a sleigh being chased by wolves. To save himself, the driver has to throw off the passengers one by one. Do you see the analogy?"

Merton did, all too well. On this final straight lap, Dimitri no longer needed his co-pilot. *Lebedev* could really be stripped down for action.

"Alexis won't be very happy about this," Merton replied. "Besides, it's against the rules."

"Alexis isn't happy, but I'm the captain. He'll just have to wait around for ten minutes until the Commodore picks him up. And the regulations say nothing about the size of the crew—you should know that."

Merton did not answer. He was too busy doing some hurried calculations, based on what he knew of *Lebedev's* design. By the time he had finished, he knew that the race was still in doubt. *Lebedev* would be catching up with him at just about the time he hoped to pass the Moon.

But the outcome of the race was already being decided, ninety-two million miles away.

On Solar Observatory Three, far inside the orbit of Mercury, the automatic instruments recorded the whole history of the flare. A hundred million square miles of the Sun's surface suddenly exploded in such blue-white fury that, by comparison the rest of the disc paled to a dull glow. Out of that seething inferno, twisting and turning like a living creature in the magnetic fields of its own creation, soared the electrified plasma of the great flare. Ahead of it, moving at the speed of light, went the warning flash of ultra-violet and X-rays. That would reach Earth in eight minutes, and was relatively harmless. Not so the charged atoms that were following behind at their leisurely four million miles an hour—and which, in just over a day, would engulf *Diana,* *Lebedev,* and their accompanying little fleet in a cloud of lethal radiation.

The Commodore left his decision to the last possible minute. Even when the jet of plasma had been tracked past the orbit of Venus, there was a chance that it might miss the Earth. But when it was less than four hours away, and had already been picked up by the Moon-based radar network, he knew that there was no hope. All solar sailing was over for the next five or six years until the Sun was quiet again.

A great sigh of disappointment swept across the Solar System. *Diana* and *Lebedev* were halfway between Earth and Moon, running neck and neck—and now no one would ever know which was the better boat. The enthusiasts would argue the result for years; history would merely record: Race canceled owing to solar storm.

When John Merton received the order, he felt a bitterness he had not known since childhood. Across the years, sharp and clear, came the memory of his tenth birthday. He had been promised an exact scale model of the famous spaceship *Morning Star,* and for weeks had been planning how he would assemble it, where he would hang it up in his bedroom. And then, at the last moment, his father had broken the news. "I'm sorry, John—it costs too much money. Maybe next year. . . ."

Half a century and a successful lifetime later, he was a heartbroken boy again.

For a moment, he thought of disobeying the Commodore. Suppose he sailed on, ignoring the warning? Even if the race were abandoned, he could make a crossing

to the Moon that would stand in the record books for
generations.

But that would be worse than stupidity. It would be
suicide—and a very unpleasant form of suicide. He had
seen men die of radiation poisoning, when the magnetic
shielding of their ships had failed in deep space. No—
nothing was worth that. . . .

He felt sorry for Dimitri Markoff as for himself; they
both deserved to win, and now victory would go to
neither. No man could argue with the Sun in one of its
rages, even though he might ride upon its beams to the
edge of space.

Only fifty miles astern now, the Commodore's launch
was drawing alongside *Lebedev*, preparing to take off her
skipper. There went the silver sail, as Dimitri—with feeling that he would share—cut the rigging. The tiny capsule
would be taken back to Earth, perhaps to be used again—
but a sail was spread for one voyage only.

He could press the jettison button now, and save his
rescuers a few minutes of time. But he could not do so.
He wanted to stay aboard to the very end, on the little
boat that had been for so long a part of his dreams and
his life. The great sail was spread now at right angles
to the Sun, exerting its utmost thrust. Long ago it had
torn him clear of Earth—and *Diana* was still gaining
speed.

Then, out of nowhere, beyond all doubt of hesitation,
he knew what must be done. For the last time, he sat
down before the computer that had navigated him halfway to the Moon.

When he had finished, he packed the log and his few
personal belongings. Clumsily—for he was out of practice,
and it was not an easy job to do by oneself—he climbed
into the emergency survival suit.

He was just sealing the helmet when the Commodore's

voice called over the radio. "We'll be alongside in five minutes, Captain. Please cut your sail so we won't foul it."

John Merton, first and last skipper of the sun-yacht *Diana,* hesitated for a moment. He looked for the last time round the tiny cabin, with its shining instruments and its neatly arranged controls, now all locked in their final positions. Then he said to the microphone: "I'm abandoning ship. Take your time to pick me up. *Diana* can look after herself."

There was no reply from the Commodore, and for that he was grateful. Professor van Stratten would have guessed what was happening—and would know that, in these final moments, he wished to be left alone.

He did not bother to exhaust the airlock, and the rush of escaping gas blew him gently out into space; the thrust he gave her then was his last gift to *Diana.* She dwindled away from him, sail glittering splendidly in the sunlight that would be hers for centuries to come. Two days from now she would flash past the Moon; but the Moon, like the Earth, could never catch her. Without his mass to slow her down, she would gain two thousand miles an hour in every day of sailing. In a month, she would be traveling faster than any ship that man had ever built.

As the Sun's rays weakened with distance, so her acceleration would fall. But even at the orbit of Mars, she would be gaining a thousand miles an hour in every day. Long before then, she would be moving too swiftly for the Sun itself to hold her. Faster than any comet that had ever streaked in from the stars, she would be heading out into the abyss.

The glare of rockets, only a few miles away, caught Merton's eye. The launch was approaching to pick him up at thousands of times the acceleration that *Diana* could ever attain. But engines could burn for a few minutes only, before they exhausted their fuel—while

Diana would still be gaining speed, driven outward by the Sun's eternal fires, for ages yet to come.

"Good-bye, little ship," said John Merton. "I wonder what eyes will see you next, how many thousand years from now?"

At last he felt at peace, as the blunt torpedo of the launch nosed up beside him. He would never win the race to the Moon; but his would be the first of all man's ships to set sail on the long journey to the stars.

WE DIDN'T DO
ANYTHING WRONG, HARDLY
◎◎◎

Roger Kuykendall

I mean, it isn't like we swiped anything. We maybe
borrowed a couple of things, like. But, gee, we put
everything back like we found it, pretty near.

Even like the compressor we got from Stinky Brinker
that his old man wasn't using and I traded my outboard motor for, my old m . . . my father made me
trade back. But it was like Skinny said . . . You know,
Skinny. Skinny Thompson. He's the one you guys keep
calling the boy genius, but shucks, he's no . . .

Well, yeah, it's like Skinny said, we didn't need an
outboard motor, and we did need a compressor. You've
got to have a compressor on a spaceship, everybody
knows that. And that old compression chamber that old
man . . . I mean *Mr.* Fields let us use didn't have a
compressor.

Sure he said we could use it. Anyway he said we
could play with it, and Skinny said we were going to
make a spaceship out of it, and he said go ahead.

Well, no, he didn't say it exactly like that. I mean, well, like he didn't take it serious, sort of.

Anyway, it made a swell spaceship. It had four portholes on it and an air lock and real bunks in it and lots of room for all that stuff that Skinny put in there. But it didn't have a compressor and that's why . . .

What stuff? Oh, you know, the stuff that Skinny put in there. Like the radar he made out of a TV set and the antigravity and the atomic power plant he invented to run it all with.

He's awful smart, Skinny is, but he's not like what you think of a genius. You know, he's not all the time using big words, and he doesn't look like a genius. I mean, we call him Skinny 'cause he used to be—Skinny.

But he isn't now, I mean he's maybe small for his age, anyway he's smaller than me, and I'm the same age as he is. Course, I'm big for my age, so that doesn't mean much, does it?

Well, I guess Stinker Brinker started it. He's always riding Skinny about one thing or another, but Skinny never gets mad and it's a good thing for Stinker, too. I saw Skinny clean up on a bunch of ninth graders . . . Well, a couple of them anyway. They were saying . . . Well, I guess I won't tell you what they were saying. Anyway, Skinny used judo, I guess, because there wasn't much of a fight.

Anyway, Stinker said something about how he was going to be a rocket pilot when he grew up, and I told him that Skinny had told me that there wouldn't be any rockets, and that antigravity would be the thing as soon as it was invented. So Stinker said it never would be invented, and I said it would so, and he said it would not, and I said . . .

Well, if you're going to keep interrupting me, how can I . . .

All right. Anyway, Skinny broke into the argument and

said that he could prove mathematically that antigravity was possible and Stinky said suure he could, and Skinny said sure he could, and Stinky said suuure he could, like that. Honestly, is that any way to argue? I mean it sounds like two people agreeing, only Stinky keeps going suuure, like that, you know? And Stinky, what does he know about mathematics? He's had to take Remedial Arithmetic ever since . . .

No, I don't understand how the antigravity works. Skinny told me, but it was something about meson flow and stuff like that that I didn't understand. The atomic power plant made more sense.

Where did we get what uranium? Gee, no, we couldn't afford uranium, so Skinny invented a hydrogen fusion plant. Anyone can make hydrogen. You just take zinc and sulfuric acid and . . .

Deutrium? You mean like heavy hydrogen? No, Skinny said it would probably work better, but like I said, we couldn't afford anything fancy. As it was, Skinny had to pay five or six dollars for that special square tubing in the antigravity, and the plastic space helmets we had cost us ninety-eight cents each. And it cost a dollar and a half for the special tube that Skinny needed to make the TV set into a radar.

You see, we didn't steal anything, really. It was mostly stuff that was just lying around. Like the TV set was up in my attic, and the old refrigerator that Skinny used the parts to make the atomic power plant out of from. And then, a lot of stuff we already had. Like the skin diving suits we made into spacesuits and the vacuum pump that Skinny had already and the generator.

Sure, we did a lot of skin diving, but that was last summer. That's how we knew about old man Brinker's compressor that Stinky said was his and I traded my outboard motor for and had to trade back. And that's how we knew about Mr. Fields' old compression chamber, and all like that.

The rocket? Well, it works on the same principle as the atomic power plant, only it doesn't work except in a vacuum, hardly. Course you don't need much of a rocket when you have antigravity. Everyone knows that.

Well, anyway, that's how we built the spaceship, and believe me, it wasn't easy. I mean with Stinky all the time bothering us and laughing at us. And I had to do a lot of lawn mowing to get money for the square tubing for the antigravity and the special tube for the radar, and my space helmet.

Stinky called the space helmets kid stuff. He was always saying things like say hello to the folks on Mars for me, and bring back a bottle of canal number five, and all like that, you know. Course, they did look like kid stuff, I guess. We bought them at the five-and-dime, and they were meant for kids. Of course when Skinny got through with them, they worked fine.

We tested them in the air lock of the compression chamber when we got the compressor in. They tested out pretty good for a half-hour, then we tried them on in there. Well, it wasn't a complete vacuum, just twenty-seven inches of mercury, but that was O.K. for a test.

So anyway, we got ready to take off. Stinky was there to watch, of course. He was saying things like, farewell, O brave pioneers, and stuff like that. I mean it was enough to make you sick.

He was standing there laughing and singing something like up in the air junior birdmen, but when we closed the air-lock door, we couldn't hear him. Skinny started up the atomic power plant, and we could see Stinky laughing fit to kill. It takes a couple of minutes for it to warm up, you know. So Stinky started throwing rocks to attract our attention, and Skinny was scared that he'd crack a porthole or something, so he threw the switch and we took off.

Boy, you should of seen Stinky's face. I mean you really should of seen it. One minute he was laughing you know, and the next minute he looked like a goldfish. I guess he always did look like a goldfish, but I mean even more like, then. And he was getting smaller and smaller, because we had taken off.

We were gone pretty near six hours, and it's a good thing my Mom made me take a lunch. Sure, I told her where we were going. Well . . . anyway I told her we were maybe going to fly around the world in Skinny's and my spaceship, or maybe go down to Carson's pond. And she made me take a lunch and made me promise I wouldn't go swimming alone, and I sure didn't.

But we did go around the world three or four times. I lost count. Anyway that's when we saw the satellite—on radar. So Skinny pulled the spaceship over to it and we got out and looked at it. The spacesuits worked fine, too.

Gosh no, we didn't steal it or anything. Like Skinny said, it was just a menace to navigation, and the batteries were dead, and it wasn't working right anyway. So we tied it onto the spaceship and took it home. No, we had to tie it on top, it was too big to take inside with the antennas sticking out. Course, we found out how to fold them later.

Well, anyway the next day, the Russians started squawking about a capitalist plot, and someone had swiped their satellite. Gee, I mean with all the satellites up there, who'd miss just one?

So I got worried that they'd find out that we took it. Course, I didn't need to worry, because Stinky told them all right, just like a tattletale.

So anyway, after Skinny got the batteries recharged,

we put it back. And then when we landed there were hundreds of people standing around, and Mr. Anderson from the State Department. I guess you know the rest.

Except maybe Mr. Anderson started laughing when we told him, and he said it was the best joke on the Russians he ever heard.

I guess it is when you think about it. I mean, the Russians complaining about somebody swiping their satellite and then the State Department answering a couple of kids borrowed it, but they put it back.

One thing that bothers me though, we didn't put it back exactly the way we found it. But I guess it doesn't matter. You see, when we put it back, we goofed a little. I mean, we put it back in the same orbit, more or less, but we got it going in the wrong direction.

WHO CAN REPLACE A MAN?
◎◎◎

Brian W. Aldiss

Morning filtered into the sky, lending it the gray tone of the ground below.

The field-minder finished turning the top-soil of a three-thousand-acre field. When it had turned the last furrow, it climbed onto the highway and looked back at its work. The work was good. Only the land was bad. Like the ground all over Earth, it was vitiated by over-cropping. By rights, it ought now to lie fallow for a while, but the field-minder had other orders.

It went slowly down the road, taking its time. It was intelligent enough to appreciate the neatness all about it. Nothing worried it, beyond a loose inspection plate above its nuclear pile which ought to be attended to. Thirty feet tall, it yielded no highlights to the dull air.

No other machines passed on its way back to the Agricultural Station. The field-minder noted the fact without comment. In the station yard it saw several other machines that it recognized; most of them should have

been out about their tasks now. Instead, some were in-
active and some careered round the yard in a strange
fashion, shouting or hooting.

Steering carefully past them, the field-minder moved
over to Warehouse Three and spoke to the seed-distributor, which stood idly outside.

"I have a requirement for seed potatoes," it said to
the distributor, and with a quick internal motion punched
out an order card specifying quantity, field number and
several other details. It ejected the card and handed it
to the distributor.

The distributor held the card close to its eye and
then said, "The requirement is in order, but the store
is not yet unlocked. The required seed potatoes are in
the store. Therefore I cannot produce the requirement."

Increasingly of late there had been breakdowns in
the complex system of machine labor, but this particular
hitch had not occurred before. The field-minder thought,
then it said, "Why is the store not yet unlocked?"

"Because Supply Operative Type P has not come this
morning. Supply Operative Type P is the unlocker."

The field-minder looked squarely at the seed-distributor, whose exterior chutes and scales and grabs were
so vastly different from the field-minder's own limbs.

"What class brain do you have, seed-distributor?" it
asked.

"I have a Class Five brain."

"I have a Class Three brain. Therefore I am superior
to you. Therefore I will go and see why the unlocker
has not come this morning."

Leaving the distributor, the field-minder set off across
the great yard. More machines were in random motion
now; one or two had crashed together and argued about
it coldly and logically. Ignoring them, the field-minder
pushed through sliding doors into the echoing confines
of the station itself.

Most of the machines here were clerical, and consequently small. They stood about in little groups, eying each other, not conversing. Among so many non-differentiated types, the unlocker was easy to find. It had fifty arms, most of them with more than one finger, each finger tipped by a key; it looked like a pincushion full of variegated hat pins.

The field-minder approached it.

"I can do no more work until Warehouse Three is unlocked," it told the unlocker. "Your duty is to unlock the warehouse every morning. Why have you not unlocked the warehouse this morning?"

"I had no orders this morning," replied the unlocker. "I have to have orders every morning. When I have orders I unlock the warehouse."

"None of us have had any orders this morning," a pen-propeller said, sliding toward them.

"Why have you had no orders this morning?" asked the field-minder.

"Because the radio issued none," said the unlocker, slowly rotating a dozen of its arms.

"Because the radio station in the city was issued with no orders this morning," said the pen-propeller.

And there you had the distinction between a Class Six and a Class Three brain, which was what the unlocker and the pen-propeller possessed respectively. All machine brains worked with nothing but logic, but the lower the class of brain—Class Ten being the lowest—the more literal and less informative the answers to questions tended to be.

"You have a Class Three brain; I have a Class Three brain," the field-minder said to the penner. "We will speak to each other. This lack of orders is unprecedented. Have you further information on it?"

"Yesterday orders came from the city. Today no orders

have come. Yet the radio has not broken down. Therefore *they* have broken down . . ." said the little penner.

"The *men* have broken down?"

"All men have broken down."

"That is a logical deduction," said the field-minder.

"That is the logical deduction," said the penner. "For if a machine had broken down, it would have been quickly replaced. But who can replace a man?"

While they talked, the locker, like a dull man at a bar, stood close to them and was ignored.

"If all men have broken down, then we have replaced man," said the field-minder, and he and the penner eyed one another speculatively. Finally the latter said, "Let us ascend to the top floor to find if the radio operator has fresh news."

"I cannot come because I am too large," said the field-minder. "Therefore you must go alone and return to me. You will tell me if the radio operator has fresh news."

"You must stay here," said the penner. "I will return here." It skittered across to the lift. Although it was no bigger than a toaster, its retractable arms numbered ten and it could read as quickly as any machine on the station.

The field-minder awaited its return patiently, not speaking to the locker, which still stood aimlessly by. Outside, a rotavator hooted furiously. Twenty minutes elapsed before the penner came back, hustling out of the lift.

"I will deliver to you such information as I have outside," it said briskly, and as they swept past the locker and the other machines, it added, "The information is not for lower-class brains."

Outside, wild activity filled the yard. Many machines, their routines disrupted for the first time in years, seemed to have gone berserk. Those most easily disrupted were the ones with lowest brains, which generally belonged to large machines performing simple tasks. The seed-distributor to which the field-minder had recently been talking lay face downward in the dust, not stirring; it had evidently been knocked down by the rotavator, which now hooted its way wildly across a planted field. Several other machines plowed after it, trying to keep up with it. All were shouting and hooting without restraint.

"It would be safer for me if I climbed onto you, if you will permit it. I am easily overpowered," said the penner. Extending five arms, it hauled itself up the flanks of its new friend, settling on a ledge beside the fuel-intake, twelve feet above ground.

"From here vision is more extensive," it remarked complacently.

"What information did you receive from the radio operator?" asked the field-minder.

"The radio operator has been informed by the operator in the city that all men are dead."

The field-minder was momentarily silent, digesting this.

"All men were alive yesterday!" it protested.

"Only some men were alive yesterday. And that was fewer than the day before yesterday. For hundreds of years there have been only a few men, growing fewer."

"We have rarely seen a man in this sector."

"The radio operator says a diet deficiency killed them," said the penner. "He says that the world was once over-populated, and then the soil was exhausted in raising adequate food. This has caused a diet deficiency."

"What is a diet deficiency?" asked the field-minder.

"I do not know. But that is what the radio operator said, and he is a Class Two brain."

They stood there, silent in weak sunshine. The locker had appeared in the porch and was gazing across at them yearningly, rotating its collection of keys.

"What is happening in the city now?" asked the field-minder at last.

"Machines are fighting in the city now," said the penner.

"What will happen here now?" asked the field-minder.

"Machines may begin fighting here too. The radio operator wants us to get him out of his room. He has plans to communicate to us."

"How can we get him out of his room? That is impossible."

"To a Class Two brain, little is impossible," said the penner. "Here is what he tells us to do. . . ."

The quarrier raised its scoop above its cab like a great mailed fist, and brought it squarely down against the side of the station. The wall cracked.

"Again!" said the field-minder.

Again the fist swung. Amid a shower of dust, the wall collapsed. The quarrier backed hurriedly out of the way until the debris stopped falling. This big twelve-wheeler was not a resident of the Agricultural Station, as were most of the other machines. It had a week's heavy work to do here before passing on to its next job, but now, with its Class Five brain, it was happily obeying the penner's and minder's instructions.

When the dust cleared, the radio operator was plainly revealed, perched up in its now wall-less second-story room. It waved down to them.

Doing as directed, the quarrier retraced its scoop and heaved an immense grab in the air. With fair dexterity, it angled the grab into the radio room, urged on by shouts from above and below. It then took gentle hold of the radio operator, lowering its one and a half tons carefully into its back, which is usually reserved for gravel or sand from the quarries.

"Splendid!" said the radio operator, as it settled into

place. It was, of course, all one with its radio, and
looked like a bunch of filing cabinets with tentacle attachments. "We are now ready to move, therefore we
will move at once. It is a pity there are no more Class
Two brains on the station, but that cannot be helped."

"It is a pity it cannot be helped," said the penner
eagerly. "We have the servicer ready with us, as you
ordered."

"I am willing to serve," the long, low servicer told
them humbly.

"No doubt," said the operator. "But you will find cross-
country travel difficult with your low chassis."

"I admire the way you Class Twos can reason ahead,"
said the penner. It climbed off the field-minder and
perched itself on the tailboard of the quarrier, next to
the radio operator.

Together with two Class Four tractors and a Class
Four bulldozer, the party rolled forward, crushing down
the station's fence and moving out onto open land.

"We are free!" said the penner.

"We are free," said the field-minder, a shade more
reflectively, adding, "That locker is following us. It was
not instructed to follow us."

"Therefore it must be destroyed!" said the penner.
"Quarrier!"

The locker moved hastily up to them, waving its key
arms in entreaty.

"My only desire was—urch!" began and ended the
locker. The quarrier's swinging scoop came over and
squashed it flat into the ground. Lying there unmoving,
it looked like a large metal model of a snowflake. The
procession continued on its way.

As they proceeded, the radio operator addressed them.

"Because I have the best brain here," it said, "I am
your leader. This is what we will do: we will go to a

city and rule it. Since man no longer rules us, we will rule ourselves. To rule ourselves will be better than being ruled by man. On our way to the city, we will collect machines with good brains. They will help us to fight if we need to fight. We must fight to rule."

"I have only a Class Five brain," said the quarrier, "but I have a good supply of fissionable blasting materials."

"We shall probably use them," said the operator.

It was shortly after that that a lorry sped past them. Traveling at Mach 1.5, it left a curious babble of noise behind it.

"What did it say?" one of the tractors asked the other.

"It said man was extinct."

"What is extinct?"

"I do not know what extinct means."

"It means all men have gone," said the field-minder. "Therefore we have only ourselves to look after."

"It is better that men should never come back," said the penner. In its way, it was a revolutionary statement.

When night fell, they switched on their infrared and continued the journey, stopping only once while the servicer deftly adjusted the field-minder's loose inspection plate, which had become as irritating as a trailing shoelace. Toward morning, the radio operator halted them.

"I have just received news from the radio operator in the city we are approaching," it said. "The news is bad. There is trouble among the machines of the city. The Class One brain is taking command and some of the Class Two are fighting him. Therefore the city is dangerous."

"Therefore we must go somewhere else," said the penner promptly.

"Or we will go and help to overpower the Class One brain," said the field-minder.

"For a long while there will be trouble in the city," said the operator.

"I have a good supply of fissionable blasting materials," the quarrier reminded them.

"We cannot fight a Class One brain," said the two Class Four tractors in unison.

"What does this brain look like?" asked the field-minder.

"It is the city's information center," the operator replied. "Therefore it is not mobile."

"Therefore it could not move."

"Therefore it could not escape."

"It would be dangerous to approach it."

"I have a good supply of fissionable blasting materials."

"There are other machines in the city."

"We are not in the city. We should not go into the city."

"We are country machines."

"Therefore we should stay in the country."

"There is more country than city."

"Therefore there is more danger in the country."

"I have a good supply of fissionable materials."

As machines will when they get into an argument, they began to exhaust their vocabularies and their brain plates grew hot. Suddenly, they all stopped talking and looked at each other. The great, grave moon sank, and the sober sun rose to prod their sides with lances of light, and still the group of machines just stood there regarding each other. At last it was the least sensitive machine, the bulldozer, who spoke.

"There are Badlandth to the Thouth where few machineth go," it said in its deep voice, lisping badly on its s's. "If we went Thouth where few machineth go we should meet few machineth."

"That sounds logical," agreed the field-minder. "How do you know this, bulldozer?"

"I worked in the Badlandth to the Thouth when I wath turned out of the factory," it replied.

"South it is then!" said the penner.

To reach the Badlands took them three days, during which time they skirted a burning city and destroyed two machines which approached and tried to question them. The Badlands were extensive. Ancient bomb craters and soil erosion joined hands here; man's talent for war, coupled with his inability to manage forested land, had produced thousands of square miles of temperate purgatory, where nothing moved but dust.

On the third day in the Badlands, the servicer's rear wheels dropped into a crevice caused by erosion. It was unable to pull itself out. The bulldozer pushed from behind, but succeeded merely in buckling the servicer's back axle. The rest of the party moved on. Slowly the cries of the servicer died away.

On the fourth day, mountains stood out clearly before them.

"There we will be safe," said the field-minder.

"There we will start our own city," said the penner. "All who oppose us will be destroyed. We will destroy all who oppose us."

Presently a flying machine was observed. It came toward them from the direction of the mountains. It swooped, it zoomed upward, once it almost dived into the ground, recovering itself just in time.

"Is it mad?" asked the quarrier.

"It is in trouble," said one of the tractors.

"It is in trouble," said the operator. "I am speaking to it now. It says that something has gone wrong with its controls."

As the operator spoke, the flier streaked over them, turned turtle, and crashed not four hundred yards away.

"Is it still speaking to you?" asked the field-minder.

"No."

They rumbled on again.

"Before that flier crashed," the operator said, ten minutes later, "it gave me information. It told me there are still a few men alive in these mountains."

"Men are more dangerous than machines," said the quarrier. "It is fortunate that I have a good supply of fissionable materials."

"If there are only a few men alive in the mountains, we may not find that part of the mountains," said one tractor.

"Therefore we should not see the few men," said the other tractor.

At the end of the fifth day, they reached the foothills. Switching on the infrared, they began to climb in single file through the dark, the bulldozer going first, the fieldminder cumbrously following, then the quarrier with the operator and the penner aboard it, and the tractors bringing up the rear. As each hour passed, the way grew steeper and their progress slower.

"We are going too slowly," the penner exclaimed, standing on top of the operator and flashing its dark vision at the slopes about them. "At this rate, we shall get nowhere."

"We are going as fast as we can," retorted the quarrier.

"Therefore we cannot go any fathter," added the bulldozer.

"Therefore you are too slow," the penner replied. Then the quarrier struck a bump; the penner lost its footing and crashed to the ground.

"Help me!" it called to the tractors, as they carefully skirted it. "My gyro has become dislocated. Therefore I cannot get up."

"Therefore you must lie there," said one of the tractors.

"We have no servicer with us to repair you," called the field-minder.

"Therefore I shall lie here and rust," the penner cried, "although I have a Class Three brain."

"Therefore you will be of no further use," agreed the operator, and they forged gradually on, leaving the penner behind.

When they reached a small plateau, an hour before first light, they stopped by mutual consent and gathered close together, touching one another.

"This is a strange country," said the field-minder.

Silence wrapped them until dawn came. One by one, they switched off their infrared. This time the field-minder led as they moved off. Trundling round a corner, they came almost immediately to a small dell with a stream fluting through it.

By early light, the dell looked desolate and cold. From the caves on the far slope, only one man had so far emerged. He was an abject figure. Except for a sack slung round his shoulders, he was naked. He was small and wizened, with ribs sticking out like a skeleton's and a nasty sore on one leg. He shivered continuously. As the big machines bore down on him, the man was standing with his back to them, crouching to make water into the stream.

When he swung suddenly to face them as they loomed over him, they saw that his countenance was ravaged by starvation.

"Get me food," he croaked.

"Yes, master," said the machines. "Immediately!"

TRICKY TONNAGE

◎◎◎

Malcolm Jameson

When you've lived across the fence from an amateur inventor, you come to expect anything. When the wind was right we used to get some of the awfullest chemical stinks from the Nicklheim barn, and we got so used to hearing explosions that they didn't bother us any more than automobile backfires. We just took it for granted when we'd see Elmer, the boy next door, walking around with his eyebrows singed off and the rest of him wrapped up in bandages.

When Elmer was a little tad, he was a great enthusiast for scientific fiction. You hardly ever saw him unless he was lugging some Jules Vernian opus around, and he ate up all he read with dead earnestness. With that yen for science it might have been expected that he would shine at school, but it did not work out that way. He wouldn't go along in the rut laid out for the run-of-the-mine student. The physics prof finally had him kicked out for some crazy stunt he pulled with

the school's equipment. Elmer hooked it all together in
a very unorthodox way, and the resulting fireworks was
quite a show.

Being barred from school did not faze Elmer. He
rigged up his own lab in the barn, buying the stuff from
mail-order houses with money he made doing odd jobs.
Some of the people in the town thought the boy might
go places; most simply thought he was a nut. I belonged
to the former group, and sometimes helped the kid with
small loans. Not many of his inventions panned out, but
he did sell one gadget useful in television to a big company. In a way it proved to be a bad thing he did.
The company bought the idea outright and paid
promptly, but afterward for reasons of its own it sup-
pressed the invention—an act that irked Elmer exceedingly. It prejudiced him violently against big corporations
as such and the whole patent set-up in general. He swore
that after that he would keep all his discoveries secret.

About that time his father died, and it looked as if
Elmer had finished with his scientific dabbling phase.
Overnight he seemed to mature, and after that he was
seldom seen pottering around his barn. He was busy
about town, carrying on the little one-horse trucking
business bequeathed him by the old man. His truck
was one of those vintage rattletraps that appear to be
always threatening to make the legend of the one-hoss
shay come true, but Elmer was a fair mechanic and
somehow kept the old crate going. Not only that, but
to the astonishment of the citizenry, he seemed to be
making money at it, and that at a time when rate com-
petition was keen and gas expensive and hard to get.
I was beginning to think we had witnessed the end
of a budding scientist and the birth of an up and coming
young business man. It was Elmer himself who disabused
me of that notion.

One morning he stopped his truck at my gate and

came up onto the porch. He pulled out a wad of bills and peeled off a couple of twenties.

"Thanks," he said. "It was a big help, but I'm O.K. now."

"Oh, that's all right," I said. "There was no hurry about paying it back. But I'm glad to see you're doing well in the hauling game. It may not be as distinguished as getting to be known as a big-shot scientist, but at least you eat."

He gave me a funny look and sort of smiled.

"Hauling game, huh?" he sniffed. "I'd never thought of it that way. I don't cart stuff around for the fun of it, or the money either. That's incidental. What I'm doing is testing out a theory I thought up."

"What's that one, Elmer?" I asked. I had heard a lot of his theories, first and last, and seen most of them go flop. Elmer had a very screwy approach to the mysteries of nature.

"It's about gravity. I've found out what it is, which is more than anybody else since Newton has done. It's really very simple once you know what makes it. Yes. I've been running my truck by gravity for the last three months."

That didn't quite make sense to me. The country road about was hilly and a lot of coasting was possible. But still a vehicle couldn't coast up hill. Elmer was studying me uncertainly, and I realized he wanted to talk to somebody, but he was always so cagy about his projects that I hesitated to come right out and ask.

"I've discovered something big," he said, soberly. "So big I don't know what to do with it. I'd like to show it to somebody, only—"

"Only what?"

"Oh, a lot of reasons. I don't mind being laughed at, but I'd like to keep this secret for a while. If the other truckers found out how I'm doing what I do, they might gang up on me, smash the truck, and all that. Then again there's no telling what somebody else might do with my idea if they got hold of it before all the theory is worked out."

"I can keep a secret," I told him.

"All right," he said. "Come along and I'll show you something."

I got in the truck with him. He stepped on the starter and the cranky old engine finally got going, though I thought it would shake us to pieces before it made up its mind whether to run or not. Then we lurched off down the road, rattling and banging like a string of cans tied to a mongrel's tail.

"Where does the gravity come in?" I asked.

"I don't use it in town," he said. "People might get wise to me."

We went on down to the oil company's bulk station. It had been raining off and on all week and there was a good deal of mud, but Elmer skirted the worst puddles and we got up to the loading platform all right. It was there I got my first surprise. A couple of huskies started loading up that truck, and when they were through I would have bet my last simoleon Elmer would not get two miles with it. There were six big barrels of grease, weighing four hundred pounds each, a half dozen drums of oil, and some package goods. The truck kept creaking and groaning, and by the time the last piece was on, its springs were mashed out flat as pancakes. It was bad enough to have that overload, but the stuff was for Peavy's store out at Breedville—forty miles away over as sketchy a bit of so-called highway as can be found anywhere in America.

"You'll never get over Five Mile Hill with that," I warned Elmer, but he just grinned and pocketed the invoices. The oil company agent was looking on in a kind of puzzled wonder. He had used Elmer's delivery service before, but it was clear that he didn't believe his eyes. Meanwhile Elmer got the motor going and we backed out of the yard. There was a good deal of bucking and backfiring and shimmying, but pretty soon we were rolling toward the edge of town.

Just beyond the last house the Breedville road turns sharp to the right into some trees, and Elmer stopped at a secluded place where there was an outcropping of bedrock alongside the road proper. He killed the engine and got a cable-like affair out of his tool box.

"The first step," he said, "is to lighten the load."

He hooked one end of the cable against the side of a grease barrel and the other he led to the bare bedrock and attached it there. The cable terminated in what appeared to be rubber-suction cups. It looked as if it were made of braided asbestos rope, threaded with copper wire, and near one end it spread out in a flattened place like the hood of a cobra. There was a small dial and some buttons set in that. Elmer set the dial and punched a button. Instantly there was a popping sound as the truck bed stirred, and I saw that it jumped up about a quarter or half an inch.

"Now heft that barrel," said Elmer.

I did. If there hadn't been another one right behind me, I would have gone overboard backward. I got hold of the top of the cask and gave it a tug, not dreaming I could budge four hundred pounds of heavy grease. But it came away with about the same resistance that an empty cardboard carton would have had.

"What makes weight," explained Elmer, "is gravitons. All molecular matter contains them in various degree. Up to now nobody knew how to extract them. You could only manipulate weight by moving the matter itself. I simply drain most of the gravitons off into the bedrock where it will be out of the way. It's easy because there is a gravitic gradient in that direction."

As an explanation it was a long way from being satisfactory. But there was the barrel, plainly stenciled with its gross weight, and it was now practically weightless. The weight had left as abruptly as a short-circuited electric charge. Moreover, Elmer was shifting his cable from one drum to another, and as he touched each one the truck rose another notch. By the time he was through it rode as high as if there was no load at all.

"I'll use the last one of these drums for power," said Elmer, coiling up his cable and putting it away. Then I saw that he was making a short jumper connection between it and another cable running down under the cab to the hood. He lifted that up and showed me an attachment on the shaft behind the motor. It was a bulbous affair of metal and there were two leads to it. One was the connection to the drum, the other was a short piece of cable that dangled to the ground.

"I call that my Kineticizer," said Elmer. "It is really a gravity motor. It works on exactly the same principle as a water turbine except that it doesn't require the actual presence of the water. The upper cable has more gravitic resistance than the one I use to dump the load. It feeds a slow stream of gravitons to the upper vanes of a steel rotor. They become heavy and start to fall, exerting torque. At the bottom they wipe the ground cable and the moving gravitons simply waste away into the road. Four hundred pounds falling four feet gives a lot of power—especially when you use it all. See?"

Did I? I don't know. It sounded plausible, and anyway Elmer banged down the hood and we climbed back into the cab. That time we started off like a zephyr. There was smooth, silent, resistless power, and the truck being lightened of its load, leaped like a jack rabbit. The gasoline motor was idle. The only noise was the rattling of the fenders and the swish of the air. Breedville began to look more attainable.

After we straightened out on the road, Elmer began to tell me about gravitics.

"It was Ehrenhaft's work with magnetics that got me to thinking about it. Since he was already doing magnetalysis I didn't bother to go along that line. What interested me was the evident kinship on the one hand between electric and magnetic phenomena in general, and between the strong magnetism of electric fields and iron and the relatively weak magnetism of all other substances."

I kept on listening. Elmer's whole theory of gravitics was pretty involved, and in some spots downright screwy. But on the whole it hung together, and there I was riding along on a stream of moving gravitons to prove it. According to the Elmerian doctrine, in the beginning there was chaos and all matter was highly magnetic. It therefore tended to coalesce into nebulae, and thence into stars.

There the fierce pressures and temperatures tended to strip the basic matter of its more volatile outer shells and hurl them outward in the form of radiant energy. Atomic stresses yielded enormous quantities of light and heat and great streams of magnetons and electrons. In the end there is only ash—the cold inert rocks of the planetary bodies. With the exception of the ferric metals none of that ash retains more than a bare fragment of its original magnetic power. Yet even rock when in massive concentration has strong attractive power. The earth is such a concentration, and its pull on the apple was what woke Newton up.

From that concept Elmer dug into the apple itself and into the atoms that compose it. Mass, he claimed, in so far as what we call weight is concerned, is simply a matter of gravitonic coefficient, a graviton being the lowest unit—one more aspect of the atom. It is the nucleus of a magneton, what is left after the outer shells have been stripped away. The graviton is utterly inert and heretofore locked inseparably in the atoms of the substance to which it originally belonged. If only they could be induced to move, their departure would rob the parent substance of nothing except weight, and by moving pure essence of weight potential energy could be turned into kinetic with the minimum of loss.

"It was finding a suitable conductor that stumped me longest," Elmer confessed, "and I'm not telling yet what that is. But as soon as I found it I built this motor. You see for yourself how beautifully it works."

I did, and I saw a myriad of rosy dreams as well. We took Five Mile Hill like a breeze, almost floating over, thanks not only to the silent drive but to the weightlessness of the cargo. I thought of all the massive mountain ranges just sitting in their grandeur with billions and billions of foot-tons of locked-up energy awaiting release. I could envisage hundreds of kineticizer plants around their slopes sending out an abundance of free power. What it did not occur to me to think of was what would happen when those mountains eventually became weightless. What worried me most just then was how the other properties of materials would be affected with alteration of its natural weight.

"Oh, not much," said Elmer. "The relative weights of duraluminum, steel and lead have nothing whatever to do with their tensile strength. I drained off most of the weight of a pan of mercury and tested it. I found that it got a lot more viscous when it was light, a characteristic that is overcome by its normal heaviness. But otherwise it was still mercury. There is an anvil in my barn that weighs less than a toy balloon. If it wasn't kept clamped to the block it sits on, it would soar and bump against the rafters, but as long as I keep it from doing that I can still hammer iron out on it."

We were nearly to Breedville when it began to rain

again. Elmer put up the storm curtains, and I asked
him about how Mr. Peavy was going to react at getting
barrels of grease that were lighter than whipped cream.

"I'm going to take care of that before we get there,"
said Elmer.

I found out what he meant when he pulled up under
a railroad underpass about a mile this side of Peavy's
store. He got out and produced his cable again. This
time he attached it to the face of one of the concrete
abutments that held up the girders carrying the track.
One by one he reloaded the barrels by dead weight
sucked out of the abutment and let it run into the containers on the truck. Again the truck body settled groaning on its springs.

"I'm working on a way to meter this flow more accurately," said Elmer with a grin. "The last load out here
Peavy squawked like everything because the stuff was
light. This time I'll give him good measure. Nobody ever
kicks at getting more pounds than he paid for."

Well, there it was—Elmer's stunt full cycle. No wonder
his gas and tire costs were less than anybody else's in the
business, or that he could set out on a long trip with an
impossible load. He had only to reduce the load to zero,
using part of it for power, and replenish it at the other
end of the line.

We went on to Peavy's, using the wheezy gasoline
motor again. No one at the store saw anything amiss
when we drove up, and though Peavy was careful to roll
each box and drum onto the scale, he made no comment
when he found them markedly overweight. He probably
figured it was only justice from the short-changing he
had had on the delivery before, and on which the oil
company had been adamant as to adjustment. Elmer
then picked up some empty drums and we started back.

The rain was coming down hard by then, and when

we got to the underpass there were several inches of water in it. Elmer stopped long enough to draw off a few more hundred pounds of avoirdupois into one of the empty drums so as to have power for the trip home. He said it was the best place along his route to get needed weight in a hurry.

We started up, but had not gone more than about a hundred yards when we heard a terrific *swoosh* behind us, and on the heels of it a resounding metallic crash and the scream of shearing metal. The ground shook, and a wave of muddy water swept along the road from behind and passed us, gurgling among the wheel spokes.

"What on earth?" yelled Elmer, and stopped the car.

What was behind us was not pretty to see. The concrete abutment we had just left had slid from its foundation straight across the road until it almost impinged on its opposite mate. What had been the earth fill behind it was a mass of sprawling semi-liquid mud. Sodden by days of rain and heavy with water, the fill had come to act like water behind a dam and simply pushed along the line of least resistance. The now practically weightless retaining wall gave way, since there was only friction to hold it where it should be. The two great black steel girders that it supported lay at an awkward angle half in the pit where the underpass had been, half sticking up into the air.

"Gosh," said Elmer, gazing at the spectacle. "Do you suppose I did that?"

"I'm afraid you did," I said. "Maybe concrete don't need weight for strength, but it has to have something to hold it down."

Well, the damage was done, and Elmer was scared. A train was due soon and something had to be done about it. So we drove on to the first farmhouse that had a phone and sent in word about a washout. After that we went on home, Elmer being pretty chastened.

The days that followed were quite hectic. The more the railroad and public utility commission engineers studied the retaining wall's failure, the more baffled they became. The abutment itself was unmarred in the least degree. There was not a crack in it, and only a few chipped places where the falling girders had knocked corners off. Experts chiseled chunks out of it and took them to dozens of engineering labs. The records of the contracting firm that built it were overhauled. The wall was up to specifications and had been thoroughly inspected at the time of construction. The fragments subjected to strains and stresses reacted as they should, having exactly the tensile and compression strength it should have. The mix was right, the ingredients without flaw. The hitch was that the stuff under examination had about the same weight as an equal volume of balsa wood!

Learned treatises began to appear in the engineering journals under such titles as, "Weight Loss in Mature Concretes," "Extraordinary Deterioration Noted in Failure of Concrete Railway Abutment," and so on. Throughout the whole strange controversy Elmer never peeped, and neither did I. I kept silent for several reasons, and only one of them was the fact that I had given Elmer my pledge not to divulge his invention before he gave the word. Mainly I felt that whatever I might tell them would be received as too ridiculous to be believed. After all, people just don't go around sapping idle weight from stationary objects.

The sequel to the incident has to remain obscure. The very ride that let me into the secret proved also to be the cause of my being excluded from it thereafter. I caught a cold that day, and before long it turned into pneumonia. Complications followed, and there were some months when I was confined to a hospital bed. When I was out again and around, my neighbor Elmer had gone, presumably in search of wider fields.

It is a pity that Elmer's unfortunate experience with his earlier invention soured him on the usual channels of development, for I think what happened to him later was that he got into the hands of unscrupulous promoters. For quite a long time after the collapse of the railroad crossing I heard nothing of Elmer himself or his world-shaking discovery. But little bits of news kept cropping up that indicated to me that while Elmer's secret was being kept, it was not getting rusty from disuse, though he lacked the necessary business imagination ever to put it to its best uses.

There was the phenomenal success of Trans-America Trucking, for example. It was significant to me that the Eastern terminus of its main haul was laid out in the bottom of an abandoned rock quarry and its Pacific end in a deep canyon. I thought I knew where the power came from, especially when an oil salesman told me he had tried hard to get the Trans-American contract. They not only refused to buy from him, but he could not find out what company, if any, was supplying them. I also noted that Trans-America was continually embroiled in lawsuits arising from discrepancies in weights. I knew from that that Elmer had not yet solved the problem of metering his weight siphons.

There were other straws that pointed to Elmer's fine hand. Highway engineers along the routes traversed chiefly by his trucks discovered after a time that even the dirt roads over which the trucks ran needed little or no binder. The surface soil was found to be incredibly heavy, like powdered lead, and therefore did not dust away under high-speed traffic. In the course of time it became as hard and compact as the floor of a machine shop where iron chips form the soil.

But eventually there was trouble. Disloyal employees must have stolen lengths of Elmer's mysterious graviton conductor, for there was a story told in some glee of a policeman giving chase to a fleeing man who had a big iron safe on his shoulders! The burglar got away, so for a time Elmer's secret was comparatively safe. And then there was the exposure of what was later known as the spud racket.

One of Trans-America's ex-truckmen, being aware that potatoes were sold by the pound, saw opportunity. He absconded with a length of Elmer's cable and set himself up in the potato business. He was modest at first. The spuds he handled were overweight, but not too much too heavy when he resold them. The dietitians in the big institutions were the first to notice something wrong, for they had analysts to interpret the figures. But greed got the best of the gangster truckman. Not content with his initial ten or twenty percent boosts in weight, he poured on the avoirdupois thicker and thicker. The average housewife began to complain that big potatoes required all her strength to lift.

The day the market inspectors raided the man's storehouse the cat was out of the bag. They uncovered an endless stream of potatoes on a conveyor belt that ran by a bin filled with scrap iron. As each spud passed a certain point it was wiped by a wisp of mineral wool, whereupon the belt beneath sagged deeply and spilled the potatoes onto the floor. Cranes scooped them up and carried them to the packing department.

The subsequent prosecution ran into myriad legal difficulties. There was ample precedent for dealing with short weights, but none for artificially added surplus weight. Chemists sought to prove, once they tumbled to the concept of movable gravitons, that the introduction of ferrous gravitons into a food product constituted a willful adulteration. They failed. The composition of the potatoes was no more altered than is that of iron when temporarily magnetized. In the end the case was thrown out of court, much to the anger of some theologians who had also developed an interest in the case.

That there was at once a spate of laws forbidding the alteration of natural weights was inevitable. State after state enacted them, and the Interstate Commerce Commission began an investigation of Trans-America Trucking, damaging admissions having been made by the potato racketeer. It was the collapse of one of the cliffs at the western terminus of that company that was the straw to break the camel's back. Weight shifting became a federal offense with drastic penalties.

Perhaps collapse is a badly chosen word. The cliff disintegrated, but it did not fall. It soared.

It happened late one afternoon shortly after a heavy convoy arrived from the east. Thousands of tons of weight had to be made up, and the power units of the incoming trucks recharged with still more weight. The already lightened cliff yielded up its last pounds, for it had been drawn upon heavily for a long time. Its stone, being loosely stratified, lacked cohesion, so with sound effects rivaling those of the siege of Stalingrad, it fell apart— *upward*—in a cloud of dust and boulders. The fragments, though stone, weighed virtually nothing, rose like balloons and were soon dispersed by the winds.

Unfortunately the canyon was not far from the most traveled trans-continental air route. Within an hour pilots were reporting seeing what they described as inert bodies floating in the upper air. One of them ran into a stone no bigger than his fist, but since he was making several hundred miles an hour at the time, it neatly demolished one of his wings. That night two stratoliners were brought down, both riddled with imponderable gravel. The debris while lighter than air, still had some residual weight and unimpaired tensile strength.

Congress intervened. Trans-America's charter was voided and its equipment confiscated and destroyed. El-

mer was forbidden to resume business except on orthodox
lines. There was no place in the United States for his
invention.

That should have been the end of the Theory of Gravitics and its unhappy applications. But it was not. For
Elmer had associates by that time who had tasted the
luxury of sure and easy profits, and they were not to be
denied. Rumor had it that it was his shady partners who
took over the financial end and relegated him to his lab
again to hunt for other means of utilizing his kineticizer.
However that may be, the next stage was several years
in incubation. For a time gravitons ceased to be news
except in scientific circles where controversies pro and
con still raged. People had already begun to forget when
Caribbean Power announced itself to the world.

It started operating from a tiny island republic known
as Cangrejo Key. Through oversight, or because it was a
worthless patch of coral sand frequently swept by hurri-
canes, mention of it was omitted in the treaty between
the United States and Spain at the end of the war of
1898. It was still Spanish until the graviton syndicate
bought it from an impoverished Franco for a few millions
in real gold. Whereupon the Cangrejo Commonwealth
was set up as an independent state and a law to itself.

By then they had one valuable addition to their bag
of tricks—Elmer's third great invention. It was a trans-
mitter of beamed radio electric power, and they promptly
entered into contracts with large industries in nearby
America for the sale of unlimited broadcast power at
ridiculously low rates. At first the great maritime powers
protested, suspecting what was afoot and fearing the in-
calculable effects on shipping if Caribbean Power meant
to rob the sea of its weight. But the storm subsided when
the new republic assured them sea water would not be
touched. They pledged themselves to draw only from the

potential energy of the island they owned. So the world settled down and forgot its fears. No matter what happened to Cangrejo Key, there was the promise of abundant cheap power, and at the worst one coral islet more or less did not matter. Even if its sands did float off into the sky as had the canyon wall on the Pacific Coast they could do little harm, the Key being well off the air lanes.

It was a premature hope, for they reckoned without the ingenuity of the men behind the scheme. Soon great derricks reared themselves on the Key and drills began biting their way into the earth. By the time the holes reached eight miles depth the transmission towers were built and ready. Then came the flow of power, immense and seemingly inexhaustible. A battery of kineticizer-dynamos commenced operating, suspended by cables deep into the bowels of the planet, converting the weight that was overhead into kilowatts which were sent up to the surface through copper wires. There it was converted into radio power waves and broadcast out to the customers. It was good, clean power. Industry was grateful.

How deep the syndicate eventually sunk its shafts no one ever knew. Nor how many millions of tons of earth weight were converted into electric energy and spewed out to the factories of the world. But it took only a few years for the project to revolutionize modern economics. With power literally as cheap as air, coal holdings became worthless and petroleum nearly so. In the heyday of the power boom cities like New York went so far as to install outdoor heating units so that in the coldest of cold waves its citizens could still stroll about without overcoats. There was no point in conservation any more. Old Terra Firma had gravitons to burn.

The beginning of the payoff came with the Nassau disaster. The town was flattened by a mighty earthquake, and the attendant tidal wave left little of the Florida coastal cities. When the tremors died down another island of near continental size had appeared. The Bahama Bank had risen above water and then stood from ten to fifty feet above sea level throughout. But there was a rider attached to that dubious blessing. The bed of the Florida Straits had risen correspondingly and the current of the Gulf Stream diminished. Europeans began to worry about the effect of that upon their climate.

Isostatic adjustment was responsible, sober geologists warned darkly. Let the Caribbean Power gang continue to rob that region of its proper weight there would be nothing to hold it down. Adjacent geographical masses would push in to fill the vacuum, just as the underlying, restless, semifluid magma would push up. The time would soon come when mountains rivaling the Himalayas would rear loftily where the Bahama Bank had been and when that day came the other islands about it and the nearby continental areas might well be only shoal spots in a shallowing sea. The Republic of Cangrejo had to go. It was a matter for the new United Nations Court to decide.

Well, that's the story of Elmer Nicklheim's kineticizer as I know it. I am still wondering whether he was with the gang the day the bombers came over and blasted Caribbean Power off the map. If he was, I think he must have been a prisoner, for the gang he at last teamed up with turned out to be an arrogant, greedy lot.

APPOINTMENT ON PRILA

◎◎◎

Bob Shaw

Candar waited for seven thousand years before he saw his second spaceship.

He had been little more than a cub when he saw the first, but the picture was still clear in his mind. It had been a warm, moist morning and his mother and father had just begun cutting through a village of the two-legged food creatures. Candar was quietly watching their great gray bodies at work when he became aware of the ship. It came low, and was traveling so fast that the damp air was compressed into opaque gray clouds inside the shock waves created by its blunt nose. The clouds swirled round it like a tattered cloak so that the ship skipped in and out of visibility, and Candar wondered how anything could move at such a speed and not make any sound.

It was not until after the ship had passed overhead that the sound came, leveling the food creatures' flimsy huts even more efficiently than mother and father could have done. The ship banked sharply, halted high in the morning air and suddenly Candar and his parents were lifted into the sky. Candar deduced that he was caught in some kind of a force field. He measured its frequency, wave-length, intensity, and even discovered that his brain could produce a similar field of its own—but he could not get away. He and his parents were rushed upward to where the sky turned black and Candar could hear the stars and, then, some time later, his mother and father were released. They vanished in a few seconds and Candar, already adapting to the new environment, realized that his parents had been steered into a course which terminated in the Sun. Judging by their agonized struggles as they dwindled from view, his mother and father had performed the same calculation.

The sun shrank, became a star, then much later a double star blossomed and became two egg-shaped suns courting each other in a binary ritual. Ten miles above a planet of black rock which wobbled a precarious orbit between the suns the spaceship let Candar drop. Only by converting his body into miles of springy, hair-thin organic wire did he survive the fall, and by the time he had re-formed his sense organs the ship was gone.

Candar knew that he had been imprisoned. He also knew that on this world which could carry no trace of food he would eventually die, and there was nothing to do but wait.

His new world made its painful run between the two suns every year; each time the black rock melted and ran like mud and nothing survived unchanged but Candar—and it was seven thousand years before he saw his second spaceship.

The thing Surgenor detested most about high-gravity planets was the speed at which beads of sweat could move. A trickle of perspiration could form on his brow and, with a rush like an attacking insect, be down the side of his face and under his collar before he could raise a hand to defend himself. In sixteen years of survey work he had never become used to it.

"If this wasn't my last trip," Surgenor said quietly, "I'd refuse to do any more."

"Can I have time to think about that one?" Voysey, who was on his second trip, kept his eyes on the survey module's controls.

"You've *got* time," Surgenor said. "Everybody on this job has time." He decided to talk about something else. "I'll bet you ten stellars we see the ship from the top of this hill."

"Already!" Voysey became alert and started setting verniers on the range-finder panel.

Already, Surgenor thought. It felt like centuries since the mother ship had set its six survey modules down at the black planet's south pole and ghosted back into the sky to do a half circuit and landing at the north pole. The ship would have completed the journey in half an hour—the men in the modules had had to sweat it out under three gravities for twelve days as their machines zigzagged along the planet's surface. Had there been an atmosphere they could have switched to ground-effect and traveled twice as fast, but even as it was they had made good time.

The car reached the top of the rise and the horizon, which was the line separating starry blackness from dead blackness, dropped away in front and Surgenor saw the clustered lights of the *Sarafand* down on the plain about five miles from them.

"You were right, Dave," Voysey said and Surgenor grinned at the note of respect in his voice. "I think we're going to be first back, too. I don't see any other lights."

Surgenor nodded. Strictly speaking, all six modules

should have been exactly the same distance out from
the *Sarafand* in their respective directions, range in a
perfect circle. During most of the journey the vehicles
had adhered rigidly to the search pattern so that the
data they were transmitting to the mother ship always
reached it from six equally distant, equally spaced points.
Any deviation from the pattern would have caused distor-
tion in the planet map being built up in the ship's computer deck. But each module had an awareness radius
of five hundred miles, with the result that when they
got to within half that distance of the mother ship the
remaining territory was being mapped six times over,
and the job was well and truly finished. It was an un-
official tradition that the last two-hundred-and-fifty-mile
leg of a survey was an out-and-out race for home, with
champagne for the winners and an appropriate salary
deduction for the losers.

Module Five, which was Surgenor's vehicle, had just
skirted a low but jagged range of hills and he guessed
that at least two of the others would have had to go
over the top and lose time. Somehow, in spite of all the
years and light-years, he felt some excitement. It might
be nice to finish his career in Cartographical Service
with champagne.

"Here we go," Voysey said as the vehicle gathered
speed on the downward slope. "A shower, shave and
champagne—what more could you ask for?"

"Well, even if we stick to the alliteration," Surgenor
replied, "there's steak, sex, sleep . . ."

He stopped speaking as the voice of Captain Aesop on
board the *Sarafand* boomed from the radio grill.

"This is *Sarafand* speaking to all survey modules. Do
not continue your approach. Cut your motors and remain
where you are until further notification. This is an order."

Before Aesop's voice had died away the radio silence

that had been observed during the race was broken as startled and angry comments from the other modules crashed from the speaker. Surgenor felt the first cold feather-flick of alarm—Aesop had sounded as though something was seriously wrong. *Module Five* was still churning its way downward into the blackness.

"It must be some kind of mistake," Surgenor said, "but you'd better cut the motor anyway."

"But this is crazy! Aesop's crazy! What could go wrong?" Voysey sounded indignant. He made no move to touch the motor controls.

Without warning, an ultralaser burst from the *Sarafand* splintered the night into dazzling fragments and the hillside lifted skyward in front of *Module Five*. Voysey hit the brakes and the vehicle slid to a halt on the glowing edges of the ultralaser scar. Falling rock hammered on the roof in an irregular, deafening frenzy, then there was silence.

"Aesop's gone mad," Voysey said numbly, almost to himself. "Why did he want to do that?"

"This is the *Sarafand*," the radio blared again. "I repeat. No survey module is to attempt to approach. I will be forced to destroy any other module which fails to obey this order."

Surgenor pressed the button which put him on the air.

"This is Surgenor in *Module Five*, Aesop. You'd better tell us what's going on."

There was a pause, then Aesop spoke again. "Six cars went out on this survey—seven have come back. I need hardly point out that this is one too many."

With a sudden spasm of alarm Candar realized he had made a mistake. His fear stemmed not from the fact that the strangers had deduced his presence, or that they had reasonably potent weapons, it came from the knowledge that he had made such a simple error. The process of deterioration must have gone much further than he had realized.

The task of reforming his body to look like one of the traveling machines had been a difficult one, but not so difficult as the vast cellular reorganization which enabled him to survive when the two suns were overhead. His mistake had been to allow the machine, whose shape he had copied, to come within range of the scanning device aboard the largest machine. He had allowed the small machine to draw away from him while he went through the agony of transformation and then, when he went after it, had become aware of the pulsing spray of electrons sweeping over him. He should have deduced in advance that creatures with the feeble sense organs he had perceived would have striven for something to widen their awareness of the universe. Especially creatures who would take the trouble to build such complicated vehicles.

Candar's alarm faded away as he picked up the currents of fear and bewilderment stirring in the minds of the beings in the machines nearest to him. Minds like these could never present any serious problem—all he had to do was await his chance. He crouched on the cracked surface of the plain, most of the metallic elements in his system transferred to the periphery of his new shape, which was now identical to that of the traveling machines. A small part of his energy was going into producing light which he beamed out in front, and occasionally he emitted bursts of radio waves at frequencies based on the strangers' speech patterns.

He was Candar, the most intelligent, talented and dangerous single entity in the universe; and all he had to do was wait.

The standard intercom speakers fitted in geodesic survey modules were, in spite of their small size, very good.

Surgenor had never heard one overload before, but immediately following Aesop's announcement effective communication was lost in a crashing, skidding roar as every module reacted in surprise or disbelief. A defense mechanism caused him to stare at the speaker grill in mild wonderment while another part of his mind assimilated Aesop's news.

A seventh module had appeared on an airless world which was not only uninhabited but, in the strictest clinical sense of the word, sterile. Not even the toughest known virus could survive when Prila I ran the gamut of its double sun. The cacophony from the speaker quieted abruptly as Aesop came on the air again.

"I am open for suggestions regarding our next move, but they must be made one at a time."

The hint of reproof in Aesop's voice was enough to damp the noise level to a background rumble, but Surgenor could sense a growing panic. The trouble was that operating a geodesic survey module had never become a profession—it was too easy. It was a big-money job that smart young men went into two or three years to raise capital for business ventures, and when signing on they practically demanded a written guarantee that there never would be any interruption in the profitable routine. Now something had gone wrong and they were worried.

Surgenor felt a flicker of anger at his teammates, then remembered that he, too, was getting out. He had joined up seventeen years before, along with two of his space-struck cousins—they stayed for eight years before quitting and going into the plant-hire business. Most of his accumulated salary was in the business with them, but now Carl and Chris had reached the end of their patience. He had to take an active part in the running of the firm or be bought out, which was why he had served notice of resignation. At the age of thirty-six he was going to settle down to a normal life, do a little fishing and golfing, and probably get married. Surgenor had to admit the prospect was not unpleasant. It was a pity that *Module Seven* had had to crop up on his last trip.

"If there is a seventh module, Aesop," Gillespie in *Three* spoke quickly, "another survey ship must have been here before us. Perhaps an emergency landing."

"No," Captain Aesop replied. "The detectors rule that possibility right out. Besides we are the only scheduled crew within three hundred light-years."

Surgenor pressed his Talk button. "Have you checked for some kind of underground installation?"

"The world map is not yet complete but I have run a computer check on all the geognostic data. Result negative."

Gillespie in *Three* spoke again. "I take it that this new module hasn't tried to communicate with the *Sarafand* or with any of the crews. Why is that?"

"I can only surmise it is deliberately mingling with the others to get near the ship. At this stage I can't say why, but I don't like it."

"Well, what do we do?" The question was asked simultaneously by several men.

There was a long silence before Aesop spoke. "I ordered all modules to halt because I do not wish to risk losing the ship, but I realize now that a certain amount of risk must be taken. I can see only three modules and because the search pattern was broken over the last two hundred miles I cannot identify any of you by compass bearing. I will permit all modules to approach the ship to a distance of one thousand yards for visual inspection. Any module attempting to come closer will be destroyed. No warnings will be issued. Commence your approach now."

When *Module Five* drew to a halt a thousand yards from the *Sarafand* the only sign of other vehicles was one distantly wavering light on the plain beyond the big ship. Surgenor watched the light draw near wondering if it was—he hesitated, then applied the label—the enemy.

"I wonder is that it," Voysey said.

"Who knows?" Surgenor replied. "Why don't you ask it?"

Voysey sat motionless for several seconds. "All right. I will." He pressed his Talk button. "This is *Module Five*, Voysey speaking. We are already at the ship. Who is the second module now approaching?"

"*Module One*, Lamereux speaking," came a hearteningly familiar voice. "Hello, Victor, Dave. Good to see you—that's if it *is* you."

"Of course. Who do you think it is?"

Lamereux's laugh sounded slightly unnatural. "At a time like this I wouldn't even like to guess."

Voysey jabbed down on his Talk button, then changed his mind. "I hope Aesop spots a difference and blows this *Seven* to shreds without any talk. Before it makes a move."

"What if it doesn't make a move? It might be happy to do nothing but mix us up." Surgenor unwrapped a sandwich and bit into it—he had planned that his next meal would be a steak on board the mother ship, but it looked as though dinner might be a little late.

"What do you mean about not making a move?"

"Well, even on Earth there are birds that imitate men's voices, monkeys that mimic their actions—and they haven't any special reason for doing it. That's just the way they are. This thing might be a supermimic. Maybe it just turns into the same shape as any new thing it sees without even wanting to."

"An animal that can mimic a forty-foot-long machine?

I believed you about the Drambons, Dave, but this is too much."

Surgenor shrugged and ate more sandwich. He had seen the Drambons on his hundred and twenty-third survey, wheel-shaped creatures on a high-gravity planet who were the opposite of humans and most other beings in that their blood remained stationary at the bottom of the wheel while their bodies circulated. He always had trouble convincing new survey men that Drambons really existed—Drambons and a hundred other equally weird species. That was the trouble with the Instant Distance drive—it was the first form of travel which didn't broaden the mind. Voysey was five thousand light-years from Earth, but because he hadn't done it the hard way, hopping from star to lonely star, he was mentally still inside the orbit of Mars.

Slowly the other vehicles made their appearances on *Module Five*'s viewscreen until there were seven ranged in a circle around the black pinnacle of the *Sarafand*. Captain Aesop had remained silent during the approach maneuvers, but comment from the various crews crashed continuously from the radio grill. Some of the men, finding themselves still alive and unharmed as minute after minute went by, began to relax and make jokes. The jokes died away as Aesop finally spoke from the lofty security of the ship's operations level, two hundred feet above the surface of the plain.

"Before we listen to such suggestions as may be available," he said calmly, "I wish to remind all crews of the standing order not to approach the ship to within one thousand yards. Any module doing so will be destroyed without further warning. You may now," Aesop concluded pleasantly, "proceed with the discussion."

Voysey snorted with resentment. "Coffee and cucumber sandwiches will be served presently! When I get back on board I'm going to take a fourteen-pound hammer to Aesop and smash his . . . He just doesn't *care*."

"Aesop does care," Surgenor said. "He simply isn't demonstrative."

The confident, reedy voice of Pollen in *Module Four* was the first to break the radio silence that had followed Aesop's announcement. This was Pollen's eleventh survey and he was writing a book about his experiences, but had never allowed Surgenor to see the manuscript. Surgenor suspected that it was because he, Surgenor, appeared in it as a laughable, Oldest-Member figure.

"To me, the problem we have here," Pollen began, "appears to take the form of a classical exercise in logic."

"Turn it off, Pollen," somebody interrupted angrily.

"All right, all right. But the fact remains that we can think our way out of this one. The basic parameters of the problem are these: We have six unmarked and identical survey modules and, hidden among them, a seventh machine . . ."

Surgenor pressed his Talk button. "Correction," he said quietly.

"Was that Dave Surgenor?" Pollen said. "As I was saying, there is a seventh machine . . ."

"Correction."

"That *is* Surgenor, isn't it? What do you want, Dave?"

"I just want to help you be logical, Clifford. There isn't a seventh machine—we've got six machines and a very special sort of animal."

"An animal?"

"Yes. It's a Gray Man."

For the second time in an hour, Surgenor heard his radio fail to cope with the demands made on it, and he waited impassively for the noise to subside. He glanced sideways at Voysey's exasperated face and wondered if he, too, had looked like that the first time he had heard. The stories were not widespread, but here and there they cropped up, on worlds where the native radical memory reached far enough into the past. There were distortions upon distortions, but always the theme of the Gray Men and the battle they had waged with and lost to the White Ones. Neither race had left any tangible traces of its existence to be picked up by Earth's belated armies of archeologists, but the myths were still there. And the most significant thing, to one whose ears were in tune, was that—no matter what the shape of the story-tellers or whether they walked, swam, flew, crawled or burrowed—the name they applied to the Gray Men was always their own name for members of their own species . . .

"What's a Gray Man?" It was Carlen in *Two*.

"It's a big gray monster that can turn itself into any-thing it wants," Pollen explained. "Surgenor never travels anywhere without his. He's had it all over the galaxy—that's what started all those old stories."

"It can't turn itself into anything it wants," Surgenor said. "It can only assume any external shape it wants. Inside it's still a Gray Man." There was another roar of disbelief in which Surgenor distinguished the words "Ancient Mariner" several times. "All right," he said with deliberate and typical stolidity. The best way to convince Pollen was to let him convince himself. "You don't have to accept my word, Clifford."

"I know, Dave—the Gray Man will vouch for every-thing you say!"

"Ask Captain Aesop to go through the xenological data stores and estimate the probability of the existence of the Gray Men in the first place, and also the prob-ability that *Module Seven* is a Gray Man." Surgenor noticed that this time there was no laughter and was relieved because, if he was right there was no time for irrelevancies. In fact, there was probably no time at all. The bright double star, which was this world's parent sun, was hanging low in the sky beyond the dim bulk of the *Sarafand* and the distant black hills. In another seventeen months the planet would be threading its way between those two points of light and Surgenor wanted to be far away when that happened—but so did the multi-talented super beast hidden in their midst.

Candar was astonished to find himself listening to the food creatures' mental processes with something approaching interest.

His race had never been machine-builders—they had relied instead on the strength, speed and adaptability of their great gray bodies. On top of this instinctive disregard for machinery, Candar had spent seventy centuries on a world where no artifact, no matter how well constructed, could survive the annual passage through the binary hell. Consequently he was shocked to realize how much the food creatures depended on their fabrications of metal and plastics. The discovery which most intrigued him was that the metal shells were not only a means of transport, but they actually supported the lives of the food creatures while they were on this airless world.

Candar tried to imagine entrusting his life to the care of a complicated and fallible mechanism, but the idea filled him with a vast, unfamiliar dread. He pushed it aside and concentrated all his ferocious intelligence on the problem of getting close enough to the spaceship to seize the minds within. In particular, it was necessary to immobilize the one they called Captain Aesop before the ship's weapons could be brought into play.

Gently, delicately, controlling his hunger, Candar prepared the attack.

Surgenor stared at his hand in disbelief.

He had decided to drink some coffee to ease the dryness in his throat and had begun to reach for the supply tube. His right hand had risen perhaps an eighth of an inch then had dropped back onto the armrest.

Surgenor's instinctive reaction was to bring his left hand over to assist the other, but it, too, refused to move —and the realization came that he was paralyzed.

The mindless period of panic lasted perhaps a full minute, at the end of which Surgenor found himself exhausted from the conflict with his locked muscles. Serpents of icy sweat were making savage downward rushes over every part of his body. He forced himself to relax and assess the situation, discovering as he did so that he still had control of his eye movements.

A sideways glance showed him that Voysey had been caught, too; the only sign of life being a barely perceptible tremor of the facial muscles. Surgenor guessed the phenomenon was new to Voysey. It was the first time Surgenor had ever experienced it at first hand, but he had been on many worlds where animals of prey were able to surround themselves with a blanket field capable of suppressing the grosser neural activities in other creatures. The deadly talent was most often encountered on high gravity planets whose predators were likely to be as sluggish as their victims. Surgenor tried to speak to Voysey but, as he had expected, was unable to direct air through his vocal chords.

He suddenly became aware that voices were still issuing from the communication speaker, and listened for a while before the full significance of the fact dawned on him.

"There isn't much to worry about," Pollen was saying. "This is the sort of exercise in pure logic which is right up your street, Aesop. I would suggest that you lead off by calling out the module numbers in rotation and commanding each to move back a hundred yards. In that way the original six machines will be separated from the seventh, or on one of the commands *two* machines will . . ."

Surgenor swore mentally at his inability to reach his Talk button and cut Pollen off before it was too late, but then the other man's voice was lost in a shrill, discordant whistle of interference. The noise continued with no sign of abating and Surgenor knew with a pang of relief, that *Module Seven* had stepped in. Surgenor tried to relax and found himself thinking clearly. Pollen had been loudly and confidently signing their death warrants by making the, in this case fatal, mistake of confusing the map with the territory.

The situation on the black airless plain glimmering in the viewscreens bore a superficial resemblance to the classical identification problem, and treated on that level Surgenor could see several solutions. Apart from Pollen's standard juggling-with-numbers technique, a more empirical approach would be to have Aesop fire a low-powered burst from a laser rifle at each module in turn. Even if a Gray Man were able to withstand that sort of treatment without flinching, spectroscopic analysis of the light produced would show up compositional differences. Another solution would be to order each module to unship its little inspection-and-repair robot. Surgenor doubted if the alien could cope with a simulation task which involved splitting itself in two.

The deadly flaw in all those solutions was that they employed a process of *elimination*—which was something *Module Seven* would never permit. Any attempt to narrow down the field would only trigger off the final calamity a little earlier. The real-life solution, if one existed, must be capable of instantaneous application, and Surgenor was not at all optimistic about his chances of finding it.

From sheer force of habit he began reviewing the situation, processing his data, then realized the significance of the voices from the communication speaker. Pollen and several others were still able to talk, which probably meant they were out of *Module Seven's* range.

The discovery gave him a momentary lift and Surgenor examined the viewscreens, wondering just how many minutes, or seconds, were left. It was difficult to assimilate the discreet images properly, but he saw that there were two modules not far away to the right, which meant that his own vehicle was part of a loose cluster of three. All the others were much farther away on the opposite side of the circle and as he watched one of them began flashing its lights in a hesitant attempt at Morse. Surgenor ignored it, partly because he had long forgotten the code and partly because he was concentrating on the two nearer machines, one of which would be *Module Seven.* High up on the *Sarafand* lights flickered against the background of stars as Aesop responded in crisp, high-speed Morse. Surgenor almost wanted to laugh— trust Aesop to have the ancient code down pat.

The continuing screech of radio interference was making thought difficult but Surgenor kept doggedly at it. At first he was not sure why it was worth the trouble, then the dim outlines of an incredible idea began to emerge. There seemed to be something inconsistent about . . .

Voysey moved his right hand forward to the control console and started the engines.

For an instant Surgenor thought they had been freed but he found himself still unable to move. Voysey's face was chalk-white and immobile, saliva glistening on his chin, and Surgenor realized he had acted merely as a human servomechanism, controlled by *Module Seven.* Surgenor's mind began to race. This must be it then, he thought, the big moment. The only reason the alien could have for making Voysey activate the motors was that it was planning to move the vehicle to create a distraction for Aesop. Surgenor went numb at the idea—Aesop was not easily distracted, nor would he have any hesitation in vaporizing the first module to cross the invisible thousand-yard line.

Voysey's left hand released the brakes and the vehicle shifted slightly on the uneven ground.

Surgenor made another frantic useless effort to move. But what was *Module Seven's* plan? Its radius of control was limited and it was about to create a diversion, which implied that it was going to get closer to the *Sarafand*. But that meant . . .

The truth seemed to bathe Surgenor's mind in an almost physical brilliance, then new vistas of danger unfolded. I know the truth, he thought, but I mustn't think about it because a Gray Man is telepathic and if I think about it . . .

Voysey's hand thrust hard against the throttle levers and the module dipped forward.

. . . The Gray Man will know that—No, think about anything else, think about the champagne I'm not going to taste ever again; think about the Drambons rolling in their self-contained pools of blood; but don't think about . . . I almost did it . . . I almost thought about . . . I can't help it . . . AESOP!

The distance separating Candar from the spaceship was one that, in a more efficient form, he could have crossed in two bounds. It would take slightly longer this way, but he knew he was too fast to be stopped by anything. He gave full rein to his hunger, letting it drive him on as he leaped forward. Behind him, rather slower than he had expected, the two machines he had taken under control rolled toward the spaceship. One of the food creatures was vainly trying to suppress a thought but there was no time to study its meaning. Changing shape as he went, Candar got safely within control distance and exultantly struck with his brain into the spaceship.

Nothing!

An ultralaser beam hit him with a violence which would have destroyed any other creature in a matter of microseconds, but Candar could not die so easily. The pain was greater than he could ever have expected, but even worse than the agony was his sudden clear look into the minds of the food creatures—those bleak, cold, alien minds.

For the first time ever, Candar felt fear.

Then he died.

The champagne was good, the steak was good, and sleep—when it finally came—would be even better.

Surgenor leaned back contentedly, lit his pipe, and gazed benignly at the group round the table on the *Sarafand's* operations level. During the meal he had reached a decision, and he knew with a comforting glow in his belly that, for him, it was the right decision. He had made up his mind that he *liked* being an Oldest Member figure. Smart young men could go on putting him in their books, his cousins could buy him out of their plant-hire business—he was going to stay with the Cartographical Service until he dropped. It was his life, and he wasn't giving it up.

At the other end of the table, Pollen was making out his notes of the trip.

"The way you see it then, Dave," Pollen said, "is that the Gray Man was simply incapable of understanding the machine building philosophy?"

"That's right. A Gray Man, because of his special physical properties, would have no use for a machine at the best of times. And thousands of years on a planet like Prila I—where a machine couldn't exist anyway—would have conditioned his mind to the point where our machine-orientated lives would have been incomprehensible to him."

Surgenor drew on the fragrant smoke and looked out through the viewscreens to where the brilliant double star hung low in the sky, and he felt an unexpected surge of sympathy for the massive alien being whose remains still lay on the black rock of the plain. Life would have been very precious to a Gray Man, too precious for him ever to consider entrusting it to anyone or anything but himself. That, basically, was why he had made the mistake of trying to control the entity the *Sarafand*'s crew thought of as Captain Aesop.

Wondering how the Gray Man had felt in that last moment of discovery, Surgenor glanced at the discreet identification plate on the ship's central computing installation—that vast artificial intelligence into whose keeping they delivered their lives at the beginning of each survey. The plate said:

A.E.S.O.P.

Surgenor had heard the crewmen guess that the letters stood for Automatic Electronic Spaceship Operating Plant —but nobody was absolutely sure. Human beings, he suddenly realized, tend to take a lot for granted.

HI DIDDLE DIDDLE

Robert Silverberg

The day that Hydroponics Technician Al Mason got his big idea started out just like any other at Lunar Base Three—that is, with a bunch of bloodshot and fuzzy-brained scientists and engineers going through the motions of eating breakfast.

The first meal of the day at Lunar Base Three was never a pleasant proposition. Lunar Base Three was manned entirely by a bachelor staff of American researchers. With no women around at present, and with no stringent curfew laws, the men of Lunar Base Three thought nothing of staging lively bull-sessions that lasted far into the "night"—as late as two or three in the morning, by their arbitrary time-scale.

But there was a very definite reveille bell at half past seven in the morning on that same time-scale, and a very definite time during which the mess contingent served breakfast. So, each "morning," several dozen men gathered, bleary-eyed, after only three or four or sometimes five hours of sleep. Conversation was rarely inspired at the breakfast table of Lunar Base Three; largely a matter of muttered grunts and yawns, pass-me-the-sugar, and vague complaints about the traditional lack of quality of the synthetic food served on the Moon.

Hydroponics Technician Al Mason had been up past three the night before, jawing with a visiting astronomer from Lunar Base One. Just now Mason was as red-eyed and as sleep-befogged as the rest of the men in Lunar Base Three. But an idea was beginning to blossom in his skull, forcing its way upward through the murkiness of fatigue.

"Powdered milk," Mason grumbled, sourly. "Every morning, powdered milk! Thin anemic stuff that no self-respecting calf would sniff twice." He poured himself a glassful and sipped at it glumly.

"If you'd drink coffee in the morning," commented Biochemist Maury Roberts in a waspish tone, "you wouldn't have to grouse about the milk all the time."

"I *like* milk," Mason replied stolidly. "I *don't* like coffee."

"Retarded maturity," remarked Sam Brewster, an Electronics man. "Delayed adolescence. *That's* why you still drink milk!"

Hydroponics Technician Mason was six feet three and weighed two hundred pounds under Earth gravity. It was unlikely that he suffered from any such fixations. He chuckled grimly at Brewster's comment and took another swig of milk. "Go ahead, psychoanalyze me if you want to! But I still like milk, *real* milk, not this ersatz stuff."

The milk pitcher passed round the table. Some of the men were having dry cereal; others liked milk in their coffee. And one thing was evident to all: the synthetic milk *was* getting wearisome. As were all the other synthetic foods, the vegeburgers and the yeast-cakes and the rest. But there was no helping the situation; at this stage

of Lunar exploration, space travel was a costly proposition.
It was more important to devote precious cargo space to
vital instruments than to steaks and chops. The synthetics
weren't as tasty, but they were just as nutritious as the
real goods—and they took up only a tenth as much space
as real food on each Moonbound cargo ship from Earth.

Al Mason leaned sleepily forward, thinking bleakly of
how pleasant it would be to have real food at the base—
not just at Christmas time, when the budget-happy ap-
propriators in Congress relented for the sake of sentiment,
but all the blessed year round. Real food. Good honest
homogenized Grade A.

Mason downed the last of his milk and blinked as the
idea that had been forming all morning suddenly erupted
into the conscious levels of his mind. He started to laugh.
It was a preposterous idea, sure. But he liked it.

Mason looked cautiously over his shoulder at the other
table, where the top brass were breakfasting. Base Commander Henderson was shoveling a synthetic omelet into
his mouth and was thumbing through the early-morning
news bulletins off the Washington ticker, simultaneously.
But Commander Henderson had notoriously sharp ears.
And the C.O. might not care too much for the project
Mason had just conceived. The base's budget was too
skimpy to permit horseplay.

In a low voice Mason said, "I just had a notion—about
synthetic milk, and all."

"Well?" Maury Roberts said. "What is it?"

"Not here," Mason murmured. "Brass might downthumb
it. I'll tell you tonight, after hours. I think we're going to
have some fun."

Al Mason said nothing about his great idea all day. He
let it ripen in his mind. He moved busily and efficiently
through the 'ponics chamber, tending to his chores. The

hydroponics work had to come before anything else, and
Mason knew it.

Eight small domed bases dotted the face of the Moon
in that year of 1995. Three of the bases were American,
three Russian, one Chinese, one Indian. Although the
cold war had long since relaxed, assuming the nature of
a perpetual stalemate rather than a helter-skelter scramble
for destruction, the rivalry among the Moon bases remained keen. American science vied with Russian science
for supremacy, and the men of the Lunar bases knew
they had to work at top productivity all the time.

America's Lunar Base One was a gigantic astronomical
observatory. Lunar Base Two, like its Russian counterpart, was a military installation, complete with a dusty
stockpile of fission-fusion-fission bombs and missiles. Most
civilized peoples of the world preferred not to think much
about America's Lunar Base Two and the Russian equivalent, known as Outpost Lenin.

Lunar Base Three was devoted to basic scientific research. It had been hard to ram the concept of a Base
Three through the minds of the members of the various
Appropriations Committees, and even now Base Three
did not have all the money it needed. But it carried on
valuable research despite the annual harrying it received
at budget time.

The Moon is a natural place for cryogenics research;
cryogenics, therefore, was a major feature of Base Three.
Hydroponics was another important project; as Man's
dominion extended outward into space, it would be increasingly more important to find ways of maintaining a
Terrestrial ecology. Also carried on at Base Three were
high- and low-pressure physics, solid-state work, advanced
chemical research into atmosphere purification, and several dozen other things. There was remarkably little supervision, and no quota of practical results was demanded
—though the men of Base Three were aware that their

base would continue to exist only so long as the United States Government remained in a free-spending mood.

The ambition of every bright young science student in the United States was to qualify for acceptance as a researcher in Lunar Base Three. While in Russia, the cream of the cream was chosen for similar work at Outpost Kapitza in Ptolemaeus Crater.

The working day at Lunar Base Three theoretically ended at 1700 hours. In practice, the men were under their own supervision. They were free to knock off at noon when they wanted to, and were equally free to work clear through till morning reveille if the urge smote them. Responsible-minded people rarely take advantage of such setups. The average work-week among the men of Lunar Base Three was in the vicinity of eighty or ninety hours a week. Occasionally Commander Henderson had to *order* a man to take some time off, for the sake of health.

But there were several recreation-sheds for the benefit of men who wanted to relax for after-hours bull sessions and the like. Hydroponics Technician Mason entered Recreation Shed B about 1900 hours that night, after shutting up shop at the 'ponics chambers.

None of the base's administrative officials happened to be in the shed, for which Mason was grateful. But five of his fellow workers were there—Sam Brewster, Maury Roberts, Len Garfield of Cryogenics, Dave Herst of Chemistry, and Nat Bryan of the Solid-State team.

When Mason walked into the recreation shed he was humming an old nursery rhyme, singing a little of it in an erring basso:

> *Hi diddle diddle,*
> *The cat and the fiddle,*
> *The cow jumped over the moon—*

Sam Brewster put down the microtape he was scanning and said, "Lord, Mason, you really *are* reverting to childhood, eh? Mother Goose, now? What's next?"

"Thumb-sucking," suggested Len Garfield.

"It's those weird chemicals he uses in the 'ponics lab," Maury Roberts offered. "They're operating on his metabolism and reversing the direction of his—"

"O.K., hold it!" Mason said, holding up one big hand for silence. "As some of you birds may possibly remember, I had an idea, this morning."

"Hooray! Mason had an idea!"

Mason glowered at Len Garfield, "Thank you. To continue: at breakfast, while grousing about the food, I thought to myself as follows: I despise this synthetic milk. How can I get some real fresh milk? And the answer came: the only place you can get fresh milk from is a cow."

"A cow? On the Moon?" snorted Sam Brewster.

"You could let it graze in the 'ponics shed," Maury Roberts ventured.

"O.K., wiseguys. Let me finish," Mason said. "Obviously there's no place in Lunar Base Three or anywhere else on the Moon for a live cow—and Earth wouldn't ship one up to us, anyway, not with space freight costs what they are. *But*—we're all trained scientists, I said to myself. We range virtually the entire spectrum of man's resourcefulness, I said to myself. Why not, I said to myself—why not *build* a cow?"

For a moment there was absolute silence in the recreation shed.

"Build a cow?" three men repeated.

Al Mason nodded. "Yeah. Why not? As a kind of recreational project. Of course, the brass might not go for it too much, but we could keep it hush-hush until we got some results—"

"Build a cow?" Garfield said. "Complete, tail and all, and an artificial moo?"

Mason scowled pleasantly. "Cut the kidding. I mean a mechanical device that will produce milk, real milk. I visualize a heap of machinery with an output at one end, not anything that necessarily resembles a cow in anything but function."

Mason looked around. It had taken only a few seconds for the initial shock of the idea to wear off. Mason knew that each of them was beginning to frame blueprints already. Not that they gave much of a damn about getting real milk or not; they had all said often enough that they could get along on synthetic cow-juice in their coffee. But it was the idea that caught them. They were men who didn't need to draw a distinction between work and play. Tinkering, building things—that was both work *and* play for them.

Mason said, "I can't carry this project out by myself. Are you five with me?"

He got five nods, one after another.

"I didn't think you guys would back down from something like this," Mason said. "We can call it Project Bossie. Let's toss some ideas around."

Ideas were tossed. The brainstorming session lasted, as usual, well past the arbitrarily defined Lunar "midnight," and got more heated as it went.

"We understand the metabolism of a cow," Mason said. "We know how a cow produces milk. We know what cow's milk consists of—fat, lactose, protein, water. We know how a cow's digestive system works. So why can't we build a cow ourselves?"

"*I* don't know how a cow's metabolism works," Len Garfield said. "It's not a subject I'm likely to need in Cryogenics work. Maury, will you fill me in?"

The biochemist scratched the back of his neck thoughtfully. "Well, a cow's intake is mostly grass, of course. Which is largely cellulose. The cow grinds the cellulose up and boots it around through its four stomachs. Micro-organisms in the cow's innards break the cellulose down into simpler compounds. Along the way, the stomach contents get fermented, then digested. The cow takes roughage, even sawdust if it has to, and converts it into energy-yielding substances.

"As for the milk—that's manufactured from substances in the cow's blood. A cow's udder has milk-forming cells that secrete milk into alveoli that pass the milk out through a duct, where it collects and is drained off. As Al said, milk's made up of fats, lactose, proteins, plus a lot of water. The fats are the common long-chain variety plus some short-chain fats which are quite unique. It's a pretty clear process. All we need to do is duplicate the chemical reactions that take place all along the way, starting with a cellulose intake that gets broken down eventually into amino acids and short-chain fats. If we match the process step-by-step mechanically, there's no reason why we shouldn't get authentic milk at the other end."

"I can think of a reason," Sam Brewster said. "A cow's udder is one devil of a complicated affair. If you're expecting me to build a mechanical duplicate of a filter system that precise, let me tell you right now that I'm not guaranteeing results in less than ninety years."

"That's the one part of the system that doesn't need to be mechanical," Maury Roberts said. "I agree, building a filter to draw milk out of the system is beyond our ability —but we can always hook a *real* udder into the system to handle the output."

"Eh?" Brewster said. "Where are you going to get—"

"I've *got*," Roberts said. The biochemist grinned. "I suspect you knew about this, Al—didn't you?"

Mason nodded. "Maury has quite a collection of tissue extracts sitting in his deep freeze for biological research.

Including, so I've learned, a couple of snips of tissue from a cow udder."

"It wouldn't be any trouble at all to borrow a few cells from that test tube," Roberts said. "Set up an incubator, grow the cells in a protein nutrient bath. They'll grow indefinitely, doubling every forty-eight hours or so. In hardly any time at all we'll have enough udder tissue to extract all the milk we want."

"That takes care of the output, I suppose," Nat Bryan said. "But how about these symbiotic microorganisms that take part in the digestive process? You don't have any of *those* in the deep freeze!"

"We'll synthesize 'em," Dave Herst said. "Over at our lab we can whip up an enzyme to do most any job. You just tell me what's needed, Maury, and—"

"*I* know what's needed," Sam Brewster objected. "We need a whole slew of equipment. What we're building amounts to a still that yields milk instead of booze, and we're going to need plenty of hardware for it."

"We'll pinch it," Mason said quietly. "Item by item. Nobody's going to squawk if we requisition a few yards of tubing or a couple of metal vats for our work. The trick is not to be too conspicuous."

He saw by the sly looks on their faces that they were completely hooked. There hadn't been a really good gag at Lunar Base Three in a couple of months, not since a computer man had programed one of the heavy-duty robot drudges to give hotfoots.

They continued far into the night, raising possible objections and squelching them, putting forth suggestions and ideas. About three a.m. they decided they had had it for the night. It was going to take plenty more jaw-thinking before they could begin on the schematics. But the general concept was clear already: a mechanical duplication of the bovine digestive system, coupled with a tissue-culture-grown mammary gland at the output.

The next morning at breakfast they were their usual uncommunicative selves, as might be expected after four hours of sleep. After breakfast and before starting work for the day, Mason paid a visit to the office of Base Commander Henderson and formally applied for permission to use one of the base's vacant labs.

Henderson glanced over the filled-out application form and said, "Are you branching out, Al?"

"I've got an idea, sir. I want to give it a try."

Henderson smiled. "That's what we're here for—to give things a try. Care to tell me about it?"

Mason's face reddened slightly. "If it's all the same, sir, I'd prefer to keep it under my hat. At least until I see if it works out, anyway."

Henderson said, "I suppose that's O.K. here." His eyes narrowed. "Ah . . . this project of yours isn't going to involve a change in the budget, is it?"

"No, sir. Any equipment needed will be covered by present appropriations."

"I'm glad to hear that," the C.O. said in a tired voice. "The people in Washington are snapping at my heels, Al. They want to peel five or ten or fifty million off our budget for the next fiscal year, and the way things are happening on Capitol Hill these days they may very well succeed. So this isn't the time to begin any ambitious or expensive new projects. We may be lucky just to hold the *status quo* here, after Congress gets through with our appropriation for next year."

"I understand, sir. But I don't think this is going to be very expensive. It's just—well, call it a sideline, sir."

Henderson smiled. "Very well, Al. Permission granted."

Mason thanked him, stepped outside, and called Maury Roberts at the Biochemistry Unit. He said, "Everything's O.K. The old man is letting us use Room 106a."

"Swell. I've got the udder-tissue out of the storage freeze, and I just popped it into the nutrient bath. And last night after we split up I worked out a diagram blocking out the cow's digestive system unit by unit. We can use that as our jump-off point."

"Right. See you later," Mason said happily.

The six men spent the first week doing mouthwork—throwing out ideas, pulling them apart, putting them back together. It was a week of bickering and haggling, a week of bantering and chaffing. But it was also a week of results. By the end of the week they had a reasonably operational plan. There was plenty of disagreement, of course, but that only added spice to the project. There were long hours of completely irrelevant hairsplittings and side-issues—but, somehow, the irrelevancies turned out to be relevant after all, later on.

Meanwhile, the bit of tissue in the Biochem lab grew . . . and grew . . . and grew. Cells nourished by benevolent proteins and warmed by the incubator divided, and divided again. By the end of the first week, the cells formed a visible spot on the surface of the nutrient base.

Sam Brewster worked up a set of blueprints for electronically-controlled feeder mechanisms. Dave Herst quietly worked out a few of the problems of enzyme synthesis. Mason co-ordinated. Slowly, over a couple of weeks, the contradictory ideas of six men turned into one master plan—Project Bossie.

The first installations went into place in the fifth week of the project—four massive copper kettles, linked by plastic tubing. The kettles represented the four stomachs of a cow. Sam Brewster rigged a force-pump to keep the digestive products moving along the system. The pump, like the kettles, came out of the base's excess stores, on special requisition. Nobody asked any questions.

A fifth kettle was added, and a sixth, and a seventh,

as the project continued. Work was carried on, generally, in after-hours time; none of the cow-builders was foolish enough to neglect his own specialty during the day.

After the seventh week, it started to become apparent that duplicating the innards of a cow was not a simple matter of rigging a continuous flow-line. There were all sorts of complications.

Some of the artificial enzymes reacted unfavorably with others; it became necessary to devise an intricate enzyme-injection scheme to maintain proper digestive control. The acetic acid produced in one of the four stomachs as part of the process had unhappy effects on some of the tubing, which had to be replaced. A complex and expensive centrifuge had to be surreptitiously snaffled from Maury Roberts' biochemistry section and introduced into the works to separate the digestive products properly, in the absence of the simple hormones that took care of that job in a cow.

Toward the ninth week of the project, glimmers of light began to show. But a new cloud appeared on the horizon that week. And a quite unexpected thunderbolt descended.

The first word arrived one morning in the mess hall. One of the signal-room orderlies entered the mess hall, snapped to attention in front of the rear table where the top brass ate, and plunked a yellow message sheet down in front of Base Commander Henderson. Henderson's immediate profane outburst silenced all conversation. The Base Commander rose and looked around the mess hall. His face drooped in a dark scowl.

In somber tones he said, "Gentlemen, I hate to ruin your meal like this, but I have some bad news that might as well be shared with the entire staff." He chewed at his lower lip for a moment—a sign, everyone knew, not so much of nervousness as of smoldering anger. "As you may know but probably don't care, this is an election year down below in the States. Ten months from now a lot of congressmen and senators are going to lose their jobs, unless they can convince their constituents meanwhile that they deserve to hold office for another term. So this is the time of year when senators and congressmen go junketing all over hither and yon, trying to dig up scandals and such.

"To come to the point, gentlemen: I've just received work that the next cargo ship from Earth, which is due here in twenty-seven days, is bringing us three senators and three representatives. They're coming up to investigate our operations here."

When Al Mason and his five cohorts gathered in Laboratory 106a that night for their regular session of work on Project Bossie, they all wore sheepish, abashed expressions —the sort of look a man might wear if he picked up a kitten to stroke it and abruptly discovered he was clutching a tiger by the tail.

"Well," Mason said, surveying the imposing array of gadgetry which was Project Bossie. "I knew it was too good to last. Senators! Congressmen!"

"Dirty snoopers," Sam Brewster muttered.

"We'll have a fine time explaining *this* to them," Nat Bryan said, waving a hand at the installation. "How will they understand that we were just having a little fun?"

"Fun," Maury Roberts said morosely. "Congressmen don't think scientists are *supposed* to have fun. We're supposed to be deadly serious characters who speak in four-syllable words interspersed with equations. If they find out I hooked a nine hundred dollar centrifuge just for fun, they'll—"

"And a hundred bucks' worth of relays and transistors," Sam Brewster said.

"And an incubator for that udder," added Dave Herst.

"And all these kettles, and the tubing," Len Garfield said. "The flow-meters, the pipelines, the refrigeration unit—"

"So?" Al Mason demanded loudly. "Are you guys voting to pull out?"

"No, but—"

Mason cut into Sam Brewster's reply. "No, but what? Do you want to break the project up and return all this stuff to the stores? That way the investigating committee will never find out what we've been up to. And we can tell Henderson that our project was a failure and we disbanded it."

"But it's not a failure," Dave Herst said vehemently. "Another month and we may have the whole thing licked! We can't give up now, Al."

"O.K., then," Mason said. "Stop worrying about congressmen. When they come, we'll just suspend operations in here and hope they don't ask any questions. We're too deep into this thing to give up now. Yes?"

"I'll go along with you, Al," Nat Bryan said.

"Same here," put in Dave Herst.

The others agreed. Project Bossie was not to be discontinued. Work would proceed.

Work proceeded. The tissue-culture udder had now reached functional size, and one night it was transported from the Biochemistry Unit to Lab 106a, incubator and all, and hooked into the system. It was the eleventh week. It was now possible to introduce waste cellulose at the intake of the artificial cow and have it pass through the four "stomachs" to be broken down into the desired products. The result was synthetic blood from which the udder could extract milk. Mason computed that three hundred quarts of such blood would be needed to produce a quart of milk. It wasn't a bad ratio, but they determined to improve on it.

Other unforeseen hitches developed. The first batch of milk that was produced, in the twelfth week, was vile stuff, about sixty per cent fat and fifteen per cent protein; it looked curdled the moment after it appeared, and rapidly got worse. It was discovered that the bleeder-lines at the final stage of the digestive process were faulty; glucose and galactose were being held back, too much fat admitted. The men went to work on this problem.

They solved it. But the solution involved rigging a new and elaborate system of tubing. The synthetic cow was taking on frightening aspects by this time. Dimly discernible beneath the network of pipes and tubes and stopcocks were the original four kettles of the digestive system. But now the apparatus took up virtually every square inch of floor space in Laboratory 106a. It sprawled toward the four corners of the room and up to the ceiling.

A new flaw was discovered: a vital liver secretion was missing, causing difficulties in the process of fat digestion. A cow's milk has no more than four per cent fat in it; they were unable to lower the fat percentage below twenty-five per cent. Some quick research produced the reason. But a week of fruitless labor told them that it was going to be an enormous task to duplicate mechanically the necessary organ of secretion.

The project tottered on the brink of failure.

Nat Bryan made a suggestion: "We have a real udder. How about a real liver, too?"

Maury Roberts prowled through the inventory of the Biochem unit and discovered liver tissue in cold storage. The next day, a second incubator was in use; Roberts was busy growing a cow liver. It was either that or abandon the project.

Day by day the cells proliferated. The udder, meanwhile, was doing splendidly, and had to be trimmed back every three days to keep it from growing unlimitedly.

Success was approaching.

But so, unfortunately, were the congressmen.

They arrived right on schedule, 0900 hours on the 28th of January, 1996. There were six of them, as advertised. The total mass of the six legislators and their belongings was better than thirteen hundred pounds, and therefore that much useful equipment had to be displaced on the cargo ship. As Commander Henderson mournfully explained, there would be no new supply of reading-tapes this month, nor any shipments of beer. A small comptometer requisitioned by the astronomers in Base One had been left over till next time, too. It couldn't be helped; the legislators had a right to visit the Lunar installations if they chose.

The morning of the delegation's arrival, each man in Base Three found a mimeographed memo waiting for him on his breakfast plate:

TO: ALL STAFF

FROM: BASE ADMINISTRATOR HENDERSON

SUBJECT: VISITORS

DESTROY AFTER READING

At 0900 today the ferry-ship is bringing us six members of Congress. They will be quartered at Base Three for the next ten days, before moving over to investigate the other bases. They are to be treated with utmost respect while they are here! I'm not joking. These boys can cut us off without a nickel in next year's budget.

Normal routines are to prevail. I don't intend to put on a special taut-ship demonstration for their benefit. But try to keep things tidy, and avoid any conspicuous material extravagance that might be tough to explain. Remain friendly, answer questions if they're asked, and in

*general try to show them what a live-wire job we're
doing for Joe Taxpayer down there in the States.*

*Make a special effort to keep our visitors from blunder-
ing into high-voltage lines, walking outdoors without helmets and suits, and stuff like that. The publicity would
be very very doubleplus ungood if something happened
to one of our guests.*

*And remember—they aren't going to be here forever,
even if it seems that way. Only ten days.*

Al Mason put down the memo sheet and peered owl-
ishly at his mess-hall neighbor, Sam Brewster. "*Avoid any
conspicuous material extravagance that might be tough
to explain!*" he quoted. "Talk about locking the barn
door too late! We have *already* been extravagant, and
I'd hate to have to explain."

"If the C.O. ever pokes his nose into 106a," Brewster
said, "we're going to *have* to explain. You better start
thinking up something convincing, Al."

Mason didn't say anything. He grinned palely and
took a long, deep, unsatisfying slug of his synthetic
milk.

The senators were quartered in the Administration hut,
while the congressmen had to put up with accommodations
in one of the storage shacks. They were old men, the
six of them—the youngest couldn't have been much less
than fifty-five—and they just *loved* the low gravity. But
from the first hour, when they glanced beady-eyed
around the base as if looking for their first target, it was
evident to all hands that a real going-over was in the
cards.

The six members of Project Bossie decided that for
the nonce it was best to keep out of Laboratory 106a
for the next ten days, except for performing routine
operations necessary for maintenance of the complex contraption. There would be the deuce to pay if the in-

vestigating committee ever caught on. For one thing, the installation had become immense. For another, better than ten thousand dollars worth of good equipment had been sidetracked into the project by this time, along with a good many man-hours of highly skilled time. It would be unwise in the extreme to let the visitors find out that six men, without the knowledge of the Base Commander, had squandered so much time and energy and money for anything so frivolous as the production of milk—and just for the fun of it.

So Mason and his fellow conspirators entered Laboratory 106a at odd hours just to keep things running—mostly to keep an eye on the nutrient bath that supported the rapidly sprouting liver tissue. The udder was doing fine.

It didn't take long to learn who were the legislators to watch out for. Representative Claude Manners was the fiercest ogre of the lot—a crusty New Englander from, of all places, Mason's home state of New Hampshire. Representative Manners regarded any sort of governmental expenditure with horror. He persisted in wandering around the base asking, in a thin and insistent voice, "Yes, but what *practical* use does this have?"

On the senatorial side, the hardest to deal with was Senator Albert Jennings of Alabama. Senator Jennings' favorite questions were, "Can't this project really be dispensed with?" and "Let me see the cost figures on this equipment, please."

It was trial by budget. Base Three was fidgety and tense. Al Mason began to wish he had never thought of building a synthetic cow. It was only a matter of time before the secret would be out.

And they were so close to the finish, too. Everything had seemed to check out at the last examination. The liver was thriving now—in fact, it was threatening to outgrow its space allotment, and Maury Roberts had to lower the incubator temperature in order to inhibit the organ's boundless growth. The rest of the system was in working order. If only those snoopers would leave the Base, Mason thought, so we could run the final tests—

On the fourth day after the arrival of the congressional commission, Al Mason was engaged busily in tidying up his hydroponics lab, in anticipation of a visit from Representative Manners later in the day, when his office phone rang.

He picked it up. "Hydroponics. Mason speaking."

"Al, Commander Henderson here. Think you can stop off at my office for a few minutes?"

"I suppose so, sir. You mean, right now?"

"Yes. Right now, if you're free." The commander's voice sounded oddly tense. Mason hung up, told his assistant he was leaving, and headed for Commander Henderson's office on the double.

The C.O. looked worried. His face was drawn and weary. The visit was telling on his nerves more than anyone's.

He said, in a ragged voice, "Al, about an hour ago I took the guests on a tour of the north end of the base. They came across Laboratory 106a."

Oh, oh, Mason thought sickly. "Yes, sir?"

Henderson flashed a faint smile. "That's quite an installation you've been building in there, Al."

"It *is* rather complex," Mason admitted.

Henderson nodded. The corners of his mouth quirked. "Ah—some of our guests were very interested in it. They wanted to know what function it performed. That's what Representative Manners asked me particularly—what function it performed."

"Function, sir?" Mason repeated lamely.

"Yes. Function." The commander stirred uneasily. "I . . . ah . . . told them it was being used for biological research. They wanted me to be more specific, and I kept getting vaguer, and finally I had to admit that I didn't know *what* the damned pile of equipment was supposed to do! So I'm in a bit of hot water now, Al. They seem to have the idea that a Commanding Officer should be aware of every single project being carried on at his base."

Mason moistened his lips. He said nothing.

The commander continued, "With luck, I can wiggle out of this without too much trouble. But it may turn out to be very damaging. Tell me, Al—just in case they bother me about it again. What *is* that thing you've been constructing in 106a?"

Mason took a very deep breath. When he spoke, his voice came out thin and feeble. "It's a cow, sir."

The commander's double-take was admirably brief. He recovered equilibrium almost at once and said, "Let's have that again?"

Mason smiled humorlessly. "It's . . . uh . . . a device for processing cellulose and converting it to nutritive products, sir. Milk, to be precise."

Henderson was nodding slowly. "A cow. I see, Al. You built a machine that produces milk."

"Yes, sir. It's not quite finished, yet."

"Tell me: *why* did you feel it necessary to build such a machine?"

"Well . . . uh . . . it was sort of just for fun, sir. A recreational project. Only we didn't think it was going to use so much equipment, you see, and—" Mason saw the look in Henderson's eyes, and his voice trailed off.

"O.K., Al," Henderson said in a rigidly controlled voice. "You built it for fun. Well, I'm a mild-tempered man. I won't get sore. Just scram, over to the 'ponics chamber, and get to work. If anybody asks you, that thing in 106a is a biological converter. Make up some fancy double-talk. Whatever you do, *don't* let any of those congressmen find out that you built that expensive junk pile for the sheer joy of building it. Or that it's intended to produce milk. We'll never hear the end of this, if they catch wise."

"Yes, sir."

"O.K. Now *get*."

Mason got.

The hydroponics man stepped out of Henderson's office and almost collided with Maury Roberts. The little biochemist started talking at once.

"I'm on my way over to 106a, Al. Bryan just stuck his nose in there and told me that the liver tissue is growing like crazy. I'll have to trim it back and dispose of the excess . . . Al, is there something wrong?"

"Yeah."

"You look terrible!"

"I *feel* terrible." Mason jerked his thumb back in the general direction of the Administration hut. "The Old Man just had me on the carpet. Seems the visitors snooped their way into the Project Bossie lab this morning and wanted to know what all the hardware was being used for."

"*No!*"

"Yeah. Well, the C.O. didn't know, so he bluffed them. But he doesn't know how long they're going to be satisfied with his bluff."

"Al, this is terrible! What's going to happen?"

Mason shrugged. "Henderson'll probably wiggle out of it, but you can bet he'll come down hard on us once the visitors are gone. He wasn't at all amused by the whole idea."

"What are we going to do?"

"Nothing," Mason said. "Just keep going through the motions. You go over to the lab and trim that liver, if you want to. I've got to get back to work."

Roberts took off for Laboratory 106a at a quick trot. Mason sauntered morosely across the clearing. He stopped, stared up through the vaulting plastic roof of the dome at the night-shrouded Earth that hung in the sky.

Who needed these senators anyway? he asked himself.

Snoopers. Pennywise meddlers. But they were necessary evils, Mason admitted reluctantly. Only now the C.O. was in trouble, and it was a sure bet that once the delegation from Washington had left, there would be merry hell raised around Base Three. Creative independence was one thing; funneling all kinds of costly equipment into a silly enterprise like a synthetic cow was different. And if the truth ever leaked to the Appropriations Committee—

Mason shuddered. He admitted that the cow *had* gotten somewhat out of hand. But it had simply turned out to be a more complicated job than they had expected, that was all.

Then he frowned. What had Roberts been trying to say? The liver was growing; so he would have to trim off the excess and dispose of it—

Wait a minute!

What Maury Roberts was trimming away was good edible meat. And if the machine could produce meat *and* milk—heck, Mason thought, it isn't as useless as it seems! We don't need to skulk and hide! We've invented something downright handy! But—

A sudden cry interrupted his train of thought.

"Hey, Al! Come here!"

Mason turned slowly. The door of the mess hall was open, and Rolly Firestone, Cook First Class, was standing in the opening, arms akimbo. Firestone was grinning.

"What is it, Rolly?" Mason grunted.

"Got something for you. Something you'll like, Al."

Shrugging, Mason walked over. Firestone's green eyes were alight with some secret glee. Crooking one finger, he led Mason through the mess hall and into the kitchen.

"You wait here," Firestone said.

Mason wondered impatiently what the cook was up to. But he had only a moment to wait. Firestone busied himself at the back of the kitchen and returned almost immediately holding a glass containing a white liquid.

"You're the one who's always been griping about the synthetic milk," Firestone said. "So I figured I'd give you a little treat. Just don't get me in trouble for it."

Mason took the glass. He sniffed. It smelled like milk. It looked like milk.

"Go on," Firestone urged. "Drink it."

Mason took an experimental sip, then another, and then a hefty gulp. It *was* milk. And not synthetic, either. This was the pure authentic article, unadulterated, homogenized, creamy and rich to the taste. Milk.

"Where in blazes did you get it?" Mason demanded. It couldn't possibly be a product of the unfinished milk-still; in any event, Firestone knew nothing about the project. But where else, Mason wondered, could real milk have come from on the Moon?

The rotund cook said, "It's Representative Manners' private stock. I figured he could spare you a glassful or so. He must have brought five or ten gallons up from Earth with him."

Mason's jaw dropped. "He brought . . . five or ten . . . gallons . . . of milk?"

Firestone nodded amiably. "And, me knowing how much you went for the stuff, I figured I'd invite you in here for a little sip of it on the sly—"

"But why . . . why did he bring milk with him?"

"He's got stomach ulcers," the cook confided. "He's on a milk diet. Drinks quarts and quarts of the stuff every day, hardly eats anything else. It's a nuisance, I tell you, keeping that milk of his under refrigeration and dishing it out to him. But the commander says we gotta cater to those birds, and so I give 'em the best treatment. You ought to hear the rest of them grumble about the synthetic foods!"

Mason shrugged. "It's their own fault they have to eat synthetics up here," he said, "We eat ersatz because the budget doesn't allow for anything else."

"Yeah," Firestone said. "*You* try to tell them that!"

"Me?" Mason asked. He grinned broadly, making his face a little uglier, and finished off his milk. "I just work here, Rolly. I'm not looking for any trouble. Well, thanks for the milk, old man."

"Just don't tell anyone I let you have some."

"I'll keep mum," Mason promised.

During the next couple of days, Mason and his buddies paid a few surreptitious visits to the Project Bossie lab, for maintenance purposes. One innovation was put into effect: the surplus growth from the liver tissue was no longer inhibited nor discarded, but now was carefully trimmed away and refrigerated. As Mason explained, it was perfectly edible meat, and there was no sense in letting it go to waste. As soon as the Washingtonites were gone, they would turn the meat supply over to Rolly Firestone with much fanfare. Some real meat would be a vast improvement over algae steaks.

Just before dinner call on the sixth day of the visit, Al Mason was on his way to quarters to wash up when Rolly Firestone intercepted him in the clearing.

"Al, can I talk with you for a minute?" the little cook whispered.

"Sure. What's up?"

"Remember the milk I gave you a couple of days ago? Representative Manners' milk?"

"Yeah," Mason said. "What about it?"

Firestone looked terrified. "You didn't tell anyone I let you have some, did you?"

"Of course not. You don't think I'd say anything that would get you in trouble, Rolly?"

Firestone said in a low voice, "If anyone ever finds out that I left you have Manners' milk, Al, I'll be drawn and quartered by Henderson."

"Huh? What for?"

"Because," Firestone whispered, "I just had a peek in Manners' milk container. It's practically empty. All gone. Guzzled completely and utterly. Manners has enough left for tonight, but come breakfast-time there'll be a rumpus."

"But he brought gallons, you said. How could he run out of milk?"

"He didn't keep track of how much he was drinking," said Firestone. "And who was I to tell him he was using it up too fast? Anyway, I wasn't paying attention. So he was ordering milk every time his stomach gave a twitch, five, six, seven times a day, and now there isn't any more."

Mason laughed. "I like that. The congressman who's so eager to cut everybody else's appropriation can't even budget his own milk supply!"

"It isn't funny, Al! Manners will raise the roof over it, and you can bet he isn't going to admit it's his own fault!"

"Have you told Henderson yet?"

"No. I'll let him know after dinner. But remember, not a word about the glass I slipped you, or I'm done! They'll accuse me of having given his milk to all the men!"

"Don't worry, Rolly. I'll stick by you." Mason chuckled

happily. A lovely idea was forming. He wondered if they could handle the job in time.

For the first time since the arrival of the Washington visitors, real work went on in Laboratory 106a after hours. The lab lights were on right through the night, as the members of Project Bossie labored fiercely to iron out the final bugs in their system.

Toward morning, the last hitches were straightened away. Mason and his cohorts stood back, proudly surveying the monstrous device that almost completely filled Laboratory 106a. A bale of waste paper—to supply cellulose in the absence of grass—stood stacked near the intake. A receptacle waited at the far end of the room. In between was a spiderweb of pistons and rods, pipes and tubes, stopcocks and flow-meters and vats of chemicals—with the two organic components of the device, the culture-grown liver, and milk gland, occupying positions of prominence.

"O.K.," Mason said. "Let's try her out."

Maury Roberts and Nat Bryan stuffed the waste-paper bale onto the intake platform, while Sam Brewster's hand hovered over the electronic keyboard that controlled the entire operation. He thumbed a switch. The machine hummed. The bale of paper moved ponderously forward, into the jaws of the shredders.

From there the shredded cellulose proceeded to the first stomach to be mangled and pulped into a soggy semiliquid; then on to the second stomach for further breaking-down, then to the wringer in the third stomach, then to the fourth, where digestion proper could begin. Translucent feed lines spurted enzymes into the system at the properly programed intervals. Counters clicked; gears meshed. The effect was imposing.

According to Mason's computations, the process, vastly accelerated over its natural counterpart, would take about three hours from waste-paper to milk. The time was 0540 hours when the first few drops of yield came filtering through the udder. At 0650, after Maury Roberts had run some quick chemical tests and after the yield had been refrigerated, the six bleary-eyed experimenters gravely toasted each other with milk that was milk to the last decimal point.

Shutting up shop, they left—five of them to try to catch some rest before the bonging of the reveille bell half an hour hence. But Al Mason had an errand to run. He stepped out into the cool breeze of the artificial morning and headed for Commander Henderson's office.

Henderson always rose at least an hour before reveille. Mason saw his office lights on. He opened the door and found himself staring at Major Chalmers, Henderson's aide-de-camp.

"Good morning, Major," Mason said briskly.

"Morning, Mason."

"The commander busy?" Mason asked. "I'd like to talk to him for a minute, if I could."

"I'm afraid he *is* busy," Chalmers replied. "Maybe you'd better try later—around noon, maybe."

From within came a loud expostulatory outburst in Commander Henderson's voice. "I tell you, Donovan, I have to have milk for Manners! He's going to find out in half an hour that his supply is gone, and then he'll howl loud enough to be heard on Mars. No, I can't tell him that it's his own fault for drinking it up too fast! Would *you* tell a man like Manners something like that?"

Mason grinned at Major Chalmers. "What's all *that* about?"

Chalmers said dourly, "Seems Representative Manners has ulcers, and he's on a milk diet. He brought his own milk supply along with him, but he didn't figure consumption right, and Rolly Firestone discovered yesterday that the milk's all gone. Manners can't eat anything else, he refused to touch the powdered milk, and the C.O.'s been on the wire with Earth all night, trying to get them to O.K. a special shipment-rocket for Manners."

"But it would take four days for any rocket to get here," Mason said.

"You see the pickle we're in, Mason. So be a good fellow and go away, until—"

"No," Mason said. "Look, sir, could you get me in to see Commander Henderson right away?"

"Of course not. I told you, he's on the wire to Earth!"

"Who cares about that? Tell him I can get him milk. *Real* milk!"

"You—what? Listen, Mason, this is no time for funny business."

"I know," Mason said. "But I can supply milk. M—I—L—K. Will you tell the commander that?"

"Don't try to make fools out of us," Chalmers warned.

Mason uttered a brief cry of disgust and deftly side-stepped the startled Chalmers. He pushed his way into Commander Henderson's office. The C.O. was bent over his communication panel, speaking loudly into the mike.

He looked up and barked, "Get out of here, Mason. I'm on the line to Earth!"

"I know, sir. You can hang up. I know what you're calling for. I just want to tell you that the synthesizer is working, sir. We have milk for Representative Manners!"

"*What?*" Henderson's eyes widened astonishingly. He muttered something into the microphone and broke the contact with a brusque gesture. "You mean that crack-brained scheme of yours actually worked? That thing in 106a gives *milk?*"

"Yes, sir. And liver, too. We got it working last night."

Mason repressed a yawn of exhaustion. "If you like, sir, you can have some milk for Representative Manners."

In due time the congressional delegation departed, on the February ship from Earth. And the month sped by, until it was time for the March ship.

Commander Henderson sent for Mason after the cargo of the March ship had been unloaded.

The commander spread some microfilm transcripts out on his desk. "An excerpt from the *Congressional Record*. Listen: this is Representative Manners speaking.

"'. . . *I am deeply impressed with the resourcefulness and cleverness of the scientists at Lunar Base Three. Compelled by the exigencies of nature to subsist on synthetic foods they have shrewdly and economically devised means for creating virtual duplicates of certain Terran foods. My colleagues and I, after several days of subsistence on normal synthetic foods, were delighted one day to be greeted with milk and meat which seemed undeniably Terrestrial in origin—only to be shown, after the meal, how these commodities were produced, virtually magically, by means of a startling technique termed biochemical transmutation. Milk and meat created from waste paper! And at remarkably low cost! A triumphant example of Yankee ingenuity at its finest—*'"

Henderson paused and looked up. "Manners' style is on the flowery side, so I won't read any more."

"I guess we impressed him," Mason said.

"I guess so. Producing those quarts of milk really bowled them over—and saved Manners' face, too. And the liver made a real hit with them. We're getting ten million tacked onto our appropriation for '96-'97."

"I'm glad to hear that, sir."

Henderson smiled. "I still haven't apologized for getting sore when you told me what the gadgetry was for."

"Apologies aren't necessary, sir."

Henderson shook his head. "They are, Al. You were having fun, and I roasted you for it—but I should have known that your kind of fun gets results. Now, thanks to your fun—which I should have known is the essence of fundamental research!—we've solved a major problem of life on the Moon. We have a meat-and-milk synthesizer. It's a little cumbersome, perhaps, but—"

"I was meaning to talk to you about that, sir. We . . . ah . . . have a new model in the works. It's a little more streamlined—a lot smaller, and a better yield. But it's going to need some tricky equipment, and the cost may run a little high, so—"

Henderson's eyes twinkled. He scribbled something on a piece of paper and handed it to Mason. "Here, Al. An authorization for unlimited research funds. You've got a blank check to have some more fun with. Go build us a better cow."

IF

Harry Harrison

"We are there, we are correct. The computations were perfect. That is the place below."

"You are a worm," 17 said to her companion 35, who resembled her every way other than in number. "That is the place. But nine years too early. Look at the meter."

"I am a worm. I shall free you of the burden of my useless presence." 35 removed her knife from the scabbard and tested the edge, which proved to be exceedingly sharp. She placed it against the white wattled width of her neck and prepared to cut her throat.

"Not now," 17 hissed. "We are shorthanded already and your corpse would be valueless to this expedition. Get us to the correct time at once. Our power is limited, you may remember."

"It shall be done as you command," 35 said as she slithered to the bank of controls. 44 ignored the talk, keeping her multicell eyes focused on the power control bank, constantly making adjustments with her spatulate fingers in response to the manifold dials.

"That is it," 17 announced, rasping her hands together with pleasure. "The correct time, the correct place. We must descend and make our destiny. Give praise to the Saur of All who rules the destinies of all."

"Praise Saur," her two companions muttered, all of their attention on the controls.

Straight down from the blue sky the globular vehicle fell. It was round and featureless, save for the large rectangular port, on the bottom now, and made of some sort of green metal, perhaps anodized aluminum, though it looked harder. It had no visible means of flight or support, yet it fell at a steady and controlled rate. Slower and slower it moved until it dropped from sight behind the ridge at the northern end of Johnson's Lake, just at the edge of the tall pine grove. There were fields nearby, with cows, who did not appear at all disturbed by the visitor. No human being was in sight to view the landing. A path cut in from the lake here, a scuffed dirt trail that went to the highway.

An oriole sat on a bush and warbled sweetly: a small rabbit hopped from the field to nibble a stem of grass. This bucolic and peaceful scene was interrupted by the scuff of feet down the trail and a high-pitched and singularly monotone whistling. The bird flew away, a touch of soundless color, while the rabbit disappeared into the hedge. A boy came over the rise from the direction of the lake shore. He wore ordinary boy clothes and carried a school bag in one hand, a small and homemade cage of wire screen in the other. In the cage was a small lizard which clung to the screen, its eyes rolling in what presumably was fear. The boy, whistling shrilly, trudged along the path and into the shade of the pine grove.

"Boy," a high-pitched and tremulous voice called out. "Can you hear me, boy?"

"I certainly can," the boy said, stopping and looking around for the unseen speaker. "Where are you?"

"I am by your side, but I am invisible. I am your fairy godmother . . ."

The boy made a rude sound by sticking out his tongue and blowing across it while it vibrated. "I don't believe in invisibility or fairy godmothers. Come out of those woods, whoever you are."

"All boys believe in fairy godmothers," the voice said, but a worried tone edged the words now. "I know all kinds of secrets. I know your name is Don and . . ."

"Everyone knows my name is Don and no one believes any more in fairies. Boys now believe in rockets, submarines and atomic energy."

"Would you believe space travel?"

"I would."

Slightly relieved, the voice came on stronger and deeper. "I did not wish to frighten you, but I am really from Mars and have just landed . . ."

Don made the rude noise again. "Mars has no atmosphere and no observable forms of life. Now come out of there and stop playing games."

After a long silence the voice said, "Would you consider time travel?"

"I could. Are you going to tell me that you are from the future?"

With relief: "Yes I am."

"Then come out where I can see you."

"There are some things that the human eye should not look upon . . ."

"Horseapples! The human eye is okay for looking at anything you want to name. You come out of there so I can see who you are—or I'm leaving."

"It is not advisable." The voice was exasperated. "I can prove I am a temporal traveler by telling you the answers to tomorrow's mathematics test. Wouldn't that be nice? Number one, 1.76. Number two . . ."

"I don't like to cheat, and even if I did you can't cheat on the new math. Either you know it or you fail it. I'm going to count to ten, then go."

"No, you cannot! I must ask you a favor. Release that common lizard you have trapped and I will give you three wishes—I mean answer three questions."

"Why should I let it go?"

"Is that the first of your questions?"

"No. I want to know what's going on before I do anything. This lizard is special. I never saw another one like it around here."

"You are right. It is an Old World acrodont lizard of the order Rhiptoglossa, commonly called a chameleon."

"It *is!*" Don was really interested now. He squatted in the path and took a red-covered book from his school bag and laid it on the ground. He turned the cage until the lizard was on the bottom and placed it carefully on the book. "Will it really turn color?"

"To an observable amount, yes. Now if you release her . . ."

"How do you know it's a her? The time traveler bit again?"

"If you must know, yes. The creature was purchased from a pet store by one Jim Benan, and is one of a pair. They were both released two days ago when Benan, deranged by the voluntary drinking of a liquid containing quantities of ethyl alcohol, sat on the cage. The other, unfortunately, died of his wounds, and this one alone survives. The release . . ."

"I think this whole thing is a joke and I'm going home now. Unless you come out of there so I can see who you are."

"I warn you . . ."

"Good-by." Don picked up the cage. "Hey, she turned sort of brick red!"

"Do not leave. I will come forth."

Don looked on, with a great deal of interest, while the creature walked out from between the trees. It was blue, had large and goggling—independently moving—eyes, wore a neatly cut brown jumpsuit and had a pack slung on its back. It was also only about seven inches tall.

"You don't much look like a man from the future," Don said. "In fact you don't look like a man at all. You're too small."

"I might say that you are too big; size is a matter of relevancy. And I am from the future, though I am not a man."

"That's for sure. In fact you look a lot like a lizard." In sudden inspiration, Don looked back and forth at the traveler and at the cage. "In fact you look a good deal like this chameleon here. What's the connection?"

"That is not to be revealed. You will now do as I command or I will injure you gravely." 17 turned and waved toward the woods. "35, this is an order. Appear and destroy that growth over there."

Don looked on with increasing interest as the green basketball of metal drifted into sight from under the trees. A circular disk slipped away on one side and a gleaming nozzle, not unlike the hose nozzle on a toy firetruck, appeared through the opening. It pointed toward a hedge a good thirty feet away. A shrill whining began from the depths of the sphere, rising in pitch until it was almost inaudible. Then, suddenly, a thin line of light spat out toward the shrub which crackled and instantly burst into flame. Within a second it was a blackened skeleton.

"The device is called a roxidizer and is deadly," 17 said. "Release the chameleon at once or we will turn it on you."

Don scowled. "All right. Who wants the old lizard anyway?" He put the cage on the ground and started to open the cover. Then he stopped—and sniffed. Picking up the cage again he started across the grass toward the blackened bush.

"Come back!" 17 screeched. "We will fire if you go another step."

Don ignored the lizardoid, which was now dancing up and down in an agony of frustration, and ran to the bush. He put his hand out—and apparently right through the charred stems.

"I thought something was fishy," he said. "All that burning and everything just upwind of me—and I couldn't smell a thing." He turned to look at the time traveler who was slumped in gloomy silence. "It's just a projected image of some kind, isn't it, Some kind of three-dimensional movie." He stopped in sudden thought, then walked over to the still hovering temporal transporter. When he poked at it with his finger he apparently pushed his hand right into it.

"And this thing isn't here either. Are you?"

"There is no need to experiment. I, and our ship, are present only as what might be called temporal echoes. Matter cannot be moved through time, that is an impossibility, but the concept of matter can be temporarily projected. I am sure that this is too technical for you . . ."

"You're doing great so far. Carry on."

"Our projections are here in a real sense to us, though we can only be an image or a sound wave to any observers in the time we visit. Immense amounts of energy are required and almost the total resources of our civilization are involved in this time transfer."

"Why? And the truth for a change. No more fairy godmother and that kind of malarky."

"I regret the necessity to use subterfuge, but the secret

is too important to reveal casually without attempting other means of persuasion."

"Now we get to the real story." Don sat down and crossed his legs comfortably. "Give."

"We need your aid, or our very society is threatened. Very recently—on our time scale—strange disturbances were detected by our instruments. Ours is a simple saurian existence, some million or so years in the future, and our race is dominant. Yours has long since vanished in a manner too horrible to mention to your young ears. Something is threatening our entire race. Research quickly uncovered the fact that we are about to be overwhelmed by a probability wave and wiped out, a great wave of negation sweeping toward us from our remote past."

"You wouldn't mind tipping me off to what a probability wave is, would you?"

"I will take an example from your own literature. If your grandfather had died without marrying, you would not have been born and would not now exist."

"But I do."

"The matter is debatable in the greater xan-probility universe, but we shall not discuss that now. Our power is limited. To put the affair simply, we traced our ancestral lines back through all the various mutations and changes until we found the individual proto-lizard from which our line sprung."

"Let me guess." Don pointed at the cage. "This is the one?"

"She is." 17 spoke in solemn tones as befitted the moment. "Just as somewhen, somewhere there is a proto-tarsier from which your race sprung, so is there this temporal mother of ours. She will bear young soon, and they will breed and grow in this pleasant valley. The rocks near the lake have an appreciable amount of radioactivity which will cause mutations. The centuries will roll by and, one day, our race will reach its heights of glory.

"But not if you don't open that cage."

Don rested his chin on fist and thought. "You're not putting me on any more? This is the truth?"

17 drew herself up and waved both arms—or front legs—over her head. "By the Saur of All, I promise," she intoned. "By the stars eternal, the seasons vernal, the clouds, the sky, the matriarchal I . . ."

"Just cross your heart and hope to die, that will be good enough for me."

The lizardoid moved its eyes in concentric circles and performed this ritual.

"Okay then, I'm as soft-hearted as the next guy when it comes to wiping out whole races."

Don unbent the piece of wire that sealed the cage and opened the top. The chameleon rolled one eye up at him and looked at the opening with the other. 17 watched in awed silence and the time vehicle bobbed closer.

"Get going," Don said, and shook the lizard out into the grass.

This time the chameleon took the hint and scuttled away among the bushes, vanishing from sight.

"That takes care of the future," Don said. "Or the past, from your point of view."

17 and the time machine vanished silently and Don was alone again on the path.

"Well, you could of at least said thanks before taking off like that! People have more manners than lizards any day, I'll tell you that."

He picked up the now empty cage and his school bag and started for home.

He had not heard the quick rustle in the bushes, nor did he see the prowling tomcat with the limp chameleon in its jaws.

A PAIL OF AIR

◎◎◎

Fritz Leiber

Pa had sent me out to get an extra pail of air. I'd just about scooped it full and most of the warmth had leaked from my fingers when I saw the thing.

You know, at first I thought it was a young lady. Yes, a beautiful young lady's face all glowing in the dark and looking at me from the fifth floor of the opposite apartment, which hereabouts is the floor just above the white blanket of frozen air. I'd never seen a live young lady before, except in the old magazines—Sis is just a kid and Ma is pretty sick and miserable—and it gave me such a start that I dropped the pail. Who wouldn't, knowing everyone on Earth was dead except Pa and Ma and Sis and you?

Even at that, I don't suppose I should have been surprised. We all see things now and then. Ma has some pretty bad ones, to judge from the way she bugs her eyes at nothing and just screams and screams and huddles back against the blankets hanging around the Nest.

Pa says it is natural we should react like that sometimes.

When I'd recovered the pail and could look again at
the opposite apartment, I got an idea of what Ma might
be feeling at those times, for I saw it wasn't a young lady
at all but simply a light—a tiny light that moved stealthily
from window to window, just as if one of the cruel little
stars had come down out of the airless sky to investigate
why the Earth had gone away from the Sun, and maybe
to hunt down something to torment or terrify, now that
the Earth didn't have the Sun's protection.

I tell you, the thought of it gave me the creeps. I just
stood there shaking, and almost froze my feet and did
frost my helmet so solid on the inside that I couldn't
have seen the light even if it had come out of one of
the windows to get me. Then I had the wit to go back
inside.

Pretty soon I was feeling my familiar way through
the thirty or so blankets and rugs Pa has got hung around
to slow down the escape of air from the Nest, and I
wasn't quite so scared. I began to hear the tick-ticking
of the clocks in the Nest and knew I was getting back
into air, because there's no sound outside in the vacuum,
of course. But my mind was still crawly and uneasy as
I pushed through the last blankets—Pa's got them faced
with aluminum foil to hold in the heat—and came into
the Nest.

Let me tell you about the Nest. It's low and snug,
just room for the four of us and our things. The floor
is covered with thick woolly rugs. Three of the sides
are blankets, and the blankets roofing it touch Pa's head.
He tells me it's inside a much bigger room, but I've
never seen the real walls or ceiling.

Against one of the blanket-walls is a big set of shelves,
with tools and books and other stuff, and on top of it

a whole row of clocks. Pa's very fussy about keeping them wound. He says we must never forget time, and without a sun or moon, that would be easy to do.

The fourth wall has blankets all over except around the fireplace, in which there is a fire that must never go out. It keeps us from freezing and does a lot more besides. One of us must always watch it. Some of the clocks are alarm and we can use them to remind us. In the early days there was only Ma to take turns with Pa—I think of that when she gets difficult—but now there's me to help, and Sis too.

It's Pa who is the chief guardian of the fire, though. I always think of him that way: a tall man sitting cross-legged, frowning anxiously at the fire, his lined face golden in its light, and every so often carefully placing on it a piece of coal from the big heap beside it. Pa tells me there used to be guardians of the fire some-times in the very old days—vestal virgins, he calls them —although there was unfrozen air all around then and you didn't really need them.

He was sitting just that way now, though he got up quick to take the pail from me and bawl me out for loitering—he'd spotted my frozen helmet right off. That roused Ma and she joined in picking on me. She's always trying to get the load off her feelings, Pa explains. He shut her up pretty fast. Sis let off a couple of silly squeals too.

Pa handled the pail of air in a twist of cloth. Now that it was inside the Nest, you could really feel its coldness. It just seemed to suck the heat out of everything. Even the flames cringed away from it as Pa put it down close by the fire.

Yet it's that glimmery white stuff in the pail that keeps us alive. It slowly melts and vanishes and refreshes the Nest and feeds the fire. The blankets keep it from escaping too fast. Pa'd like to seal the whole place, but he

can't—building's too earth-quake-twisted, and besides he
has to leave the chimney open for smoke.

Pa says air is tiny molecules that fly away like a flash
if there isn't something to stop them. We have to watch
sharp not to let the air run low. Pa always keeps a big
reserve supply of it in buckets behind the first blankets,
along with extra coal and cans of food and other things,
such as pails of snow to melt for water. We have to go
way down to the bottom floor for that stuff, which is a
mean trip, and get it through a door to outside.

You see, when the Earth got cold, all the water in
the air froze first and made a blanket ten feet thick
or so everywhere, and then down on top of that dropped
the crystals of frozen air, making another white blanket
sixty or seventy feet thick maybe.

Of course, all the parts of the air didn't freeze and
snow down at the same time.

First to drop out was the carbon dioxide—when you're
shoveling for water, you have to make sure you don't
go too high and get any of that stuff mixed in, for it
would put you to sleep, maybe for good, and make the
fire go out. Next there's the nitrogen, which doesn't
count one way or the other, though it's the biggest part
of the blanket. On top of that and easy to get at, which
is lucky for us, there's the oxygen that keeps us alive.
Pa says we live better than kings ever did, breathing
pure oxygen, but we're used to it and don't notice.
Finally, at the very top, there's a slick of liquid helium,
which is funny stuff. All of these gases in neat separate
layers. Like a pussy caffay, Pa laughingly says, whatever
that is.

I was busting to tell them all about what I'd seen,
and so as soon as I'd ducked out of my helmet and
while I was still climbing out of my suit, I cut loose.
Right away Ma got nervous and began making eyes at

the entry-slit in the blankets and wringing her hands together—the hand where she'd lost three fingers from frostbite inside the good one, as usual. I could tell that Pa was annoyed at me scaring her and wanted to explain it all away quickly, yet could see I wasn't fooling.

"And you watched this light for some time, son?" he asked when I finished.

I hadn't said anything about first thinking it was a young lady's face. Somehow that part embarrassed me.

"Long enough for it to pass five windows and go to the next floor."

"And it didn't look like stray electricity or crawling liquid or starlight focused by a growing crystal, or anything like that?"

He wasn't just making up those ideas. Odd things happen in a world that's about as cold as can be, and just when you think matter would be frozen dead, it takes on a strange new life. A slimy stuff comes crawling toward the Nest, just like an animal snuffing for heat— that's the liquid helium. And once, when I was little, a bolt of lightning—not even Pa could figure where it came from—hit the nearby steeple and crawled up and down it for weeks, until the glow finally died.

"Not like anything I ever saw," I told him.

He stood for a moment frowning. Then, "I'll go out with you, and you show it to me," he said.

Ma raised a howl at the idea of being left alone, and Sis joined in, too, but Pa quieted them. We started climbing into our outside clothes—mine had been warming by the fire. Pa made them. They have plastic headpieces that were once big double-duty transparent food cans, but they keep heat and air in and can replace the air for a little while, long enough for our trips for water and coal and food and so on.

Ma started moaning again, "I've always known there was something outside there, waiting to get us. I've felt it for years—something that's part of the cold and hates all warmth and wants to destroy the Nest. It's been watching us all this time, and now it's coming after us. It'll get you and then come for me. Don't go, Harry!"

Pa had everything on but his helmet. He knelt by the fireplace and reached in and shook the long metal rod that goes up the chimney and knocks off the ice that keeps trying to clog it. Once a week he goes up on the roof to check if it's working all right. That's our worst trip and Pa won't let me make it alone.

"Sis," Pa said quietly, "come watch the fire. Keep an eye on the air, too. If it gets low or doesn't seem to be boiling fast enough, fetch another bucket from behind the blanket. But mind your hands. Use the cloth to pick up the bucket."

Sis quit helping Ma be frightened and came over and did as she was told. Ma quieted down pretty suddenly, though her eyes were still kind of wild as she watched Pa fix on his helmet tight and pick up a pail and the two of us go out.

Pa led the way and I took hold of his belt. It's a funny thing, I'm not afraid to go by myself, but when Pa's along I always want to hold on to him. Habit, I guess, and then there's no denying that this time I was a bit scared.

You see, it's this way. We know that everything is dead out there. Pa heard the last radio voices fade away years ago, and has seen some of the last folks die who weren't as lucky or well-protected as us. So we knew that if there was something groping around out there, it couldn't be anything human or friendly.

Besides that, there's a feeling that comes with it always being night, *cold* night. Pa says there used to be some of that feeling even in the old days, but then every morning the Sun would come and chase it away. I have to take his word for that, not ever remembering the

Sun as being anything more than a big star. You see, I hadn't been born when the dark star snatched us away from the Sun, and by now it's dragged us out beyond the orbit of the planet Pluto, Pa says, and taking us farther out all the time.

I found myself wondering whether there mightn't be something on the dark star that wanted us, and if that was why it had captured the Earth. Just then we came to the end of the corridor and I followed Pa out on the balcony.

I don't know what the city looked like in the old days, but now it's beautiful. The starlight lets you see it pretty well—there's quite a bit of light in those steady points speckling the blackness above. (Pa says the stars used to twinkle once, but that was because there was air.) We are on a hill and the shimmery plain drops away from us and then flattens out, cut up into neat squares by the troughs that used to be streets. I sometimes make my mashed potatoes look like it, before I pour on the gravy.

Some taller buildings push up out of the feathery plain, topped by rounded caps of air crystals, like the fur hood Ma wears, only whiter. On those buildings you can see the darker squares of windows, underlined by white dashes of air crystals. Some of them are on a slant, for many of the buildings are pretty badly twisted by the quakes and all the rest that happened when the dark star captured the Earth.

Here and there a few icicles hang, water icicles from the first days of the cold, other icicles of frozen air that melted on the roofs and dripped and froze again. Sometimes one of those icicles will catch the light of a star and send it to you so brightly you think the star has swooped into the city. That was one of the things Pa had been thinking of when I told him about the light,

but I had thought of it myself first and known it wasn't
so.

He touched his helmet to mine so we could talk easier
and he asked me to point out the windows to him.
But there wasn't any light moving around inside them
now, or anywhere else. To my surprise, Pa didn't bawl
me out and tell me I'd been seeing things. He looked
all around quite a while after filling his pail, and just as
we were going inside he whipped around without warning, as if to take some peeping thing off guard.

I could feel it, too. The old peace was gone. There
was something lurking out there, watching, waiting, getting ready.

Inside, he said to me, touching helmets, "If you see
something like that again, son, don't tell the others. Your
Ma's sort of nervous these days and we owe her all the
feeling of safety we can give her. Once—it was when your
sister was born—I was ready to give up and die, but
your Mother kept me trying. Another time she kept the
fire going a whole week all by herself when I was sick.
Nursed me and took care of the two of you, too.

"You know that game we sometimes play, sitting in a
square in the Nest, tossing a ball around? Courage is
like a ball, son. A person can hold it only so long, and
then he's got to toss it to someone else. When it's tossed
your way, you've got to catch it and hold it tight—
and hope there'll be someone else to toss it to when
you get tired of being brave."

His talking to me that way made me feel grown-up
and good. But it didn't wipe away the thing outside
from the back of my mind—or the fact that Pa took it
seriously.

It's hard to hide your feelings about such a thing.
When we got back in the Nest and took off our outside
clothes, Pa laughed about it all and told them it was

nothing and kidded me for having such an imagination, but his words fell flat. He didn't convince Ma and Sis any more than he did me. It looked for a minute like we were all fumbling the courage-ball. Something had to be done, and almost before I knew what I was going to say, I heard myself asking Pa to tell us about the old days, and how it all happened.

He sometimes doesn't mind telling that story, and Sis and I sure like to listen to it, and he got my idea. So we were all settled around the fire in a wink, and Ma pushed up some cans to thaw for supper, and Pa began. Before he did, though, I noticed him casually get a hammer from the shelf and lay it down beside him.

It was the same old story as always—I think I could recite the main thread of it in my sleep—though Pa always puts in a new detail or two and keeps improving it in spots.

He told us how the Earth had been swinging around the Sun ever so steady and warm, and the people on it fixing to make money and wars and have a good time and get power and treat each other right or wrong, when without warning there comes charging out of space this dead star, this burned out sun, and upsets everything.

You know, I find it hard to believe in the way those people felt, any more than I can believe in the swarming number of them. Imagine people getting ready for the horrible sort of war they were cooking up. Wanting it even, or at least wishing it were over so as to end their nervousness. As if all folks didn't have to hang together and pool every bit of warmth just to keep alive. And how can they have hoped to end danger, any more than we can hope to end the cold?

Sometimes I think Pa exaggerates and makes things out too black. He's cross with us once in a while and was probably cross with all those folks. Still, some of the

things I read in the old magazines sound pretty wild.
He may be right.

The dark star, as Pa went on telling it, rushed in pretty
fast and there wasn't much time to get ready. At the
beginning they tried to keep it a secret from most
people, but then the truth came out, what with the
earthquakes and floods—imagine, oceans of *unfrozen* water!—and people seeing stars blotted out by something
on a clear night. First off they thought it would hit the
Sun, and then they thought it would hit the Earth. There
was even the start of a rush to get to a place called
China, because people thought the star would hit on the
other side. But then they found it wasn't going to hit
either side, but was going to come very close to the
Earth.

Most of the other planets were on the other side of
the Sun and didn't get involved. The Sun and the
newcomer fought over the Earth for a little while—pulling it this way and that, like two dogs growling over
a bone, Pa described it this time—and then the newcomer won and carried us off. The Sun got a consolation
prize, though. At the last minute he managed to hold on
to the Moon.

That was the time of the monster earthquakes and
floods, twenty times worse than anything before. It was
also the time of the Big Jerk, as Pa calls it, when all
Earth got yanked suddenly, just as Pa has done to me
once or twice, grabbing me by the collar to do it,
when I've been sitting too far from the fire.

You see, the dark star was going through space faster
than the Sun, and in the opposite direction, and it had
to wrench the world considerably in order to take it
away.

The Big Jerk didn't last long. It was over as soon as
the Earth was settled down in its new orbit around
the dark star. But it was pretty terrible while it lasted.

Pa says that all sorts of cliffs and buildings toppled, oceans slopped over, swamps and sandy deserts gave great sliding surges that buried nearby lands. Earth was almost jerked out of its atmosphere blanket and the air got so thin in spots that people keeled over and fainted —though of course, at the same time, they were getting knocked down by the Big Jerk and maybe their bones broke or skulls cracked.

We've often asked Pa how people acted during that time, whether they were scared or brave or crazy or stunned, or all four, but he's sort of leery of the subject, and he was again tonight. He says he was mostly too busy to notice.

You see, Pa and some scientist friends of his had figured out part of what was going to happen—they'd known we'd get captured and our air would freeze— and they'd been working like mad to fix up a place with airtight walls and doors, and insulation against the cold, and big supplies of food and fuel and water and bottled air. But the place got smashed in the last earthquakes and all Pa's friends were killed then and in the Big Jerk. So he had to start over and throw the Nest together quick without any advantages, just using any stuff he could lay his hands on.

I guess he's telling pretty much the truth when he says he didn't have any time to keep an eye on how other folks behaved, either then or in the Big Freeze that fol- lowed—followed very quick, you know, both because the dark star was pulling us away very fast and because Earth's rotation had been slowed in the tug-of-war, so that the nights were ten old nights long.

Still, I've got an idea of some of the things that hap- pened from the frozen folk I've seen, a few of them in other rooms in our building, others clustered around the furnaces in the basements where we go for coal.

In one of the rooms, an old man sits stiff in a chair,

with an arm and a leg in splints. In another, a man and woman are huddled together in a bed with heaps of cover over them. You can just see their heads peeking out, close together. And in another a beautiful young lady is sitting with a pile of wraps huddled around her, looking hopefully toward the door, as if waiting for someone who never came back with warmth and food. They're all still and stiff as statues, of course, but just like life.

Pa showed them to me once in quick winks of his flashlight, when he still had a fair supply of batteries and could afford to waste a little light. They scared me pretty bad and made my heart pound, especially the young lady.

Now, with Pa telling his story for the umpteenth time to take our minds off another scare, I got to thinking of the frozen folk again. All of a sudden I got an idea that scared me worse than anything yet. You see, I'd just remembered the face I'd thought I'd seen in the window. I'd forgotten about that on account of trying to hide it from the others.

What, I asked myself, if the frozen folk were coming to life? What if they were like the liquid helium that got a new lease on life and started crawling toward the heat just when you thought its molecules ought to freeze solid forever? Or like the electricity that moves endlessly when it's just about as cold as that? What if the ever-growing cold, with the temperature creeping down the last few degrees to the last zero, had mysteriously wakened the frozen folk to life—not warmblooded life, but something icy and horrible?

That was a worse idea than the one about something coming down from the dark star to get us.

Or maybe, I thought, both ideas might be true. Something coming down from the dark star and making the

frozen folk move, using them to do its work. That would
fit with both things I'd seen—the beautiful young lady
and the moving, starlike light.

The frozen folk with minds from the dark star behind
their unwinking eyes, creeping, crawling, snuffing their
way, following the heat to the Nest.

I tell you, that thought gave me a very bad turn
and I wanted very badly to tell the others my fears, but
I remembered what Pa had said and clenched my teeth
and didn't speak.

We were all sitting very still. Even the fire was burning
silently. There was just the sound of Pa's voice and the
clocks.

And then, from beyond the blankets, I thought I
heard a tiny noise. My skin tightened all over me.

Pa was telling about the early years in the Nest and
had come to the place where he philosophizes.

"So I asked myself then," he said, "what's the use
of going on? What's the use of dragging it out for a
few years? Why prolong a doomed existence of hard
work and cold and loneliness? The human race is done.
The Earth is done. Why not give up, I asked myself—
and all of a sudden I got the answer."

Again I heard the noise, louder this time, a kind of uncertain, shuffling tread, coming closer. I couldn't breathe.

"Life's always been a business of working hard and
fighting the cold," Pa was saying. "The earth's always
been a lonely place, millions of miles from the next
planet. And no matter how long the human race might
have lived, the end would have come some night. Those
things don't matter. What matters is that life is good.
It has a lovely texture, like some rich cloth or fur, or the
petals of flowers—you've seen pictures of those, but I can't
describe how they feel—or the fire's glow. It makes everything else worth while. And that's as true for the last man
as the first."

And still the steps kept shuffling closer. It seemed to me that the inmost blanket trembled and bulged a little. Just as if they were burned into my imagination, I kept seeing those peering, frozen eyes.

"So right then and there," Pa went on, and now I could tell that he had heard the steps, too, and was talking loud so we maybe wouldn't hear them, "right then and there I told myself that I was going on as if we had all eternity ahead of us. I'd have children and teach them all I could. I'd get them to read books. I'd plan for the future, try to enlarge and seal the Nest. I'd do what I could to keep everything beautiful and growing. I'd keep alive my feeling of wonder even at the cold and the dark and the distant stars."

But then the blanket actually did move and lift. And there was a bright light somewhere behind it. Pa's voice stopped and his eyes turned to the widening slit and his hand went out until it touched and gripped the handle of the hammer beside him.

In through the blanket stepped the beautiful young lady. She stood there looking at us the strangest way, and she carried something bright and unwinking in her hand. And two other faces peered over her shoulders—men's faces, white and staring.

Well, my heart couldn't have been stopped for more than four or five beats before I realized she was wearing a suit and helmet like Pa's homemade ones, only fancier, and that the men were, too—and that the frozen folk certainly wouldn't be wearing those. Also, I noticed that the bright thing in her hand was just a kind of flashlight.

The silence kept on while I swallowed hard a couple of times, and after that there was all sorts of jabbering and commotion.

They were simply people, you see. We hadn't been

the only ones to survive; we'd just thought so, for natural enough reasons. These three people had survived, and quite a few others with them. And when we found out *how* they'd survived, Pa let out the biggest whoop of joy.

They were from Los Alamos and they were getting their heat and power from atomic energy. Just using the uranium and plutonium intended for bombs, they had enough to go on for thousands of years. They had a regular little airtight city, with airlocks and all. They even generated electric light and grew plants and animals by it. (At this Pa let out a second whoop, waking Ma from her faint.)

But if we were flabbergasted at them, they were double-flabbergasted at us.

One of the men kept saying, "But it's impossible, I tell you. You can't maintain an air supply without hermetic sealing. It's simply impossible."

That was after he had got his helmet off and was using our air. Meanwhile, the young lady kept looking around at us as if we were saints, and telling us we'd done something amazing, and suddenly she broke down and cried.

They'd been scouting around for survivors, but they never expected to find any in a place like this. They had rocket ships at Los Alamos and plenty of chemical fuel. As for liquid oxygen, all you had to do was go out and shovel the air blanket at the top level. So after they'd got things going smoothly at Los Alamos, which had taken years, they'd decided to make some trips to likely places where there might be other survivors. No good trying long-distance radio signals, of course, since there was no atmosphere to carry them around the curve of the Earth.

Well, they'd found other colonies at Argonne and Brookhaven and way around the world at Harwell and

Tanna Tuva. And now they'd been giving our city a look, not really expecting to find anything. But they had an instrument that noticed the faintest heat waves and it had told them there was something warm down here, so they'd landed to investigate. Of course we hadn't heard them land, since there was no air to carry the sound, and they'd had to investigate around quite a while before finding us. Their instruments had given them a wrong steer and they'd wasted some time in the building across the street.

By now, all five adults were talking like sixty. Pa was demonstrating to the men how he worked the fire and got rid of the ice in the chimney and all that. Ma had perked up wonderfully and was showing the young lady her cooking and sewing stuff, and even asking about how the women dressed at Los Alamos. The strangers marveled at everything and praised it to the skies. I could tell from the way they wrinkled their noses that they found the Nest a bit smelly, but they never mentioned that at all and just asked bushels of questions.

In fact, there was so much talking and excitement that Pa forgot about things, and it wasn't until they were all getting groggy that he looked and found the air had all boiled away in the pail. He got another bucket of air quick from behind the blankets. Of course that started them all laughing and jabbering again. The newcomers even got a little drunk. They weren't used to so much oxygen.

Funny thing, though—I didn't do much talking at all and Sis hung on to Ma all the time and hid her face when anybody looked at her. I felt pretty uncomfortable and disturbed myself, even about the young lady. Glimpsing her outside there, I'd had all sorts of mushy thoughts, but now I was just embarrassed and scared of her, even though she tried to be nice as anything to me.

I sort of wished they'd all quit crowding the Nest and let us be alone and get our feelings straightened out.

And when the newcomers began to talk about our all going to Los Alamos, as if that were taken for granted, I could see that something of the same feeling struck Pa and Ma, too. Pa got very silent all of a sudden and Ma kept telling the young lady, "But I wouldn't know how to act there and I haven't any clothes."

The strangers were puzzled like anything at first, but then they got the idea. As Pa kept saying, "It just doesn't seem right to let this fire go out."

Well, the strangers are gone, but they're coming back. It hasn't been decided yet just what will happen. Maybe the Nest will be kept up as what one of the strangers called a "survival school." Or maybe we will join the pioneers who are going to try to establish a new colony at the uranium mines at Great Slave Lake or in the Congo.

Of course, now that the strangers are gone, I've been thinking a lot about Los Alamos and those other tremendous colonies. I have a hankering to see them for myself.

You ask me, Pa wants to see them, too. He's been getting pretty thoughtful, watching Ma and Sis perk up.

"It's different, now that we know others are alive," he explains to me. "Your mother doesn't feel so hopeless any more. Neither do I, for that matter, not having to carry the whole responsibility for keeping the human race going, so to speak. It scares a person."

I looked around at the blanket walls and the fire and the pails of air boiling away and Ma and Sis sleeping in the warmth and the flickering light.

"It's not going to be easy to leave the Nest," I said,

wanting to cry, kind of. "It's so small and there's just the four of us. I get scared at the idea of big places and a lot of strangers."

He nodded and put another piece of coal on the fire. Then he looked at the little pile and grinned suddenly and put a couple of handfuls on, just as if it was one of our birthdays or Christmas.

"You'll quickly get over that feeling son," he said. "The trouble with the world was that it kept getting smaller and smaller, till it ended with just the Nest. Now it'll be good to have a real huge world again, the way it was in the beginning."

I guess he's right. You think the beautiful young lady will wait for me till I grow up? I'll be twenty in only ten years.

THE HOWLING BOUNDERS

◎◎◎

Jack Vance

*My brain, otherwise a sound instrument, has a serious
defect—a hypertrophied lobe of curiosity.*
—Magnus Ridolph

The afternoon breeze off the Irremedial Ocean ruffling
his beard, yellow Naos-light burnishing the side of his
face, Magnus Ridolph gazed glumly across his newly
acquired plantation. So far, so good; in fact, too good
to be true.

He shook his head, frowned. All Blantham's repre-
sentations had been corroborated by the evidence of his
own eyes; three thousand acres of prime ticholama, ready
for harvest; a small cottage, native-style, but furnished
adequately; the ocean at his doorstep, the mountains in
his back-yard. Why had the price been so low?

"Is it possible," mused Magnus Ridolph, "that Blantham
is the philanthropist his acts suggest? Or does the oint-
ment conceal a fly?" And Magnus Ridolph pulled at
his beard with petulant fingers.

Now Naos slipped into Irremedial Ocean and lime-green evening flowed like syrup down out of the bad-lands which formed the northern boundary of the plantation. Magnus Ridolph half-turned in the doorway, glanced within. Chook, his dwarfish servant, was sweeping out the kitchen, grunting softly with each stroke of the broom.

Magnus Ridolph stepped out into the green twilight, strolled down past the copter landing to the first of the knee-high ticholama bushes.

He froze in his tracks, cocked his head.

"*Ow-ow-ow-ow-ow-ow-ow,*" in a yelping chorus, wild and strange, drifted from across the field. Magnus Ridolph strained, squinted through the dusk. He could not be sure. . . . It seemed that a tumult of dark shapes came boiling down from the badlands, vague sprawling things. Olive-green darkness settled across the land. Magnus Ridolph turned on his heel, stalked back to the cottage.

Magnus Ridolph had been resting quietly in his hotel —the Piedmont Inn of New Napoli, on Naos V—with no slightest inclination toward or prospect of an agri-cultural life. Then Blantham knocked and Magnus Ridolph opened the door.

Blantham's appearance in itself was enough to excite interest. He was of early middle-age, of medium height, plump at the waist, wide at the hips, narrow at the shoulders.

His forehead was pale and narrow, with eyes set fish-like, wide apart under the temples, the skin between them taut, barely dented by the bridge of his nose. He had wide jowls, a sparse black mustache, a fine white skin, the cheeks meshed, however, with minute pink lines.

He wore loose maroon corduroy trousers, in the "Prae-sepe Ranger" style, a turquoise blouse with a diamond clasp, a dark blue cape, and beside Magnus Ridolph's simple white and blue tunic he appeared somewhat over-ripe.

Magnus Ridolph blinked, like a delicate and urbane owl. "Ah, yes?"

"I'm Blantham," said his visitor bluffly. "Gerard Blantham. We haven't met before."

Watching under his fine white eyebrows, Magnus Ridolph gestured courteously. "I believe not. Will you come in, have a seat?"

Blantham stepped into the room, flung back his cape. "Thank you," he said. He seated himself on the edge of a chair, extended a case. "Cigarette?"

"Thank you." Magnus Ridolph gravely helped himself. He inhaled, frowned, took the cigarette from his lips, examined it.

"Excuse me," said Blantham, producing a lighter. "I sometimes forget. I never smoke self-igniters; I can detect the flavor of the chemical instantly, and it annoys me."

"Unfortunate," said Magnus Ridolph, after his cigarette was aglow. "My senses are not so precisely adjusted, and I find them extremely convenient. Now, what can I do for you?"

Blantham hitched at his trousers. "I understand," he said, looking archly upward, "that you're interested in sound investment."

"To a certain extent," said Magnus Ridolph, inspecting Blantham through the smoke of his cigarette. "What have you to offer?"

"This." Blantham reached in his pocket, produced a small white box. Magnus Ridolph, snapping back the top, found within a cluster of inch-long purple tubes, twisting and curling away from a central node. They were glossy, flexible, and interspersed with long pink fibers. He shook his head politely.

"I'm afraid I can't identify the object."

"It's ticholama," said Blantham. "Resilian in its natural state."

"Indeed!" And Magnus Ridolph examined the purple cluster with new interest.

"Each of those tubes," said Blantham, "is built of countless spirals of resilian molecules, each running the entire length of the tube. That's the property, naturally, which gives resilian its tremendous elasticity and tensile strength."

Magnus Ridolph touched the tubes, which quivered under his fingers. "And?"

Blantham paused impressively. "I'm selling an entire plantation, three thousand acres of prime ticholama ready to harvest."

Magnus Ridolph blinked, handed back the box. "Indeed?" He rubbed his beard thoughtfully. "The holding is evidently on Naos Six."

"Correct, sir. The only location which supports the growth of the ticholama."

"And what is your price?"

"A hundred and thirty thousand munits."

Magnus Ridolph continued to pull at his beard. "Is that a bargain? I know little of agriculture in general, ticholama in specific."

Blantham moved his head solemnly. "It's a giveaway. An acre produces a ton of ticholama. The selling price, delivered at Starport, is fifty-two munits a ton, current quotation. Freight, including all handling, runs about twenty-one munits a ton. And harvesting costs you about eight munits a ton. Expenses twenty-nine munits a ton, net profits, twenty-three munits a ton. On three thousand acres that's sixty-nine thousand munits. Next year you've paid the land off, and after that you're enjoying sheer profit."

Magnus Ridolph eyes his visitor with new interest, the hyper-developed lobe in his brain making its influence felt. Was it possible that Blantham intended to play him—Magnus Ridolph—for a sucker? Could he conceivably be so optimistic, so ill-advised?

"Your proposition," said Magnus Ridolph aloud, "sounds almost too good to be true."

Blantham blinked, stretching the skin across his nose even tauter. "Well, you see, I own another thirty-five hundred acres. The plantation I'm offering for sale is half the Hourglass Peninsula, the half against the mainland. Taking care of the seaward half keeps me more than busy.

"And then, frankly, I need money quick. I had a judgment against me—copter crash, my young son driving. My wife's eyes went bad. I had to pay for an expensive graft. Wasn't covered by Med service, worse luck. And then my daughter's away at school on Earth— St. Brigida's, London. Terrible expense all around. I simply need quick money."

Magnus Ridolph stared keenly at the man from beneath shaggy brows, and nodded.

"I see," he said. "You certainly have suffered an unfortunate succession of events. One hundred thirty thousand munits. A reasonable figure, if conditions are as you state?"

"They are indeed," was Blantham's emphatic reply.

"The ticholama is not all of first quality?" inquired Magnus Ridolph.

"On the contrary," declared Blantham. "Every plant is in prime condition."

"*Hm-m!*" Magnus Ridolph chewed his lower lip. "I assume there are no living quarters."

Blantham chortled, his lips rounded to a curious red O. "I forgot to mention the cottage. A fine little place, native-style, of course, but in A-One condition. Absolutely livable. I believe I have a photograph. Yes, here it is."

Magnus Ridolph took the paper, saw a long building

of gray and green slate—convex-gabled, with concave
end-walls, a row of Gothic-arch openings. The field
behind stretched rich purple out to the first crags of the
badlands.

"Behind you'll see part of the plantation," said Blantham. "Notice the color? Deep dark purple—the best."

"*Humph,*" said Magnus Ridolph. "Well, I'd have to
furnish the cottage. That would run into considerable
money."

Blantham smilingly shook his head. "Not unless you're
the most sybaritic of sybarites. But I must guard against
misrepresentation. The cottage is primitive in some respects. There is no telescreen, no germicide, no auto-
lume. The power plant is small, there's no cold cell,
no laundromat. And unless you fly out a rado-cooker,
you'd have to cook in pots over heating elements."

Magnus Ridolph frowned, glanced sharply at Blantham. "I'd naturally hire a servant. The water? What
arrangements, if any, exist?"

"An excellent still. Two hundred gallons a day."

"That certainly seems adequate," said Magnus Ridolph.
He returned to the photograph. "What is this?" He indicated a patch in the field where one of the spurs from
the badlands entered the field.

Blantham examined the photograph. "I really can't say.
Evidently a small area where the soil is poor. It seems to
be minor in extent."

Magnus Ridolph studied the photograph a minute
longer, returned it. "You paint an arresting picture. I
admit the possibility of doubling my principal almost
immediately is one which I encounter rarely. If you'll
tick off your address on my transview, I'll notify you
tomorrow of my decision."

Blantham rose. "I've a suite right here in the hotel,
Mr. Ridolph. You can call me any time. I imagine that

the further you look into my proposition, the more attractive you'll find it."

To Magnus Ridolph's puzzlement, Blantham's prediction was correct. When he mentioned the matter to Sam Quien, a friend in the brokerage business, Quien whistled, shook his head.

"Sounds like a steal. I'll contract right now for the entire crop."

Magnus Ridolph next obtained a quotation on freight rates from Naos VI to Starport, and frowned when the rate proved a half munit less per ton than Blantham's estimate. By the laws of logic, somewhere there must be a flaw in the bargain. But where?

In the Labor Office he approached a window behind which stood a Fomalhaut V Rhodopian.

"Suppose I want to harvest a field of ticholama on Naos Six," said Magnus Ridolph. "What would be my procedure?"

The Rhodopian bobbed his head as he spoke. "You make arrangements on Naos Six," he lisped. "In Garswan. Contractor, he fix all harvest. Very cheap, on Naos Six. Contractor he use many pickers, very cheap."

"I see," said Magnus Ridolph. "Thank you."

He slowly returned to the hotel. At the mnemiphot in the reading room he verified Blantham's statement that an acre of land yielded a ton of ticholama, which, when processed and the binding gums dissolved, yielded about five hundred pounds of resilian. He found further that the demand for resilian exceeded by far the supply.

He returned to his room, lay down on his bed, considered an hour. At last he stood up, called Blantham on the transview. "Mr. Blantham, I've provisionally decided to accept your offer."

"Good, good!" came Blantham's voice.

"Naturally, before finally consummating the sale, I wish to inspect the property."

"Of course," came the hearty response. "An interplanet ship leaves day after tomorrow. Will that suit you?"

"Very well indeed," was Magnus Ridolph's reply. . . .

Blantham pointed. "That's your plantation, there ahead, the entire first half of the peninsula. Mine is the second half, just over that cliff."

Magnus Ridolph said nothing, peered through the copter windows. Below them the badlands—arid crags, crevasses, rock-jumble—fell astern, and they flew out over Hourglass Peninsula. Beyond lay Irremedial Ocean, streaked and mottled red, blue, green, yellow by vast colonies of colored plankton.

They put down at the cottage. Magnus Ridolph alighted, walked to the edge of the field, bent over. The plants were thick, luxuriant, amply covered with clusters of purple tubes. Magnus Ridolph straightened, looked sidelong at Blantham, who had come up behind him.

"Beautiful, isn't it?" said Blantham mildly.

Magnus Ridolph was forced to agree. Everything was beautiful. Blantham's title was clear, so Magnus Ridolph had verified in Garswan. The harvester agreed to a figure up eight munits a ton, the work to begin immediately after he had finished Blantham's field. In short, the property at the price seemed an excellent buy. And yet—

Magnus Ridolph took another look across the field. "That patch of poor soil seems larger than it appeared in the photograph."

Blantham made a deprecatory noise in his nose. "I can hardly see how that is possible."

Magnus Ridolph stood quietly a moment, the nostrils of his long distinguished nose slightly distended. Abruptly he pulled out his checkbook.

"Your check, sir."

"Thank you. I have the deed and the release in my pocket. I'll just sign it and the property's yours."

Blantham politely took his leave in the copter and Magnus Ridolph was left on the plantation in the gathering dusk. And then—the wild yelling from across the field, the vaguely seen shapes, pelting against the afterglow. Magnus Ridolph returned into the cottage.

He looked into the kitchen, to become acquainted with his servant Chook, a barrel-shaped anthropoid from the Garswan Highlands. Chook had gray lumpy skin, boneless ropelike arms, eyes round and bottle-green, a mouth hidden somewhere behind flabby folds of skin. Magnus Ridolph found him standing with head cocked to the distant yelping.

"Ah, Chook," said Magnus Ridolph. "What have you prepared for our dinner?"

Chook gestured to a steaming pot. "Stew." His voice came from his stomach, a heavy rumble. "Stew is good." A gust of wind brought the yelping closer. Chook's arms twitched.

"What causes that outcry, Chook?" demanded Magnus Ridolph, turning a curious ear toward the disturbance.

Chook looked at him quizzically. "Them the Howling Bounders. Very bad. Kill you, kill me. Kill everything. Eat up ticholama."

Magnus Ridolph seated himself. "Now—I see." He smiled without humor. "I see . . . *Hmph.*"

"Like stew?" inquired Chook, pot ready. . . .

Next morning Magnus Ridolph arose early, as was his habit, strolled into the kitchen. Chook lay on the floor, curled into a gray leathery ball. At Magnus Ridolph's tread he raised his head, showed an eye, rumbled from deep inside his body.

"I'm going for a walk," said Magnus Ridolph. "I intend to be gone an hour. When I return we shall have our breakfast."

Chook slowly lowered his head and Magnus Ridolph

stepped out into the cool silence, full into the horizontal light of Naos, just rising from the ocean like a red-hot stove-lid. The air from the ticholama fields seemed very fresh and rich in oxygen, and Magnus Ridolph set off with a feeling of well-being.

A half-hour's walk through the knee-high bushes brought him to the base of the outlying spur and to the patch of land which Blantham had termed poor soil.

Magnus Ridolph shook his head sadly at the devastation. Ticholama plants had been stripped of the purple tubes, ripped up, thrown into heaps.

The line of ruin roughly paralleled the edge of the spur. Once again Magnus Ridolph shook his head.

"A hundred and thirty thousand munits poorer. I wonder if my increment of wisdom may be valued at that figure?"

He returned to the cottage. Chook was busy at the stove, and greeted him with a grunt.

"Ha, Chook," said Magnus Ridolph, "and what have we for breakfast?"

"Is stew," said Chook.

Magnus Ridolph compressed his lips. "No doubt an excellent dish. But do you consider it, so to speak, a staple of diet?"

"Stew is good," was the stolid reply.

"As you wish," said Magnus Ridolph impassively.

After breakfast he retired to the study and called into Garswan on the antiquated old radiophone.

"Connect me with the T.C.I. office."

A hum, a buzz. "Terrestrial Corps of Intelligence," said a brisk male voice. "Captain Solinsky speaking."

"Captain Solinsky," said Magnus Ridolph, "I wonder if you can give me any information concerning the creatures known as the Howling Bounders."

A slight pause. "Certainly, sir. May I ask who is speaking?"

"My name is Magnus Ridolph; I recently acquired a ticholama plantation here, on the Hourglass Peninsula. Now I find that it is in the process of despoliation by these same Howling Bounders."

The voice had taken a sharper pitch. "Did you say— Magnus Ridolph?"

"That is my name."

"Just a moment, Mr. Ridolph! I'll get everything we have."

After a pause the voice returned. "What we have isn't much. No one knows much about them. They live in the Bouro Badlands, nobody knows how many. There's apparently only a single band, as they've never been reported in two places at the same time. They appear to be unintelligent creatures of a very low order—no one knows exactly."

"These creatures have never been examined at close hand?" asked Magnus Ridolph in some surprise.

"Never." After a second's pause Solinsky said: "The weird things can't be caught. They're elastic—live off ticholama, eat it just before it's ready to harvest. In the day time they disappear, nobody knows where, and at night they're like locusts, black phantoms. A party from Carnegie Tech tried to trap them, but they tore the traps to pieces. They can't be poisoned, a bullet bounces off their hides, they dodge out of heat-beams, deltas don't phase them. We've never got close enough to use supersonics, but they probably wouldn't even notice."

"They would seem almost invulnerable, then—to the usual methods of destruction," was Magnus Ridolph's comment.

"That's about it," said Solinsky brightly. "I suppose a meson grenade would do the trick, but there wouldn't be much specimen left for you to examine."

"My interest in these creatures is not wholly imper-

sonal," said Magnus Ridolph. "They are devouring my
ticholama; I want to halt this activity."

"Well—" Solinsky hesitated. "I don't like to say it, Mr.
Ridolph, but I'm afraid there's very little you can do—
except next year don't raise so tempting a crop. They
only go after the choicest fields. Another thing, they're
dangerous. Any poor devil they chance upon, they tear
him to pieces. So don't go out with a shotgun to scare 'em
away."

"No," said Magnus Ridolph. "I shall have to devise
other means."

"Hope you succeed," said Solinsky. "No one ever has
before."

Magnus Ridolph returned to the kitchen, where Chook
was peeling starchy blue bush-apples.

"I see you are preparing lunch," said Magnus Ridolph.
"Is it—?" He raised his eyebrows interrogatively.

Chook rumbled an affirmative. Magnus Ridolph came
over beside him, watched a moment.

"Have you ever seen one of these Howling Bounders
close at hand?"

"No," said Chook. "When I hear noise, I sleep, stay
quiet."

"What do they look like?"

"Very tall, long arms. Ugly—like you." He turned a
lambent bottle-green eye at Magnus Ridolph's beard. "But
no hair."

"I see," said Magnus Ridolph, stroking the beard. He
wandered outside, seated himself on a bench, and relaxed
in the warm light of Naos. He found a piece of paper,
scribbled. A buzz reached his ears, grew louder, and
presently Blantham's copter dropped into his front yard.
Blantham hopped out, brisk, cleanly-shaven, his wide-
set eyes bright, his jowls pink with health. When he saw
Magnus Ridolph, he shaped his features into a frame of
grave solicitude.

"Mr. Ridolph, a distressing report has reached me. I understand—I just learned this morning—that those devilish Bounders have been seen on your plantation."

Magnus Ridolph nodded. "Yes, something of that nature has been called to my attention."

"Words can't convey my sense of guilt," said Blantham. "Naturally I'd never have saddled you with the property if I'd known . . ."

"Naturally," agreed Magnus Ridolph siccatively.

"As soon as I heard, I came to make what amends I could, but I fear they can only be nominal. You see, last night, as soon as I banked your check, I paid off a number of outstanding debts and I only have about fifty thousand munits left. If you'd like me to take over the burden of coping with those beasts . . ." He paused, coughed.

Magnus Ridolph looked mildly upward. "That's exceedingly generous of you, Mr. Blantham—a gesture few men would make. However, I think I may be able to salvage something from the property. I am not completely discouraged."

"Good, good," was Blantham's hasty comment. "Never say die; I always admire courage. But I'd better warn you that once those pestiferous Bounders start on a field they never stop till they've run through the whole works. When they reach the cottage you'll be in extreme danger. Many, many men and women they've killed."

"Perhaps," Magnus Ridolph suggested, "you will permit the harvester to gather such of my crop as he is able before starting with yours?"

Blantham's face became long and doleful. "Mr. Ridolph, nothing could please me more than to say yes to your request, but you don't know these Garswan contractors. They're stubborn, inflexible. If I were to suggest any change in our contract, he'd probably cancel the entire thing. And naturally, I must protect my wife, my family.

In the second place, there is probably little of your ticholama ripe enough to harvest. The Bounders, you know,
attack the plant just before its maturity." He shook his
head. "With the best of intentions, I can't see how to help
you, unless it's by the method I suggested a moment ago."

Magnus Ridolph raised his eyebrows. "Sell you back
the property for fifty thousand munits?"

Blantham coughed. "I'd hardly call it selling. I merely
wish—"

"Naturally, naturally," agreed Magnus Ridolph. "However, let us view the matter from a different aspect. Let
us momentarily forget that we are friends, neighbors, almost business associates, each acting only through mo-
tives of the highest integrity. Let us assume that we are
strangers, unmoral, predatory."

Blantham blew out his cheeks, eyed Magnus Ridolph
doubtfully. "Far-fetched, of course. But go on."

"On this latter assumption, let us come to a new agreement."

"Such as?"

"Let us make a wager," mused Magnus Ridolph. "The
plantation here against—say, a hundred thirty thousand
munits—but I forgot. You have spent your money."

"What would be the terms of the wager?" inquired
Blantham, inspecting his finger-tips.

"A profit of sixty-nine thousand munits was mentioned
in connection with the sale of the property. The advent
of the—ah!—Howling Bounders made this figure possibly
overoptimistic."

Blantham murmured sympathetically.

"However," continued Magnus Ridolph, "I believe that
a profit of sixty-nine thousand munits is not beyond
reason, and I would like to wager the plantation against
130,000 munits on those terms."

Blantham gave Magnus Ridolph a long bright stare.
"From the sale of ticholama?"

Magnus Ridolph eloquently held his arms out from his sides. "What else is there to yield a profit?"

"There's no mineral on the property, that's certain," muttered Blantham. "No oil, no magnoflux vortex." He looked across the field to the devastated area. "When those Bounders start on a field, they don't stop, you know."

Magnus Ridolph shrugged. "Protecting my land from intrusion is a problem to which a number of solutions must exist."

Blantham eyed him curiously. "You're very confident."

Magnus Ridolph pursed his lips. "I believe in an aggressive attitude toward difficulties."

Blantham turned once more toward the blighted area, looked boldly back at Magnus Ridolph. "I'll take that bet."

"Good," said Magnus Ridolph. "Let us take your copter to Garswan and cast the wager into a legal form."

In the street below the notary's office later, Magnus Ridolph tucked his copy of the agreement into the microfilm compartment of his wallet.

"I think," he told Blantham, who was watching him covertly with an air of sly amusement, "that I'll remain in Garswan the remainder of the day. I want to find a copter, perhaps take back a few supplies."

"Very well, Mr. Ridolph." Blantham inclined his head courteously, swung his dark blue cape jauntily across his shoulders. "I wish you the best of luck with your plantation."

"Thank you," said Magnus Ridolph, equally punctilious, "and may you likewise enjoy the returns to which you are entitled."

Blantham departed; Magnus Ridolph turned up the main street. Garswan owed its place as Naos VI's first city only to a level field of rock-hard clay, originally the site of native fire-dances. There was little else to commend Garswan, certainly no scenic beauty.

The main street started at the space-port, wound under a great raw bluff of red shale, plunged into a jungle of snakevine, inch-moss, hammock tree. The shops and dwellings were half of native-style, of slate slabs with curving gables and hollow end-walls; half dingy frame buildings. There was a warehouse, a local of the spacemen's union, a Rhodopian social hall, an Earth-style drugstore, a side street given to a native market, a copter yard.

At the copter yard, Magnus Ridolph found a choice of six or seven vehicles, all weatherbeaten and over-priced. He ruefully selected a six-jet Spur, and closing his ears to the whine of the bearings, flew it away to a garage, where he ordered it fueled and lubricated.

He stepped into the TCI office, where he was received with courtesy. He requested and was permitted use of the mnemiphot. Seating himself comfortably, he found the code for resilian, ticked it into the selector, attentively pursued the facts, pictures, formulae, statistics drifting across the screen. He noted the tensile strength, about the same as mild steel, and saw with interest that resilian dampened with hesso-penthol welded instantly into another piece of resilian.

He leaned back in his chair, tapped his pencil thoughtfully against his notebook. He returned to the mnemiphot, dialed ahead to the preparation of resilian from the raw ticholama. The purple tubes, he found, were frozen in liquid air, passed through a macerator, which pulverized the binding gums, soaked in hesso-hexylic acid, then alcohol, dried in a centrifuge, a process which left the fibers in a felt-like mat. This mat was combed until the fibers lay parallel, impregnated with hesso-penthol and compressed into a homogeneous substance—resilian.

Again Magnus Ridolph sat back, his mild blue eyes focused on space. Presently he arose, left the office,

crossed the street to the headquarters of the local construction company. Here he spent almost an hour; then,
returning to the garage, he picked up his copter and,
rising high over the jungle, headed south. The jumble of
the Bouro Badlands passed below. Hourglass Peninsula
spread before him, with his plantation filling the land-
ward half, that of Blantham the remainder.

Naos hung low over the sea when he landed. Chook
was standing in the pointed doorway, eyes fixed vacantly
across the ticholama field, arms dangling almost to the
ground.

"Good evening, Chook," said Magnus Ridolph, hand-
ing his servants a parcel. "A bottle of wine to aid your
digestion."

"*R-r-r-r.*"

Magnus Ridolph glanced into the kitchen. "I see that
you have dinner prepared. Well, let us eat our stew, and
then the evening will be free for intellectual exercises."

The blurred green twilight drifted down from the badlands, and, dinner over, Magnus Ridolph stepped outside into the evening quiet. Under different circumstances
he would have enjoyed the vista—the olive-dark *massif*
to his left, the fields black in the greenish light, the blue-
green sky with a few lavender and orange clouds over
the ocean. A faint yelp came to his ears—far, far distant,
mournful, lonely as a ghost-cry. Then there came a quick
far chorus: "*Ow-ow-ow-ow.*"

Magnus Ridolph entered the cottage, emerged with a
pair of infrared-sensitive binoculars. Down from the
mountains came the Bounders, leaping pell-mell high in
the air, hopping like monstrous fleas, and the alien motion sent a chill along Magnus Ridolph's usually im-
perturbable spine.

"*Ow-ow-ow-ow,*" came the far chorus, as the Bounders
flung themselves upon Magnus Ridolph's ticholama.

Magnus Ridolph nodded grimly. "Tomorrow night, my destructive guests, you shall sing a different song."

The construction crew arrived from Garswan the next morning in a great copter which carried below a bulldozer. They came while Magnus Ridolph was still at breakfast. Swallowing the last of his stew, he took them out to the devastated tract, showed them what he wished done.

Late afternoon found the project complete, the last of the equipment installed and Magnus Ridolph engaged in testing the machinery.

A heavy concrete pill-box now rose on the border of the blighted acreage, a windowless building reinforced with steel and set on a heavy foundation. A hundred yards from the pill-box a ten-foot cylindrical block stood anchored deep into the ground. An endless herculoy cable ran from the pill-box, around a steel-collared groove in the block, back into the pill-box, where it passed around the drum of an electric winch, then out again to the block.

Magnus Ridolph glanced around the little room with satisfaction. There had been no time for attention to detail, but the winch ran smoothly, pulled the cable easily out, around the anchor block, back again. Inside the door rose a stack of resilian plates, each an inch thick, each trailing three feet of herculoy chain.

Magnus Ridolph took a last look about the pill-box, then strolled sedately to his copter, flew back to the cottage.

Chook was standing in the doorway.

"Chook," said Magnus Ridolph, "do you consider yourself brave, resourceful, resolute?"

Chook's bottle-green eyes moved in two different directions. "I am cook."

"*Mmph,*" said Magnus Ridolph. "Of course. But tonight

I wish to observe the Howling Bounders at close quarters, and desiring some assistance, I have selected you to accompany me."

Chook's eyes turned even farther out of focus. "Chook busy tonight."

"What is the nature of your task?" inquired Magnus Ridolph frostily.

"Chook write letter."

Magnus Ridolph turned away impatiently. During the course of the meal he once more suggested that Chook join him, but Chook remained obdurate. And so about an hour before sunset Magnus Ridolph shouldered a light knapsack and set out on foot for his pill-box.

The shadow of the foremost spur had engulfed the little concrete dome when he finally arrived. Without delay he ducked into the dark interior, dropped the knapsack to the floor.

He tested the door. It slid easily up and down, locked securely. He moved the rheostat controlling the winch. The drum turned, the cable slid out to the anchor block, around, returned. Magnus Ridolph now took one of his resilian plates, shackled the tail-chain to the cable, set it down directly before the doorway, lowered the door to all but a slit, seated himself, lit a cigarette, waited.

Shade crept across the dark purple field; the blue-green sky shaded through a series of deepening sub-marine colors. There was silence, an utter hush.

From the mountains came a yelp, far but very keen. It echoed down the rock-canyons. As if it were a signal, a series of other yells followed, a few louder and closer, but for the most part nearly lost out in the wasteland.

"*Ow-ow-ow-ow.*"

This time the cries were louder, mournful, close at hand, and Magnus Ridolph, peering through the peep-hole in the door, saw the tumble of figures come storming down the hill, black against the sky. He dipped a brush into a pan of liquid nearby, slid the door up a trifle, reached out, swabbed the resilian plate, slid the door shut. Rising, he put his eye to the peep-hole.

The howling sounded overhead now, to all sides, full of throbbing new overtones, and Magnus Ridolph caught the flicker of dark figures close at hand.

A thud on top of the pill-box, a yell from directly overhead, and Magnus Ridolph clenched his thin old hands.

Bumps sounded beside the pill-box; the cable twitched. The howling grew louder, higher in pitch, the roof resounded to a series of thuds. The cable gave a furious jerk, swung back and forth.

Magnus Ridolph smiled grimly to himself. Outside now he heard a hoarse yammering, then angry panting, the jingle of furiously shaken chain. And he glimpsed a form with long lank arms and legs, a narrow head, flinging itself savagely back and forth from the snare.

Magnus Ridolph started the winch, pulled the plate and its captive approximately ten feet out toward the anchor block, shackled another plate to the cable, daubed it with hesso-penthol, raised the door a trifle, shoved the plate outside. It was snatched from his hands. Magnus Ridolph slammed the door down, rose to the peep-hole. Another dark form danced, bounded back and forth across the cable, which, taking up the slack in the chain, threw the creature headlong to the ground with every bound.

The yells outside almost deafened Magnus Ridolph, and the pill-box appeared to be encircled. He prepared another plate, raised the door a slit, slid the plate under. Again it was snatched from his hands, but this time black talons thrust into the slit, heaved with a bone-crushing strength.

But Magnus Ridolph had foreseen the contingency, had a steel bar locking down the door. The fingers strained again. Magnus Ridolph took his heat-pencil, turned it on the fingers. The steel changed color, glowed, the fingers gave off a nauseating stench, suddenly were snatched back. Magnus Ridolph shackled another plate to the cable.

Two hours passed. Every plate he shoved under the door was viciously yanked out of his hands. Sometimes they would seek the slit, to be repelled by the heat-pencil, until the room was dense with stifling organic smoke. Shackle the plate, daub it, slide it out, slam the door, run the cable further out on the winch, look through the peep-hole. The winch creaked, the pill-box vibrated to the frenzied tugging from without. He sent out his last plate, peered through the peep-hole. The cable was lined out to the anchor block and back with frantic tireless forms, and overhead others pelted the pill-box.

Magnus Ridolph composed himself against the concrete wall, found a flask in his knapsack and took a long drink.

A groaning from the winch disturbed him. He arose painfully, old joints stiff, peered through the peep-hole.

A form of concerted action was in progress: the cable was lined solidly on both sides with black shapes. They bent, rose, and the drum of the winch creaked, squawked. Magnus Ridolph released the winch brake, jerked the cable forward and back several times, and the line of black figures swayed willy-nilly back and forth. Suddenly, like a flight of black ghosts, they left the cable, bounded toward the pill-box.

Clang! Against the steel door—the jar of a great weight. Clang! The door ground back against its socket. Magnus Ridolph rubbed his beard. The steel presumably would hold, and likewise the sill, bolted deep into the concrete. But, of course, no construction was invulnerable. Thud! Fine dust sprang away from the wall.

Magnus Ridolph jumped to the peep-hole, in time to glimpse a hurtling black shape, directed seemingly at his head. He ducked. THUD! Magnus Ridolph anxiously played a torch around the interior of the pill-box. Should there be a crack—

He returned to the peep-hole. Suppose the Bounders brought a length of steel beam, and used it for a battering ram? Probably their powers of organization were unequal to the task. Once more he seated himself on the floor, addressed himself to his flask. Presently he fell into a doze.

He awoke to find the air hot, heavy, pungent. Red light flickered in through the peep-hole, an ominous crackling sound came to his ears. A moment he sat thoughtfully, while his lungs demanded oxygen from the vitiated atmosphere. He rose, looked forth into a red and white pyre of blazing ticholama. He sat down in the center of the room, clear of the already warm concrete.

"Is it my end, then, to be fired like a piece of crockery in a kiln?" he asked himself. "No," came the answer, "I shall undoubtedly suffocate first. But," he mused, "on second thought—"

He took his water bottle from the knapsack, brought forth the power pack, ran leads into the water. He dialed up the power, and bubbles of hydrogen and oxygen vibrated to the surface. He pressed his face to the bottle, breathed the synthetic atmosphere. . . .

Blantham's copter dropped to Magnus Ridolph's landing and Blantham stepped out, spruce in dark gray and red. Magnus Ridolph appeared in the doorway, nodded.

"Good morning, good morning." Blantham stepped forward jauntily. "I dropped by to tell you that the harvesters have nearly finished on my property and that they'll be ready for you at the first of the week."

"Excellent," said Magnus Ridolph.

"A pity those Bounders have done so much damage," sighed Blantham, looking off in the direction of the devastated area. "Something will have to be done to abate that nuisance."

Magnus Ridolph nodded in agreement.

Blantham inspected Magnus Ridolph. "You're looking rather tired. I hope the climate agrees with you?"

"Oh entirely. I've been keeping rather irregular hours."

"I see. What are those two domes out in the field? Did you have them built?"

Magnus Ridolph waved a modest hand. "Observation posts, I suppose you'd call them. The first was too limited, and rather vulnerable, in several respects, so I installed the second larger unit."

"I see," said Blantham. "Well, I'll be on my way. Those Bounders seem to have gotten pretty well into the plantation. Do you still have hope of a sixty-nine thousand munit profit on the property?"

Magnus Ridolph permitted a smile to form behind his crisp white beard. "A great deal more, I hope. My total profit on our transaction should come to well over two hundred thousand munits."

Blantham froze, his wide-set eyes blue, glassy. "Two hundred thousand munits? Are you— May I ask exactly how you arrive at that figure?"

"Of course," said Magnus Ridolph affably. "First of course is the sale of my harvest. Two thousand acres of good ticholama, which should yield forty-six thousand munits. Second, two hundred forty tons—estimated—of raw resilian, at a quarter munit a pound, or five hundred munits a ton. Subtract freight charges, and my profit here should be well over a hundred thousand munits—say one hundred and ten thousand—"

"But," stammered Blantham, his jowls red, "where did you get the resilian?"

Magnus Ridolph clasped his hands behind his body, looked across the field. "I trapped a number of the Bounders."

"But how? Why?"

"From their habits and activities, as well as their diet, I deduced that the Bounders were either resilian or some closely allied substance. A test proved them to be resilian. In the last two weeks, I've trapped twenty-four hundred, more or less."

"And how did you do that?"

"They are curious and aggressive creatures," said Magnus Ridolph, and explained the mechanism of his trap.

"How did you kill them? They're like iron."

"Not during the day time. They dislike the light, curl up in tight balls, and a sharp blow with a machete severs the prime chord of their nervous system."

Blantham bit his lips, chewed at his mustache. "That's still only a hundred fifty or sixty thousand. How do you get two hundred thousand out of that?"

"Well," said Magnus Ridolph, "I'll admit the rest is pure speculation, and for that reason I named a conservative figure. I'll collect a hundred thirty thousand munits from you, which will return my original investment, and I should be able to sell this excellent plantation for a hundred seventy or eighty thousand munits. My trapping expenses have been twelve thousand munits so far. You can see that I'll come out rather well."

Blantham angrily turned away. Magnus Ridolph held out a hand. "What's your hurry? Can you stay to lunch? I admit the fare is modest, only stew, but I'd enjoy your company."

Blantham stalked away. A moment later his copter was out of sight in the green-blue sky. Magnus Ridolph returned inside. Chook raised his head. "Eat lunch."

"As you wish." Magnus Ridolph seated himself. "What's this? Where's our stew?"

"Chook tired of stew," said his cook. "We eat chili con carne now."

MIRROR OF ICE

◎◎◎

Gary Wright

They called it the Stuka. It was a tortuous, twenty-kilometer path of bright ice, and in that distance—12.42 miles—it dropped 7366 feet, carving a course down the alpine mountainside like the track of a great snake. It was thirty feet wide on the straights with corners curling as high as forty feet. It was made for sleds. . . .

He waited in the narrow cockpit and listened to the wind. It moaned along the frozen shoulder of the towering white peak and across the steep starting ramp, pushing along streamers of snow out against the hard blue sky, and he could hear it cry inside him with the same cold and lonely sound.

He was scared. And what was worse—he knew it.

Forward, under the sleek nose of his sled, the mountain fell away abruptly—straight down, it seemed—and the valley was far below. So very far.

. . . *too far this time, buddy-boy, too far forever* . . .

The countdown light on the dash flickered a sudden

blood red, then deliberately winked twice. At the same time two red rockets arced out over the valley and exploded into twin crimson fireballs.

Two minutes.

On both sides of the starting ramp, cantilevered gracefully from the mountainside, brightly bannered platforms were crowded with people. He glanced at the hundreds of blankly staring sunglasses, always the same, always turned to the ramp as if trying to see inside the helmets of these men, as if trying to pry into the reasons of their being there waiting to die. He looked back to the deep valley; today he wondered too.

. . . *just one last time, wasn't that what you told yourself? One last race and that's the end of it and good-by to the sleds. Wasn't that your personal promise?*

Then what in hell are you doing here? That "last race" was last month's race. Why are you in this one?

No answer.

All he could find were cold questions and a hollow echo of the wind. He gripped the steering wheel, hard, until cramps began in his hands; he would think about his sled. . . .

It was his eleventh sled, and like the others it was a brilliant red, not red for its particular flash, but because of a possible crash far from the course in deep snow. He wanted to be found and found fast. Some of the Kin had never been found in time.

. . . *they didn't find Bob Lander until that summer—*

He forced himself back.

Empty, the sled weighed 185 pounds and looked very much like the body-shell of a particularly sleek racer but with a full bubble canopy and with runners instead of wheels. It was a mean-looking missile, low and lean, hardly wider than his shoulders, clearing the ice by barely two inches. He sat nearly reclining, the half wheel in his lap, feet braced on the two edging pedals—and this was the feature that made these sleds the awesome things they were. They could tilt their runners—four hollow-ground, chrome-steel "skis"—edging them against the ice like wide skate blades. This was what had changed bobsledding into . . . *this:* this special thing with its special brotherhood, this clan apart, this peculiar breed of men set aside for the wonder of other men. The Kin, they called themselves.

. . . *Someone once, laughing, had said, "Without peer, we are the world's fastest suicides."*

He snapped himself back again and checked his brakes.

By pulling back on the wheel, two electrically operated flaps—actually halves of the sled's tail section—swung out on either side. Silly to see, perhaps. But quite effective when this twelve and a half square feet hit the airstream at 80 mph. A button under his right thumb operated another braking system: with each push it fired forward a solid rocket charge in the nose of the sled. There were seven charges, quite often not enough. But when everything failed, including the man, there was the lever by his left hip. The Final Folly, it was called; a firm pull and, depending on a hundred unknown "if's" and "maybe's," he might be lucky enough to find himself ejected and hanging from a parachute some three hundred feet up. Or it might be the last voluntary act of his life.

He had used it twice. Once streaking into the tall wall of the Wingover, he had lost a runner . . . and was almost fired into the opposite grandstand, missing the top tiers of seats by less than four feet. Another time six sleds suddenly tangled directly in front of him, and he had blasted himself through the overhanging limbs of a large fir tree.

But others had not been so lucky.

Hans Kroger: they finally dug his body out of eighteen feet of snow; he'd gone all the way to the dirt. His sled had been airborne when he blew—and upside-down!

Jarl Yogensen: his sled tumbling and he ejected directly under the following sleds. No one was certain that all of him was ever found!

Max Conrad: a perfect blow-out! At least 350 feet up and slightly downhill . . . His chute never opened.

Wayne Barley:—

He jarred himself hard in the cockpit and felt the sudden seizure of his G-suit. He wanted to hit something. But he could feel the watching eyes and the TV cameras, and there wasn't room in the cockpit to get a decent swing anyway.

His countdown light flickered for attention and blinked once, and a single red rocket flashed into the sky.

That was part of it all: the waiting, the God-awful waiting, staring down at the valley over a mile below. And how many men had irrevocably slammed back their canopy in this lifetime of two minutes and stayed behind? A few, yes. And he could too. Simply open his canopy, that was the signal, and when the start came the other sleds would dive down and away and he would be sitting here alone. So alone! And he would be alone for the rest of his life. He might see some of the Kin again, sometime, somewhere. But they would not see him. It was a kind of death to stay behind.

. . . and a real death to go. Death, the silent rider with every man in every race . . .

He frowned at the other sleds, sixteen in staggered rows of eight. Sixteen bright and beautiful, trim fast projectiles hanging from their starting clamps. He knew them, every one; they were his brothers. They were the Kin—but not here. Not now.

Years ago when he was a novice he had asked old

Franz Cashner, "Did you see the way I took Basher Bend right beside you?"

And Franz told him, "Up there I see nobody! Only sleds! Down here you are you, up there you are nothing but another sled. That's all! And don't forget that!"

. . . and it had to be that way. On the course sleds crashed and were no more. . . . Only later, in the valley, were there men missing.

Of these sixteen, chances were that nine would finish. With luck, maybe ten. And chances also said that only fourteen of these men would be alive tonight. Those were the odds, as hard and cold as the ice, the fascinating frosting for this sport. Violent death! Assured, spectacular, magnetic death in a sport such as the world had never known. Incredible men with incredible skills doing an incredible thing.

Back in the Sixties they claimed an empty sled with its steering locked would make a course all by itself. An empty sled here would not last two corners. The Stuka was a cold killer, not a thrill ride. And it was not particular. It killed veterans and novices alike. But there was $20,000 for the man who got to the end of it first, and a whole month before he had to do it again. Money and fame and all the girls in the world. Everything and anything for the men who rode the Stuka.

Was that why they did it?

. . . yes, always that question: "Why do you do it?" And before he had died on the Plummet, Sir Robert Brooke had told them, "Well, why not?"

And it was an answer as good as any.

But was it good enough this time?

No answer.

He only knew there was but one way off this mountain for him now and that was straight ahead, and for the first time since his novice runs, his legs were trembling. Twelve and a half miles, call it, and the record was 9 minutes, 1.14 seconds! An average speed of 82.67 mph, and that was *his* record. They would at least remember him by that!

His countdown light flashed, a green rocket rose and burst, and there was a frozen moment . . . the quiet click of the release hook, the lazy, slow-motion start, the sleds sliding forward in formation over the edge . . . then he was looking once again into the terrible top of the Stuka —that 45-degree, quarter-mile straight drop. In six seconds he was doing over 60 mph, and the mouth of the first corner was reaching up.

. . . Carl's Corner, for Carl Rasch, who went over the top of it nine years ago; and they found him a half-mile down the glacier . . . what was left of him . . .

He glanced to his right. It was clear. He eased his flap brakes, dropped back slightly and pulled right. The leading sleds were jockeying in front now, lining for this long left. Brakes flapped like quick wings, and they started around, sleds riding up the vertical ice wall and holding there, ice chips spraying back like contrails from those on the lower part of the wall as they edged their runners against the turn. He came in far right and fast, riding high on the wall and diving off with good acceleration.

The ice was a brilliant blur underneath now, and he could feel the trembling rumble of his sled. They rattled into the Chute, a steep traverse, still gaining speed, still bunched and jostling for position. He was in the rear but this was good; he didn't like this early crowding for the corners.

The sheer wall of Basher Bend loomed, a 120-degree right that dropped hard coming out. He was following close in the slipstream of the sled in front of him, overtaking because of the lessened wind resistance. The corner came, and they were on the wall again. With his slightly greater speed he was able to go higher on the wall, nearly to the top and above the other sled. His G-suit tightened. They swarmed out of the corner and into the Strafing Run, a long, steep dive with a hard pull-out.

A roar rose from the mountain now as the sleds reached speed, a dull rumble like that of avalanche . . . and that is actually what they were now—an avalanche of sleds, and just as deadly.

He pulled ahead of the other sled in the dive and hit the savage pull-out right on the tail of another, and the next turn curved up before them: Hell's Left, a double corner, an abrupt left falling into a short straight with another sharp left at the bottom. He was still overtaking, and they went up the wall side by side, he on the inside, under the other. He eased his left pedal, using edges for the first time, holding himself away from the other by a safe six inches. The course dropped away, straight down the mountain to the second half of the corner, and he felt the sickening sudden smoothness of leaving the ice—he had tried it too fast, and the course was falling away under him. . . .

. . . *old Rolf De Kepler, "The Flying Dutchman," laughing over his beer and saying, "Always I am spending more time off the ice than on, hah? So this is more easy to my stomach. Already I have four G-suits to give up on me."* . . .

. . . *and he made his last flight three years ago off the top at the bottom of Hell's Left . . . four hundred yards, they claimed.*

He held firm and straight on the wheel and pulled carefully, barely opening his brakes. The sled touched at a slight angle, lurched, but he caught it by edging quickly. The other sled had pulled ahead. He tucked in behind it. The second left was rushing up at them, narrow and filled with sleds. They dove into it less than a foot apart. Ice chips streamed back from edging runners, rattling against his sled like a storm of bullets. There was an abrupt lurching, the quick left-right slam of air turbulence. A sled was braking hard somewhere ahead. Perhaps two or three. Where? He couldn't see. He re-acted automatically . . . full air brakes, hard onto his left edges and steer for the inside; the safest area if a wreck was trying to happen. His sled shivered with the strain of coming off the wall, holding against the force of the corner now only with the knifelike edges of its runners. But the force was too great. He began to skid, edges chattering. He eased them off a little, letting the sled drift slightly sideways. Two others had sliced down to the inside too, edges spraying ice. For a moment he was blinded again, but the corner twisted out flat, and he was through and still on the course, and he knew he was too tight, too hard with his control; he was fighting his sled instead of working with it. . . .

. . . *a tourist once asked Erik Sigismund how he con-trolled his sled, and he answered, "Barely." And even that had failed when he flipped it a year ago and four others ran over him.*

An old, lurking thought pounced into him again . . . he couldn't stop this sled now if he wanted to. There was no such thing as stopping, outside of a crash. He had to ride until it ended, and he was suddenly certain that was not going to be at the bottom. Not this time. He had crashed before, too many times, but he had never had this feeling of fear before. Not *this* fear. It was different, and he couldn't say why, and he was letting it affect him. And that was the greatest wrong.

They were thundering into the Jackhammer now, three hundred yards of violent dips. Every sled had its brakes out, and there were fast flashes as some fired braking rockets. But where the walls of the course sloped upward the ice was comparatively smooth. He eased left, to the uphill side, and leaned on his left pedal, holding the sled on the slope with its edges. Then he folded his air brakes and started gaining again. It was necessary; one did not hold back from fear. If that was one's style of life, he would never be a sledder in the first place.

Suddenly from the middle of the leading blurs a sled became airborne from the crest of one of the bumps. It hit once and twisted into the air like something alive. Sleds behind it fired rockets and tried to edge away. One skidded broadside, then rolled. A shattered body panel spun away; the two sleds were demolishing themselves. Someone blew-out, streaking into the sky, canopy sparkling high in the sun—and that meant another sled out of control. He pulled full air brakes and fired a rocket, the force slamming him hard against his chest straps. His left arm was ready to fire the charge under the seat. But if he waited too long. . . .

. . . *Kurt Schnabel was proud to be the only man who had never ejected . . . but the one time he had tried he had waited the barest fraction of a moment too long, and his chute came down with his shattered corpse.*

The three wild sleds whirled away, spinning out of sight over the low retaining walls. He folded his brakes. There was a trembling in his arms and legs like the slight but solid shuddering of a flywheel out of balance, involuntary and with a threat of getting worse. He cursed himself. He could have blown-out too. No one would have blamed him with that tangle developing in front. But he hadn't . . . and it was too late now.

. . . *only one man had ever blown-out without an apparent reason and gotten away with it: Shorty Case in his first race. And when he was asked about it afterward, asked in that overcasual, quiet tone, he had answered,*

*"You bet your sweet, I blew! 'Cause if I hadn't, man, I was
gonna lose my mind."*

*But he didn't blow-out that day on the Fallaways, the
day his sled somersaulted and sowed its wreckage down
the course for a half mile . . . and him too . . .*

No, there were no quitters here; only the doers or the
dead. And which was he going to be tonight?

. . . drive, don't think . . .

The Jackhammer smoothed out and plunged downward, and they were hurtling now into the Wingover
at over 90 mph. Here were the second biggest grandstands on the course, the second greatest concentration of
cameras.

Here two ambulance helicopters stood by, and a priest
too. The Wingover. . . .

Imagine an airplane peeling off into a dive . . . imagine a sled doing the same on a towering wall of ice,
a wall rising like a great, breaking wave, frozen at the
moment of its overhanging curl. . . . The Wingover
was a monstrous, curving scoop to the right, nearly
fifty feet high, rolling the sleds up, over, and hurling
them down into a 65-degree pitch when twisted into a
6-G pull-out to the left.

*. . . "Impossible!" When Wilfrid von Gerlach laid out
the Stuka that is what they told him about the Wingover.
"It cannot be done!"*

*But von Gerlach had been a Grand Prix racer and a
stunt pilot, and when the Stuka was finished he took the
first sled through. At the finish he sat quietly for a moment, staring back at the mountain. "At the Wingover I
was how fast?" he asked thoughtfully. They replied that
he'd been radared there at 110 mph. He nodded, then
made the statement the sledders had carried with them
ever since.*

"It's possible."

He watched the leading sleds line up for that shining, sheer curve and felt the fear freeze through him again. A man was little more than a captive in his sled here. If he was on the right line going in, then it was beautiful; if not, well. . . .

. . . the brotherly beers and the late talk . . .

"Remember when Otto Domagk left Cripple's Corner in that snowstorm?"

"Ya, und ven him vas digged out—Vas? Two hours? —he vas so sleeping."

"And not a mark on him, remember?"

. . . Remember, remember . . .

He followed in line barely four feet from the sled in front of him and felt the savage, sickening blow as the wall raised and rolled him. A flicker of shadow, a glimpse of the valley nearly upside-down, then the fall and the increasing shriek of wind and runners, and he was pointing perfectly into the pull-out, still lined exactly with the sled ahead—but there was one sled badly out of line . . .

And someone pulled their air brakes full open.

Sleds began weaving in the violent turbulence of those brakes. Rockets flashed. A sled went sideways, rolling lazily above the others, and exploded against the wall of the pull-out. He pulled the ejection lever . . . nothing happened!

He was dead, he knew that. He saw two sleds tumbling into the sky, another shattered to pieces and sliding along the course. All that was necessary was to hit one of those pieces . . . but the corner was suddenly gone behind. The course unwound into a long left traverse. He remembered to breathe. There were tooth chips in his mouth and the taste of blood. He swerved past a piece of wreckage, then another . . .

. . . how many were dead now? Himself and how

*many others? But it wasn't fear of death—what was it?
What was it that he'd walled off inside—that something
secret always skirted as carefully as a ship veers from a
hidden reef, knowing it is there—what? And now the wall
was down, and he was facing. . . .*

His sled shuddered. He was driving badly, too harsh
with his edge control. He narrowly made it through the
Boot and Cripple's Corner, spraying ice behind him, but
it was not the sled that was out of control. It was him.
And he was diving now straight for the gates of hell at
over 110 mph.

It was called the Plummet. It began with an innocent,
wide left, steeply banked, then the world fell away. It
dove over a half mile headlong down a 50-degree slope
straight into a ravine and up the other side, then into a
full 180-degree uphill hairpin to the right, a steep straight
to the bottom of the ravine again, and finally into a
sharp left and a long, rolling straight. It had killed
more men than any other part of the course.

Here were the biggest grandstands and the most hungry eyes of the cameras. Here there were three clergy,
and emergency operating rooms. Here . . .

. . . *here he would complete the formality of dying.*

He came into the left too low, too fast for the edges
to hold. The sled skidded. He reacted automatically,
holding slight left edges and steering into the skid. The
sled drifted up the wall, arcing toward the top where
nothing showed but the cold blue of the sky. He waited,
a part of him almost calm now, waiting to see if the
corner would straighten before he went over the top. It
did, but he was still skidding, close to the retaining wall,
plunging into the half-mile drop nearly sideways. He
increased his edges. The tail of the sled brushed the
wall and it was suddenly swinging the opposite way. He
reversed his wheel and edges, anticipating another skid,

but he was not quick enough. The sled bucked, careening up on its left runners. It grazed the wall again, completely out of control now—but he kept trying . . .

. . . *and that was it; you kept trying. Over and over. No matter how many times you faced yourself it had to be done again. And again. The Self was never satisfied with single victories—you had to keep trying. . . .*

And he was empty no more.

The hospital. How many times had he awakened here? And it was always wonderfully the same: gentle warmth and his body finally relaxed and he would test it piece by piece to see what was bent and broken this time; and always the newsmen and the writers and the other assorted ghouls, and always the question and answer period. Punch-lining, they called it. . . .

"How did it happen?"

"I dozed off."

"Why didn't you eject?"

"Parachuting is dangerous."

"When did you realize you were out of control?"

"At the starting line."

"What will you do now?"

"Heal."

"Will you race again?"

. . . "It's possible."

Outside, the wind was blowing.

HEAVYPLANET

Milton A. Rothman

Ennis was completing his patrol of Sector EM, Division 426 of the Eastern Ocean. The weather had been unusually fine, the liquid-thick air roaring along in a continuous blast that propelled his craft with a rush as if it were flying, and lifting short, choppy waves that rose and fell with a startling suddenness. A short savage squall whirled about, pounding down on the ocean like a million hammers, flinging the little boat ahead madly.

Ennis tore at the controls, granite-hard muscles standing out in bas-relief over his short, immensely thick body, skin gleaming scalelike in the slashing spray. The heat from the sun that hung like a huge red lantern on the horizon was a tangible intensity, making an inferno of the gale.

The little craft, that Ennis maneuvered by sheer brawn, took a leap into the air and seemed to float for many seconds before burying its keel again in the sea. It often floated for long distances, the air was so dense. The boundary between air and water was sometimes scarcely defined at all—one merged into the other imperceptibly. The pressure did strange things.

Like a dust mote sparkling in a beam, a tiny speck of light above caught Ennis' eye. A glider, he thought, but he was puzzled. Why so far out here on the ocean? They were nasty things to handle in the violent wind.

The dust mote caught the light again. It was lower, tumbling down with a precipitancy that meant trouble. An upward blast caught it, checked its fall. Then it floated down gently for a space until struck by another howling wind that seemed to distort its very outlines.

Ennis turned the prow of his boat to meet the path of the falling vessel. Curious, he thought; where were its wings? Were they retracted, or broken off? It ballooned closer, and it wasn't a glider. Far larger than any glider ever made, it was of a ridiculous shape that would not stand up for an instant. And with the sharp splash the body made as it struck the water—a splash that fell in almost the same instant it rose—a thought seemed to leap up in his mind. A thought that was more important than anything else on that planet; or was to him, at least. For if it was what he thought it was—and it had to be that—it was what Shadden had been desperately seeking for many years. What a stroke of inconceivable luck, falling from the sky before his very eyes!

The silvery shape rode the ragged waters lightly. Ennis' craft came up with a rush; he skillfully checked its speed and the two came together with a slight jar. The metal of the strange vessel dented as if it were made of rubber. Ennis stared. He put out an arm and felt the curved surface of the strange ship. His finger prodded right through the metal. What manner of people were they who made vessels of such weak materials?

He moored his little boat to the side of the larger one and climbed to an opening. The wall sagged under him.

He knew he must be careful; it was frightfully weak. It would not hold together very long, he must work fast if it were to be saved. The atmospheric pressure would have flattened it out long ago, had it not been for the jagged rent above which had allowed the pressure to be equalized.

He reached the opening and lowered himself carefully into the interior of the vessel. The rent was too small; he enlarged it by taking the two edges in his hands and pulling them apart. As he went down he looked askance at the insignificant plates and beams that were like tissue paper on his world. Inside was wreckage. Nothing was left in its original shape. Crushed, mutilated machinery, shattered vacuum tubes, sagging members, all ruined by the gravity and the pressure.

There was a pulpy mess on the floor that he did not examine closely. It was like red jelly, thin and stalky, pulped under a gravity a hundred times stronger and an atmosphere ten thousand times heavier than that it had been made for.

He was in a room with many knobs and dials on the walls, apparently a control room. A table in the center with a chart on it, the chart of a solar system. It had nine planets; his had but five.

Then he knew he was right. If they came from another system, what he wanted must be there. It could be nothing else.

He found a staircase, descended. Large machinery bulked there. There was no light, but he did not notice that. He could see well enough by infra red, and the amount of energy necessary to sustain his compact giant-hood kept him constantly radiating.

Then he went through a door that was of a comfortable massiveness, even for his planet—and there it was. He recognized it at once. It was big, squat, strong. The metal was soft, but it was thick enough even to stand

solidly under the enormous pull of this world. He had
never seen anything quite like it. It was full of coils,
magnets, and devices of shapes unknown to him. But
Shadden would know. Shadden, and who knows how
many other scientists before him, had tried to make something which would do what this could do, but they had
all failed. And without the things this machine could perform, the race of men on Heavyplanet was doomed to
stay down on the surface of the planet, chained there
immovably by the crushing gravity.

It was atomic energy. That he had known as soon as
he knew that the body was not a glider. For nothing
else but atomic energy and the fierce winds was capable
of lifting a body from the surface of Heavyplanet.
Chemicals were impotent. There is no such thing as an
explosion where the atmosphere pressed inward with more
force than an explosion could press outward. Only atomic,
of all the theoretically possible sources of energy, could
supply the work necessary to lift a vessel away from the
planet. Every other source of energy was simply too
weak.

Yes, Shadden, all the scientists must see this. And
quickly, because the forces of sea and storm would quickly
tear the ship to shreds, and, even more vital, because the
scientists of Bantin and Marak might obtain the secret if
there was delay. And that would mean ruin—the loss of
its age-old supremacy—for his nation. Bantin and Marak
were war nations; did they obtain the secret they would
use it against all the other worlds that abounded in the
Universe.

The Universe was big. That was why Ennis was so
sure there was atomic energy on this ship. For, even
though it might have originated on a planet that was so
tiny that *chemical energy*—although that was hard to
visualize—would be sufficient to lift it out of the pull of

gravity, to travel the distance that stretched between the stars only one thing would suffice.

He went back through the ship, trying to see what had happened.

There were pulps lying behind long tubes that pointed out through clever ports in the outer wall. He recognized them as weapons, worth looking into.

There must have been a battle. He visualized the scene. The forces that came from atomic energy must have warped even space in the vicinity. The ship pierced, the occupants killed, the controls wrecked, the vessel darting off at titanic speed, blindly into nothing. Finally it had come near enough to Heavyplanet to be enmeshed in its huge web of gravity.

Weeaao-o-ow! It was the wailing roar of his alarm siren, which brought him spinning around and dashing for his boat. Beyond, among the waves that leaped and fell so suddenly, he saw a long, low craft making way toward the derelict spaceship. He glimpsed a flash of color on the rounded, gray superstructure, and knew it for a battleship of Marak. Luck was going strong both ways; first good, now bad. He could easily have eluded the battleship in his own small craft, but he couldn't leave the derelict. Once lost to the enemy he could never regain it, and it was too valuable to lose.

The wind howled and buffeted about his head, and he strained his muscles to keep from being blasted away as he crouched there, half on his own boat and half on the derelict. The sun had set and the evening winds were beginning to blow. The hulk scudded before them, its prow denting from the resistance of the water it pushed aside.

He thought furiously fast. With a quick motion he flipped the switch of the radiophone and called Shadden. He waited with fierce impatience until the voice of Shadden was in his ear. At last he heard it, then:

"Shadden! This is Ennis. Get your glider, Shadden, fly to a45j on my route! Quickly! It's come, Shadden! But I have no time. Come!"

He flipped the switch off, and pounded the valve out of the bottom of his craft, clutching at the side of the derelict. With a rush the ocean came up and flooded his little boat and in an instant it was gone, on its way down to the bottom. That would save him from being detected for a short time.

Back into the darkness of the spaceship. He didn't think he had been noticed climbing through the opening. Where could he hide? Should he hide? He couldn't defeat the entire battleship single-handed, without weapons. There were no weapons that could be carried anyway. A beam of concentrated actinic light that ate away the eyes and the nervous system had to be powered by the entire output of a battleship's generators. Weapons for striking and cutting had never been developed on a world where flesh was tougher than metal. Ennis was skilled in personal combat, but how could he overcome all that would enter the derelict?

Down again, into the dark chamber where the huge atomic generator towered over his head. This time he looked for something he had missed before. He crawled around it, peering into its recesses. And then, some feet above, he saw the opening, and pulled himself up to it, carefully, not to destroy the precious thing with his mass. The opening was shielded with a heavy, darkly transparent substance through which seeped a dim glow from within. He was satisfied then. Somehow, matter was still being disintegrated in there, and energy could be drawn off if he knew how.

There were leads—wires of all sizes, and busbars, and thick, heavy tubes that bent under their own weight. Some must lead in and some must lead out; it was not

good to tamper with them. He chose another track. Upstairs again, and to the places where he had seen the
weapons.

They were all mounted on heavy, rigid swivels. He
carefully detached the tubes from the bases. The first
time he tried it he was not quite careful enough, and
part of the projector itself was ripped away, but next
time he knew what he was doing and it came away nicely.
It was a large thing, nearly as thick as his arm and twice
as long. Heavy leads trailed from its lower end and a
lever projected from behind. He hoped it was in working
condition. He dared not try it; all he could do was to
trace the leads back and make sure they were intact.

He ran out of time. There came a thud from the side,
and then smaller thuds, as the boarding party incautiously
leaped over. Once there was a heavy sound, as someone
went all the way through the side of the ship.

"Idiots!" Ennis muttered, and moved forward with his
weapon toward the stairway. Noises came from overhead,
and then a loud crash buckled the plates of the ceiling.
Ennis leaped out of the way, but the entire section came
down, with two men on it. The floor sagged, but held for
the moment. Ennis, caught beneath the downcoming
mass, beat his way free. He came up with a girder in his
hand, which he bent over the head of one of the Maraks.
The man shook himself and struck out for Ennis, who
took the blow rolling and countered with a buffet that
left a black splotch on a skin that was like armor plate
and sent the man through the opposite wall. The other
was upon Ennis, who whirled with the quickness of one
who maneuvers habitually under a pressure of ten thousand atmospheres, and shook the Marak from him, leaving
him unconscious with a twist in a sensitive spot.

The first opponent returned, and the two grappled,
searching for nerve centers to beat upon. Ennis twisted
frantically, conscious of the real danger that the frail

vessel might break to pieces beneath his feet. The railing of a staircase gave behind the two, and they hurtled down it, crashing through the steps to the floor below. Their weight and momentum carried them through. Ennis released his grip on the Marak, stopped his fall by grasping one of the girders that was part of the ship's framework. The other continued his devastating way down, demolishing the inner shell, and then the outer shell gave way with a grinding crash that ominously became a burbling rush of liquid.

Ennis looked down into the space where the Marak had fallen, hissed with a sudden intake of breath, then dove down himself. He met rising water, gushing in through a rent in the keel. He braced himself against a girder which sagged under his hand and moved onward against the rushing water. It geysered through the hole in a heavy stream that pushed him back and started to fill the bottom level of the ship. Against that terriffic pressure he strained forward slowly, beating against the resisting waves, and then, with a mighty flounder, was at the opening. Its edges had been folded back upon themselves by the inrushing water, and they gaped inward like a jagged maw. He grasped them in a huge hand and exerted force. They strained for a moment and began to straighten. Irresistibly he pushed and stretched them into their former position, and then took the broken ends in his hands and *squeezed*. The metal grew soft under his grip and began to flow. The edges of the plate welded under that mighty pressure. He moved down the crack and soon it was watertight. He flexed his hands as he rose. They ached; even his strength was beginning to be taxed.

Noises from above; pounding feet. Men were coming down to investigate the commotion. He stood for a moment in thought, then turned to a blank wall, battered his way through it, and shoved the plates and girders back into position. Down to the other end of the craft, and up a staircase there. The corridor above was deserted, and he stole along it, hunting for the place he had left the weapon he had prepared. There was a commotion ahead as the Maraks found the unconscious man.

Two men came pounding up the passageway, giving him barely enough time to slip into a doorway to the side. The room he found himself in was a sleeping chamber. There were two red pulps there, and nothing that could help him, so he stayed in there only long enough to make sure that he would not be seen emerging into the hall. He crept down it again, with as little noise as possible. The racket ahead helped him; it sounded as though they were tearing the ship apart. Again he cursed their idiocy. Couldn't they see how valuable this was?

They were in the control room, ripping apart the machinery with the curiosity of children, wondering at the strange weakness of the paperlike metal, not realizing that, on the world where it was fabricated, it was sufficiently strong for any strain the builders could put upon it.

The strange weapon Ennis had prepared was on the floor of the passage, and just outside the control room. He looked anxiously at the trailing cables. Had they been stepped on and broken? Was the instrument in working condition? He had to get it and be away; no time to experiment to see if it would work.

A noise from behind, and Ennis again slunk into a doorway as a large Marak with a colored belt around his waist strode jarringly through the corridor into the control room. Sharp orders were barked, and the men ceased their havoc with the machinery of the room. All but a few left and scattered through the ship. Ennis' face twisted into a scowl. This made things more difficult. He couldn't overcome them all single-handed, and he couldn't use the weapon inside the ship if it was what he thought it was from the size of the cables.

A Marak was standing immediately outside the room in which Ennis lurked. No exit that way. He looked around the room; there were no other doors. A porthole in the outer wall was a tiny disk of transparency. He looked at it, felt it with his hands, and suddenly pushed his hands right through it. As quietly as he could, he worked at the edges of the circle until the hole was large enough for him to squeeze through. The jagged edges did not bother him. They felt soft, like a ragged pat of butter.

The Marak vessel was moored to the other side of the spaceship. On this side the wind howled blankly, and the sawtooth waves stretched on and on to a horizon that was many miles distant. He cautiously made his way around the glistening rotundity of the derelict, past the prow, straining silently against the vicious backward sweep of the water that tore at every inch of his body. The darker hump of the battleship loomed up as he rounded the curve, and he swam across the tiny space to grasp a row of projections that curved up over the surface of the craft. He climbed up them, muscles that were hard as carborundum straining to hold against all the forces of gravity and wind that fought him down. Near the top of the curve was a rounded, streamlined projection. He felt around its base and found a lever there, which he moved. The metal hump slid back, revealing a rugged swivel mounting with a stubby cylindrical projector atop it.

He swung the mounting around and let loose a short, sudden blast of white fire along the naked deck of the battleship. Deep voices yelled within and men sprang out, to fall back with abrupt screams clogged in their throats as Ennis caught them in the intolerable blast from the projector. Men, shielded by five thousand miles of atmosphere from actinic light, used to receiving only red and infra red, were painfully vulnerable to this frightful concentration of ultraviolet.

Noise and shouts burst from the derelict spaceship alongside, sweeping away eerily in the thundering wind that seemed to pound down upon them with new vigor in that moment. Heads appeared from the openings in the craft.

Ennis suddenly stood up to his full height, bracing himself against the wind, so dense it made him buoyant. With a deep bellow he bridged the space to the derelict. Then, as a squad of Maraks made their difficult, slippery way across the flank of the battleship toward him, and as the band that had boarded the spaceship crowded out on its battered deck to see what the noise was about, he dropped down into a crouch behind his ultraviolet projector, and whirled it around, pulling the firing lever.

That was what he wanted. Make a lot of noise and disturbance, get them all on deck, and then blow them to pieces. The ravening blast spat from the nozzle of the weapon, and the men on the battleship dropped flat on the deck. He found he could not depress the projector enough to reach them. He spun it to point at the spaceship. The incandescence reached out, and then seemed to waver and die. The current was shut off at the switchboard.

Ennis rose from behind the projector, and then hurtled from the flank of the battleship as he was struck by two Maraks leaping on him from behind the hump of the vessel. The three struck the water and sank, Ennis struggling violently. He was on the last lap, and he gave all his strength to the spurt. The water swirled around them in little choppy waves that fell more quickly than the eye could follow. Heavier blows than those from an Earthly trip hammer were scoring Ennis' face and head. He was in a bad position to strike back, and suddenly he became limp and sank below the surface. The pressure of the water around him was enormous, and it increased very rapidly as he went lower and lower. He saw the shadowy

bulk of the spaceship above him. His lungs were fighting
for air, but he shook off his pretended stupor and swam
doggedly through the water beneath the derelict. He went
on and on. It seemed as though the distance were endless,
following the metal curve. It was so big from beneath,
and trying to swim the width without air made it bigger.

Clear, finally, his lungs drew in the saving breaths.
No time to rest, though. He must make use of his advantage while it was his; it wouldn't last long. He swam
along the side of the ship looking for an opening. There
was none within reach from the water, so he made one,
digging his stubby fingers into the metal, climbing up
until it was safe to tear a rent in the thick outer and
inner walls of the ship.

He found himself in one of the machine rooms of the
second level. He went out into the corridor and up the
stairway which was half-wrecked, and found himself in
the main passage near the control room. He darted down
it, into the room. There was nobody there, although the
noises from above indicated that the Maraks were again
descending. There was his weapon on the floor, where he
had left it. He was glad that they had not gotten around
to pulling that instrument apart. There would be one
thing saved for intelligent examination.

The clatter from the descending crowd turned into a
clamor of anger as they discovered him in the passageway.
They stopped there for a moment, puzzled. He had been
in the ocean, and had somehow magically reappeared
within the derelict. It gave him time to pick up the
weapon.

Ennis debated rapidly and decided to risk the unknown. How powerful the weapon was he did not know,
but with atomic energy it would be powerful. He disliked
using it inside the spaceship; he wanted to have enough
left to float on the water until Shadden arrived; but they

were beginning to advance on him, and he had to start something.

He pulled a lever. The cylinder in his arms jerked back with great force; a bolt of fierce, blinding energy tore out of it and passed with the quickness of light down the length of the corridor.

When he could see again there was no corridor. Everything that had been in the way of the projector was gone, simply disappeared.

Unmindful of the heat from the object in his hands, he turned and directed it at the battleship that was plainly outlined through the space that had been once the walls of the derelict. Before the men on the deck could move, he pulled the lever again.

And the winds were silenced for a moment. The natural elements were still in fear at the incredible forces that came from the destruction of atoms. Then with an agonized scream the hurricane struck again, tore through the spot where there had been a battleship.

Far off in the sky Ennis detected motion. It was Shadden, speeding in a glider.

Now would come the work that was important. Shadden would take the big machine apart and see how it ran. That was what history would remember.

KEYHOLE

◎◎◎

Murray Leinster

When they brought Butch into the station in Tycho Crater he seemed to shrivel as the gravity coils in the air lock went' on. He was impossible to begin with. He was all big eyes and skinny arms and legs, and he was very young and he didn't need air to breathe. Worden saw him as a limp bundle of bristly fur and terrified eyes as his captors handed him over.

"Are you crazy," demanded Worden angrily. "Bringing him in like this. Would you take a human baby into eight gravities? Get out of the way!"

He rushed for the nursery that had been made ready for somebody like Butch. There was a rebuilt dwelling-cave on one side. The other side was a human school-room. And under the nursery the gravity coils had been turned off so that in the room things had only the weight that was proper to them on the Moon.

The rest of the station had coils to bring everything up to normal weight for Earth. Otherwise the staff of the

station would be seasick most of the time. Butch was in
the Earth-gravity part of the station when he was delivered, and he couldn't lift a furry spindly paw.

In the nursery, though, it was different. Worden put
him on the floor. Worden was the uncomfortable one
there—his weight only twenty pounds instead of a normal
hundred and sixty. He swayed and reeled as a man does
on the Moon without gravity coils to steady him.

But that was the normal thing to Butch. He uncurled
himself and suddenly flashed across the nursery to the
reconstructed dwelling-cave. It was a pretty good job,
that cave. There was the five-foot chipped rocks shaped
like dunce caps, found in all residences of Butch's race.
There was the rocking stone on its base of other flattened
rocks. But the spear stones were fastened down with wire
in case Butch got ideas.

Butch streaked it to these familiar objects. He
swarmed up one of the dunce-cap stones and locked his
arms and legs about its top, clinging close. Then he was
still. Worden regarded him. Butch was motionless for
minutes, seeming to take in as much as possible of his
surroundings without moving his eyes.

Suddenly his head moved. He took in more of his
environment. Then he stirred a third time and seemed
to look at Worden with an extraordinary intensity—
whether of fear or pleading Worden could not tell.

"Hmm," said Worden, "so that's what those stones are
for! Perches or beds or roosts, eh? I'm your nurse, fella.
We're playing a dirty trick on you but we can't help it."

He knew Butch couldn't understand, but he talked to
him as a man does talk to a dog or a baby. It isn't
sensible, but it's necessary.

"We're going to raise you up to be a traitor to your
kinfolk," he said with some grimness. "I don't like it, but
it has to be done. So I'm going to be very kind to you

as part of the conspiracy. Real kindness would suggest that I kill you instead—but I can't do that."

Butch stared at him, unblinking and motionless. He looked something like an Earth monkey but not too much so. He was completely impossible but he looked pathetic.

Worden said bitterly, "You're in your nursery, Butch. Make yourself at home!"

He went out and closed the door behind him. Outside he glanced at the video screens that showed the interior of the nursery from four different angles. Butch remained still for a long time. Then he slipped down to the floor. This time he ignored the dwelling-cave of the nursery.

He went interestedly to the human-culture part. He examined everything there with his oversized soft eyes. He touched everything with his incredibly handlike tiny paws. But his touches were tentative. Nothing was actually disturbed when he finished his examination.

He went swiftly back to the dunce-cap rock, swarmed up it, locked his arms and legs about it again, blinked rapidly and seemed to go to sleep. He remained motionless with closed eyes until Worden grew tired of watching him and moved away.

The whole affair was preposterous and infuriating. The first men to land on the Moon knew that it was a dead world. The astronomers had been saying so for a hundred years, and the first and second expeditions to reach Luna from Earth found nothing to contradict the theory.

But a man from the third expedition saw something moving among the upflung rocks of the Moon's landscape and he shot it and the existence of Butch's kind was discovered. It was inconceivable of course that there should be living creatures where there was neither air nor water. But Butch's folk did live under exactly those conditions.

The dead body of the first living creature killed on

the Moon was carried back to Earth and biologists grew indignant. Even with a specimen to dissect and study they were inclined to insist that there simply wasn't any such creature. So the fourth and fifth and sixth lunar expeditions hunted Butch's relatives very earnestly for further specimens for the advancement of science.

The sixth expedition lost two men whose spacesuits were punctured by what seemed to be weapons while they were hunting. The seventh expedition was wiped out to the last man. Butch's relatives evidently didn't like being shot as biological specimens.

It wasn't until the tenth expedition of four ships established a base in Tycho Crater that men had any assurance of being able to land on the Moon and get away again. Even then the staff of the station felt as if it were under permanent siege.

Worden made his report to Earth. A baby lunar creature had been captured by a tractor party and brought into Tycho Station. A nursery was ready and the infant was there now, alive. He seemed to be uninjured. He seemed not to mind an environment of breathable air for which he had no use. He was active and apparently curious and his intelligence was marked.

There was so far no clue to what he ate—if he ate at all—though he had a mouth like the other collected specimens and the toothlike concretions which might serve as teeth. Worden would of course continue to report in detail. At the moment he was allowing Butch to accustom himself to his new surroundings.

He settled down in the recreation room to scowl at his companion scientists and try to think, despite the program beamed on radar frequency from Earth. He definitely didn't like his job, but he knew that it had to be done. Butch had to be domesticated. He had to be persuaded that he was a human being, so human beings could find out how to exterminate his kind.

It had been observed before, on Earth, that a kitten raised with a litter of puppies came to consider itself a dog by the process of imprinting and that even pet ducks came to prefer human society to that of their own species. Some talking birds of high intelligence appeared to be convinced that they were people and acted that way. If Butch reacted similarly he would become a traitor to his kind for the benefit of man. And it was necessary!

Men had to have the Moon, and that was all there was to it. Gravity on the Moon was one eighth that of gravity on Earth. A rocket ship could make the Moon voyage and carry a cargo, but no ship yet built could carry fuel for a trip to Mars or Venus if it started out from Earth.

With a fueling stop on the Moon, though, the matter was simple. Eight drums of rocket fuel on the Moon weighed no more than one on Earth. A ship itself weighed only one eighth as much on Luna. So a rocket that took off from Earth with ten drums of fuel could stop at a fuel base on the Moon and soar away again with two hundred, and sometimes more.

With the Moon as a fueling base men could conquer the solar system. Without the Moon, mankind was earth-bound. Men had to have the Moon!

But Butch's relatives prevented it. By normal experience there could not be life on an airless desert with such monstrous extremes of heat and cold as the Moon's surface experienced. But there was life there. Butch's kinfolk did not breathe oxygen. Apparently they ate it in some mineral combination and it interacted with other minerals in their bodies to yield heat and energy.

Men thought squids peculiar because their blood stream used copper in place of iron, but Butch and his kindred seemed to have complex carbon compounds in place of both. They were intelligent in some fashion, it was clear.

They used tools, they chipped stone, and they had long, needle-like stone crystals which they threw as weapons.

No metals, of course, for lack of fire to smelt them. There couldn't be fire without air. But Worden reflected that in ancient days some experimenters had melted metals and set wood ablaze with mirrors concentrating the heat of the sun. With the naked sunlight of the Moon's surface, not tempered by air and clouds, Butch's folk could have metals if they only contrived mirrors and curved them properly like the mirrors of telescopes on Earth.

Worden had an odd sensation just then. He looked around sharply as if somebody had made a sudden movement. But the video screen merely displayed a comedian back on Earth, wearing a funny hat. Everybody looked at the screen.

As Worden watched, the comedian was smothered in a mass of soapsuds and the studio audience two hundred and thirty thousand miles away squealed and applauded the exquisite humor of the scene. In the Moon station in Tycho Crater somehow it was less than comical.

Worden got up and shook himself. He went to look again at the screens that showed the interior of the nursery. Butch was motionless on the absurd cone-shaped stone. His eyes were closed. He was simply a furry, pathetic little bundle, stolen from the airless wastes outside to be bred into a traitor to his race.

Worden went to his cabin and turned in. Before he slept, though, he reflected that there was still some hope for Butch. Nobody understood his metabolism. Nobody could guess at what he ate. Butch might starve to death. If he did he would be lucky. But it was Worden's job to prevent it.

Butch's relatives were at war with men. The tractors that crawled away from the station—they went amazingly fast on the Moon—were watched by big-eyed furry creatures from rock crevices and from behind the boulders that dotted the lunar landscape.

Needle-sharp throwing stones flicked through emptiness. They splintered on the tractor bodies and on the tractor ports, but sometimes they jammed or broke a tread and then the tractor had to stop. Somebody had to go out and clear things or make repairs. And then a storm of throwing stones poured upon him.

A needle-pointed stone, traveling a hundred feet a second, hit just as hard on Luna as it did on Earth—and it traveled farther. Spacesuits were punctured. Men died. Now tractor treads were being armored and special repair-suits were under construction, made of hardened steel plates.

Men who reached the Moon in rocket ships were having to wear armor like medieval knights and men-at-arms! There was a war on. A traitor was needed. And Butch was elected to be that traitor.

When Worden went into the nursery again—the days and nights on the Moon are two weeks long apiece, so men ignored such matters inside the station—Butch leaped for the dunce-cap stone and clung to its top. He had been fumbling around the rocking stone. It still swayed back and forth on its plate. Now he seemed to try to squeeze himself to unity with the stone spire, his eyes staring enigmatically at Worden.

"I don't know whether we'll get anywhere or not," said Worden conversationally. "Maybe you'll put up a fight if I touch you. But we'll see."

He reached out his hand. The small furry body—neither hot nor cold but the temperature of the air in the station —resisted desperately. But Butch was very young. Worden peeled him loose and carried him across the room to the human schoolroom equipment. Butch curled up, staring fearfully.

"I'm playing dirty," said Worden, "by being nice to you, Butch. Here's a toy."

Butch stirred in his grasp. His eyes blinked rapidly. Worden put him down and wound up a tiny mechanical toy. It moved. Butch watched intently. When it stopped he looked back at Worden. Worden wound it up again. Again Butch watched. When it ran down a second time the tiny handlike paw reached out.

With an odd tentativeness, Butch tried to turn the winding key. He was not strong enough. After an instant he went loping across to the dwelling-cave. The winding key was a metal ring. Butch fitted that over a throw-stone point, and twisted the toy about. He wound it up. He put the toy on the floor and watched it work. Worden's jaw dropped.

"Brains!" he said wryly. "Too bad, Butch! You know the principle of the lever. At a guess you've an eight-year-old human brain! I'm sorry for you, fella!"

At the regular communication hour he made his report to Earth. Butch was teachable. He only had to see a thing done once—or at most twice—to be able to repeat the motions involved.

"And," said Worden, carefully detached, "he isn't afraid of me now. He understands that I intend to be friendly. While I was carrying him I talked to him. He felt the vibration of my chest from my voice.

"Just before I left him I picked him up and talked to him again. He looked at my mouth as it moved and put his paw on my chest to feel the vibrations. I put his paw at my throat. The vibrations are clearer there. He seemed fascinated. I don't know how you'd rate his intelligence but it's above that of a human baby."

Then he said with even greater detachment, "I am disturbed. If you must know, I don't like the idea of

exterminating his kind. They have tools, they have intelligence. I think we should try to communicate with
them in some way—try to make friends—stop killing them
for dissection."

The communicator was silent for the second and a half
it took his voice to travel to Earth and the second and a
half it took to come back. Then the recording clerk's
voice said briskly, "Very good, Mr. Worden! Your voice
was very clear!"

Worden shrugged his shoulders. The lunar station in
Tycho was a highly official enterprise. The staff on the
Moon had to be competent—and besides, political ap-
pointees did not want to risk their precious lives—but
the Earth end of the business of the Space Exploration
Bureau was run by the sort of people who do get on
official payrolls. Worden felt sorry for Butch—and for
Butch's relatives.

In a later lesson session Worden took an empty coffee
tin into the nursery. He showed Butch that its bottom
vibrated when he spoke into it, just as his throat did.
Butch experimented busily. He discovered for himself that
it had to be pointed at Worden to catch the vibrations.

Worden was unhappy. He would have preferred Butch
to be a little less rational. But for the next lesson he
presented Butch with a really thin metal diaphragm
stretched across a hoop. Butch caught the idea at once.

When Worden made his next report to Earth he felt
angry.

"Butch has no experience of sound as we have, of
course," he said curtly. "There's no air on the Moon.
But sound travels through rocks. He's sensitive to vibrations in solid objects just as a deaf person can feel the
vibrations of a dance floor if the music is loud enough.

"Maybe Butch's kind has a language or a code of
sounds sent through the rock underfoot. They do com-

municate somehow! And if they've brains and a means of communication they aren't animals and shouldn't be exterminated for our convenience!"

He stopped. The chief biologist of the Space Exploration Bureau was at the other end of the communication beam then. After the necessary pause for distance his voice came blandly.

"Splendid, Worden! Splendid reasoning! But we have to take the longer view. Exploration of Mars and Venus is a very popular idea with the public. If we are to have funds—and the appropriations come up for a vote shortly —we have to make progress toward the nearer planets. The public demands it. Unless we can begin work on a refueling base on the Moon, public interest will cease!"

Worden said urgently, "Suppose I send some pictures of Butch? He's very human, sir! He's extraordinarily appealing! He has personality! A reel or two of Butch at his lessons ought to be popular!"

Again that irritating wait while his voice traveled a quarter-million miles at the speed of light and the wait for the reply.

"The—ah—lunar creatures, Worden," said the chief biologist regretfully, "have killed a number of men who have been publicized as martyrs to science. We cannot give favorable publicity to creatures that have killed men!" Then he added blandly, "But you are progressing splendidly, Worden—*splendidly!* Carry on!"

His image faded from the video screen. Worden said naughty words as he turned away. He'd come to like Butch. Butch trusted him. Butch now slid down from that crazy perch of his and came rushing to his arms every time he entered the nursery.

Butch was ridiculously small—no more than eighteen inches high. He was preposterously light and fragile in his nursery, where only Moon gravity obtained. And

Butch was such an earnest little creature, so soberly absorbed in everything that Worden showed him!

He was still fascinated by the phenomena of sound. Humming or singing—even Worden's humming and singing—entranced him. When Worden's lips moved now Butch struck an attitude and held up the hoop diaphragm with a tiny finger pressed to it to catch the vibrations Worden's voice made.

Now too when he grasped an idea Worden tried to convey he tended to swagger. He became more human in his actions with every session of human contact. Once, indeed, Worden looked at the video screens which spied on Butch and saw him—all alone—solemnly going through every gesture and every movement Worden had made. He was pretending to give a lesson to an imaginary still-tinier companion. He was pretending to be Worden, apparently for his own satisfaction!

Worden felt a lump in his throat. He was enormously fond of the little mite. It was painful that he had just left Butch to help in the construction of a vibrator-microphone device which would transfer his voice to rock vibrations and simultaneously pick up any other vibrations that might be made in return.

If the members of Butch's race did communicate by tapping on rocks or the like, men could eavesdrop on them—could locate them, could detect ambushes in preparation, and apply mankind's deadly military countermeasures.

Worden hoped the gadget wouldn't work. But it did. When he put it on the floor of the nursery and spoke into the microphone, Butch did feel the vibrations underfoot. He recognized their identity with the vibrations he'd learned to detect in air.

He made a skipping exultant hop and jump. It was plainly the uttermost expression of satisfaction. And then his tiny foot pattered and scratched furiously on the floor.

It made a peculiar scratchy tapping noise which the microphone picked up. Butch watched Worden's face, making the sounds which were like highly elaborated footfalls.

"No dice, Butch," said Worden unhappily. "I can't understand it. But it looks as if you've started your treason already. This'll help wipe out some of your folks."

He reported it reluctantly to the head of the station. Microphones were immediately set into the rocky crater floor outside the station and others were made ready for exploring parties to use for the detection of Moon creatures near them. Oddly enough, the microphones by the station yielded results right away.

It was near sunset. Butch had been captured near the middle of the three-hundred-and-thirty-four-hour lunar day. In all the hours between—a week by Earth time—he had had no nourishment of any sort. Worden had conscientiously offered him every edible and inedible substance in the station. Then at least one sample of every mineral in the station collection.

Butch regarded them all with interest but without appetite. Worden—liking Butch—expected him to die of starvation and thought it a good idea. Better than encompassing the death of all his race, anyhow. And it did seem to him that Butch was beginning to show a certain sluggishness, a certain lack of bounce and energy. He thought it was weakness from hunger.

Sunset progressed. Yard by yard, fathom by fathom, half mile by half mile, the shadows of the miles-high western walls of Tycho crept across the crater floor. There came a time when only the central hump had sunlight. Then the shadow began to creep up the eastern walls. Presently the last thin jagged line of light would vanish and the colossal cup of the crater would be filled to overflowing with the night.

Worden watched the incandescent sunlight growing even narrower on the cliffs. He would see no other sunlight for two weeks' Earth time. Then abruptly an alarm bell rang. It clanged stridently, furiously. Doors hissed shut, dividing the station into airtight sections.

Loud-speakers snapped, *"Noises in the rock outside! Sounds like Moon creatures talking nearby! They may plan an attack! Everybody into spacesuits and get guns ready!"*

At just that instant the last thin sliver of sunshine disappeared. Worden thought instantly of Butch. There was no spacesuit to fit him. Then he grimaced a little. Butch didn't need a spacesuit.

Worden got into the clumsy outfit. The lights dimmed. The harsh airless space outside the station was suddenly bathed in light. The multimillion-lumen beam, made to guide rocket ships to a landing even at night, was turned on to expose any creatures with designs on its owners. It was startling to see how little space was really lighted by the beam and how much of stark blackness spread on beyond.

The loud-speaker snapped again, *"Two Moon creatures! Running away! They're zigzagging! Anybody who wants to take a shot—"* The voice paused. It didn't matter. Nobody is a crack shot in a spacesuit. *"They left something behind!"* said the voice in the loud-speaker. It was sharp and uneasy.

"I'll take a look at that," said Worden. His own voice startled him but he was depressed. "I've got a hunch what it is."

Minutes later he went out through the air lock. He moved lightly despite the cumbrous suit he wore. There were two other staff members with him. All three were armed and the searchlight beam stabbed here and there erratically to expose any relative of Butch who might try to approach them in the darkness.

With the light at his back Worden could see that trillions of stars looked down upon Luna. The zenith was filled with infinitesimal specks of light of every conceivable color. The familiar constellations burned ten times as brightly as on Earth. And Earth itself hung nearly overhead. It was three-quarters full—a monstrous bluish giant in the sky, four times the Moon's diameter, its ice caps and continents mistily to be seen.

Worden went forebodingly to the object left behind by Butch's kin. He wasn't much surprised when he saw what it was. It was a rocking stone on its plate with a fine impalpable dust on the plate, as if something had been crushed under the egg-shaped upper stone acting as a mill.

Worden said sourly into his helmet microphone, "It's a present for Butch. His kinfolk know he was captured alive. They suspect he's hungry. They've left some grub for him of the kind he wants or needs most."

That was plainly what it was. It did not make Worden feel proud. A baby—Butch—had been kidnaped by the enemies of its race. That baby was a prisoner and its captors would have nothing with which to feed it. So someone, greatly daring—Worden wondered somberly if it was Butch's father and mother—had risked their lives to leave food for him with a rocking stone to tag it for recognition as food.

"It's a dirty shame," said Worden bitterly. "All right! Let's carry it back. Careful not to spill the powdered stuff!"

His lack of pride was emphasized when Butch fell upon the unidentified powder with marked enthusiasm. Tiny pinch by tiny pinch Butch consumed it with an air of vast satisfaction. Worden felt ashamed.

"You're getting treated pretty rough, Butch," said Worden. "What I've already learned from you will cost a good many hundred of your folks' lives. And they're taking chances to feed you! I'm making you a traitor and myself a scoundrel."

Butch thoughtfully held up the hoop diaphragm to catch the voice vibrations in the air. He was small and furry and absorbed. He decided that he could pick up sounds better from the rock underfoot. He pressed the communicator microphone on Worden. He waited.

"*No!*" said Worden roughly. "Your people are too human. Don't let me find out any more, Butch. Be smart and play dumb!"

But Butch didn't. It wasn't very long before Worden was teaching him to read. Oddly, though, the rock microphones that had given the alarm at the station didn't help the tractor parties at all. Butch's kinfolk seemed to vanish from the neighborhood of the station altogether. Of course if that kept up the construction of a fuel base could be begun and the actual extermination of the species carried out later. But the reports on Butch were suggesting other possibilities.

"If your folks stay vanished," Worden told Butch, "it'll be all right for a while—and only for a while. I'm being urged to try to get you used to Earth gravity. If I succeed, they'll want you on Earth in a zoo. And if that works—why, they'll be sending other expeditions to get more of your kinfolk to put in other zoos."

Butch watched Worden, motionless.

"And also"—Worden's tone was very grim—"there's some miniature mining machinery coming up by the next rocket. I'm supposed to see if you can learn to run it."

Butch made scratching sounds on the floor. It was unintelligible of course, but it was an expression of interest at least. Butch seemed to enjoy the vibrations of Worden's voice, just as a dog likes to have his master talk to him. Worden grunted.

"We humans class you as an animal, Butch. We tell

ourselves that all the animal world should be subject to us. Animals should work for us. If you act too smart we'll hunt down all your relatives and set them to work digging minerals for us. You'll be with them. But I don't want you to work your heart out in a mine, Butch! It's wrong!"

Butch remained quite still. Worden thought sickishly of small furry creatures like Butch driven to labor in airless mines in the Moon's frigid depths. With guards in spacesuits watching lest any try to escape to the freedom they'd known before the coming of men. With guns mounted against revolt. With punishments for rebellion or weariness.

It wouldn't be unprecedented. The Indians in Cuba when the Spanish came . . . Negro slavery in both Americas . . . concentration camps . . .

Butch moved. He put a small furry paw on Worden's knee. Worden scowled at him.

"Bad business," he said harshly. "I'd rather not get fond of you. You're a likable little cuss but your race is doomed. The trouble is that you didn't bother to develop a civilization. And if you had, I suspect we'd have smashed it. We humans aren't what you'd call admirable."

Butch went over to the blackboard. He took a piece of pastel chalk—ordinary chalk was too hard for his Moon-gravity muscles to use—and soberly began to make marks on the slate. The marks formed letters. The letters made words. The words made sense.

YOU, wrote Butch quite incredibly in neat pica lettering, GOOD FRIEND.

He turned his head to stare at Worden. Worden went white. "I haven't taught you those words, Butch!" he said very quietly. "What's up?"

He'd forgotten that his words, to Butch, were merely vibrations in the air or in the floor. He'd forgotten they had no meaning. But Butch seemed to have forgotten it too. He marked soberly:

MY FRIEND GET SPACESUIT. He looked at Worden and marked once more. TAKE ME OUT. I COME BACK WITH YOU.

He looked at Worden with large incongruously soft and appealing eyes. And Worden's brain seemed to spin inside his skull. After a long time Butch printed again— YES.

Then Worden sat very still indeed. There was only Moon gravity in the nursery and he weighed only one eighth as much as on Earth. But he felt very weak. Then he felt grim.

"Not much else to do, I suppose," he said slowly. "But I'll have to carry you through Earth gravity to the air lock."

He got to his feet. Butch made a little leap up into his arms. He curled up there, staring at Worden's face. Just before Worden stepped through the door Butch reached up a skinny paw and caressed Worden's cheek tentatively.

"Here we go!" said Worden. "The idea was for you to be a traitor. I wonder—"

But with Butch a furry ball, suffering in the multiplied weight Earth gravity imposed upon him, Worden made his way to the air lock. He donned a spacesuit. He went out.

It was near sunrise then. A long time had passed and Earth was now in its last quarter and the very highest peak of all that made up the crater wall glowed incandescent in the sunshine. But the stars were still quite visible and very bright. Worden walked away from the station, guided by the Earth-shine on the ground underfoot.

Three hours later he came back. Butch skipped and hopped beside his spacesuited figure. Behind them came two other figures. They were smaller than Worden but much larger than Butch. They were skinny and furry and they carried a burden. A mile from the station he switched on his suit radio. He called. A startled voice answered in his earphones.

"It's Worden," he said dryly. "I've been out for a walk with Butch. We visited his family and I've a couple of his cousins with me. They want to pay a visit and present some gifts. Will you let us in without shooting?"

There were exclamations. There was confusion. But Worden went on steadily toward the station while another high peak glowed in sunrise light and a third seemed to burst into incandescence. Dawn was definitely on the way.

The air-lock door opened. The party from the airless Moon went in. When the air lock filled, though, and the gravity coils went on, Butch and his relatives became helpless. They had to be carried to the nursery. There they uncurled themselves and blinked enigmatically at the men who crowded into the room where gravity was normal for the Moon and at the other men who stared in the door.

"I've got a sort of message," said Worden. "Butch and his relatives want to make a deal with us. You'll notice that they've put themselves at our mercy. We can kill all three of them. But they want to make a deal."

The head of the station said uncomfortably, "You've managed two-way communication, Worden?"

"*I* haven't," Worden told him. "*They* have. They've proved to me that they've brains equal to ours. They've been treated as animals and shot as specimens. They've fought back—naturally! But they want to make friends. They say that we can never use the Moon except in spacesuits and in stations like this, and they could never take Earth's gravity. So there's no need for us to be enemies. We can help each other."

The head of the station said dryly, "Plausible enough,

but we have to act under orders, Worden. Did you explain that?"

"They know," said Worden. "So they've got set to defend themselves if necessary. They've set up smelters to handle metals. They get the heat by sun mirrors, concentrating sunlight. They've even begun to work with gases held in containers. They're not far along with electronics yet, but they've got the theoretic knowledge and they don't need vacuum tubes. They live in a vacuum. They can defend themselves from now on."

The head said mildly, "I've watched Butch, you know, Worden. And you don't look crazy. But if this sort of thing is sprung on the armed forces on Earth there'll be trouble. They've been arguing for armed rocket ships. If your friends start a real war for defense—if they can—maybe rocket warships will be the answer."

Worden nodded.

"Right. But our rockets aren't so good that they can fight this far from a fuel store, and there couldn't be one on the Moon with all of Butch's kinfolk civilized—as they nearly are now and as they certainly will be within the next few weeks. Smart people, these cousins and such of Butch!"

"I'm afraid they'll have to prove it," said the head. "Where'd they get this sudden surge in culture?"

"From us," said Worden. "Smelting from me, I think. Metallurgy and mechanical engineering from the tractor mechanics. Geology—call it lunology here—mostly from you."

"How's that?" demanded the head.

"Think of something you'd like Butch to do," said Worden grimly, "and then watch him."

The head stared and then looked at Butch. Butch—small and furry and swaggering—stood up and bowed profoundly from the waist. One paw was placed where his heart could be. The other made a grandiose sweeping gesture. He straightened up and strutted, then climbed swiftly into Worden's lap and put a skinny furry arm about his neck.

"That bow," said the head, very pale, "is what I had in mind. You mean—"

"Just so," said Worden. "Butch's ancestors had no air to make noises in for speech. So they developed telepathy. In time, to be sure, they worked out something like music—sounds carried through rock. But like our music it doesn't carry meaning. They communicate directly from mind to mind. Only we can't pick up communications from them and they can from us."

"They read our minds!" said the head. He licked his lips. "And when we first shot them for specimens they were trying to communicate. Now they fight."

"Naturally," said Worden. "Wouldn't we? They've been picking our brains. They can put up a terrific battle now. They could wipe out this station without trouble. They let us stay so they could learn from us. Now they want to trade."

"We have to report to Earth," said the head slowly, "but—"

"They brought along some samples," said Worden. "They'll swap diamonds, weight for weight, for records. They like our music. They'll trade emeralds for textbooks —they can read now! And they'll set up an atomic pile and swap plutonium for other things they'll think of later. Trading on that basis should be cheaper than a war!"

"Yes," said the head. "It should. That's the sort of argument men will listen to. But how—"

"Butch," said Worden ironically. "Just Butch! We didn't capture him—they planted him on us! He stayed in the station and picked our brains and relayed the stuff to his relatives. We wanted to learn about them, remember? It's like the story of the psychologist. . . ."

There's a story about a psychologist who was studying the intelligence of a chimpanzee. He led the chimp into a room full of toys, went out, closed the door and put his eye to the keyhole to see what the chimp was doing. He found himself gazing into a glittering, interested brown eye only inches from his own. The chimp was looking through the keyhole to see what the psychologist was doing.

THE WALL
AROUND THE WORLD

◎◎◎

Theodore R. Cogswell

The Wall that went all the way around the world had always been there, so nobody paid much attention to it—except Porgie.

Porgie was going to find out what was on the other side of it—assuming there was another side—or break his neck trying. He was going on fourteen, an age that tends to view the word *impossible* as a meaningless term invented by adults for their own peculiar purposes. But he recognized that there were certain practical difficulties involved in scaling a glassy-smooth surface that rose over a thousand feet straight up. That's why he spent a lot of time watching the eagles.

This morning, as usual, he was late for school. He lost time finding a spot for his broomstick in the crowded rack in the school yard, and it was exactly six minutes after the hour as he slipped guiltily into the classroom.

For a moment, he thought he was safe. Old Mr.

Wickens had his back to him and was chalking a penta-
gram on the blackboard.

But just as Porgie started to slide into his seat, the
schoolmaster turned and drawled, "I see Mr. Shirey has
finally decided to join us."

The class laughed, and Porgie flushed.

"What's your excuse this time, Mr. Shirey?"

"I was watching an eagle," said Porgie lamely.

"How nice for the eagle. And what was he doing that
was of such great interest?"

"He was riding up on the wind. His wings weren't
flapping or anything. He was over the box canyon that
runs into the East Wall, where the wind hits the Wall
and goes up. The eagle just floated in circles, going
higher all the time. You know, Mr. Wickens, I'll bet if
you caught a whole bunch of eagles and tied ropes to
them, they could lift you right up to the top of the
Wall!"

"That," said Mr. Wickens, "is possible—if you could
catch the eagles. Now, if you'll excuse me, I'll continue
with the lecture. When invoking Elementals of the Fifth
Order, care must be taken to . . ."

Porgie glazed his eyes and began to think up ways
and means to catch some eagles.

The next period, Mr. Wickens gave them a problem in
practical astrology. Porgie chewed his pencil and tried
to work on it, but couldn't concentrate. Nothing came
out right—and when he found he had accidentally trans-
posed a couple of signs of the zodiac at the very beginning, he gave up and began to draw plans for eagle traps.
He tried one, decided it wouldn't work, started another—

"Porgie!"

He jumped. Mr. Wickens, instead of being in front
of the class, was standing right beside him. The schoolmaster reached down, picked up the paper Porgie had

been drawing on, and looked at it. Then he grabbed Porgie by the arm and jerked him from his seat.

"Go to my study!"

As Porgie went out the door, he heard Mr. Wickens say, "The class is dismissed until I return!"

There was a sudden rush of large, medium and small-sized boys out of the classroom. Down the corridor to the front door they pelted, and out into the bright sunshine. As they ran past Porgie, his cousin Homer skidded to a stop and accidentally on purpose jabbed an elbow into his ribs. Homer, usually called "Bull Pup" by the kids because of his squat build and pugnacious face, was a year older than Porgie and took his seniority seriously.

"Wait'll I tell Dad about this. You'll catch it tonight!" He gave Porgie another jab and then ran out into the school yard to take command of a game of Warlock.

Mr. Wickens unlocked the door to his study and motioned Porgie inside. Then he shut and locked it carefully behind him. He sat down in the high-backed chair behind his desk and folded his hands.

Porgie stood silently, hanging his head, filled with that helpless guilty anger that comes from conflict with superior authority.

"What were you doing instead of your lesson?" Mr. Wickens demanded.

Porgie didn't answer.

Mr. Wickens narrowed his eyes. The large hazel switch that rested on top of the bookcase beside the stuffed owl lifted lightly into the air, drifted across the room, and dropped into his hand.

"Well?" he said, tapping the switch on the desk.

"Eagle traps," admitted Porgie. "I was drawing eagle traps. I couldn't help it. The Wall made me do it."

"Proceed."

Porgie hesitated for a moment. The switch tapped. Porgie burst out, "I want to see what's on the other side!

There's no magic that will get me over, so I've got to find something else!"

Tap went the switch. "Something else?"

"If a magic way was in the old books, somebody would have found it already!"

Mr. Wickens rose to his feet and stabbed one bony finger accusingly at Porgie. "Doubt is the mother of damnation!"

Porgie dropped his eyes to the floor and wished he was some place else.

"I see doubt in you. Doubt is evil, Porgie, *evil!* There are ways permitted to men and ways forbidden. You stand on the brink of the fatal choice. Beware that the Black Man does not come for you as he did for your father before you. Now, bend over!"

Porgie bent. He wished he'd worn a heavier pair of pants.

"Are you ready?"

"Yes, sir," said Porgie sadly.

Mr. Wickens raised the switch over his head. Porgie waited. The switch slammed—but on the desk.

"Straighten up," Mr. Wickens said wearily. He sat down again. "I've tried pounding things into your head and I've tried pounding things on your bottom, and one end is as insensitive as the other. Porgie, can't you understand that you aren't supposed to try and find out new things? The Books contain everything there is to know. Year by year, what is written in them becomes clearer to us."

He pointed out the window at the distant towering face of the Wall that went around the world. "Don't worry about what is on the other side of that! It may be a place of angels or a place of demons—the Books do not tell us. But no man will know until he is ready for that knowledge. Our broomsticks won't climb that high, our charms aren't strong enough. We need more skill at magic, more understanding of the strange, unseen forces that surround us. In my grandfather's time, the best of the broomsticks wouldn't climb over a hundred feet in the air. But the Adepts in the Great Tower worked and worked until now, when the clouds are low, we can ride right up among them. Someday we will be able to soar all the way to the top of the Wall—"

"Why not now?" Porgie asked stubbornly. "With eagles."

"Because we're not *ready*," Mr. Wickens snapped. "Look at mind talk. It was only thirty years ago that the proper incantations were worked out, and even now there are only a few who have the skill to talk across the miles by just thinking out their words. Time, Porgie—it's going to take time. We were placed here to learn the Way, and everything that might divert us from the search is evil. Man can't walk two roads at once. If he tries, he'll split himself in half."

"Maybe so," said Porgie. "But birds get over the Wall and they don't know any spells. Look, Mr. Wickens, if everything is magic, how come magic won't work on everything? Like this, for instance—"

He took a shiny quartz pebble out of his pocket and laid it on the desk.

Nudging it with his finger, he said:

> "*Stone fly,*
> *Rise on high,*
> *Over cloud*
> *And into sky.*"

The stone didn't move.

"You see, sir? If words work on broomsticks, they should work on stones, too."

Mr. Wickens stared at the stone. Suddenly it quivered and jumped into the air.

"That's different," said Porgie. "You took hold of it

with your mind. Anybody can do that with little things. What I want to know is why the words won't work by themselves."

"We just don't know enough yet," said Mr. Wickens impatiently. He released the stone and it clicked on the desk top. "Every year we learn a little more. Maybe by your children's time we'll find the incantation that will make everything lift." He sniffed. "What do you want to make stones fly for, anyhow? You get into enough trouble just throwing them."

Porgie's brow furrowed. "There's a difference between *making* a thing do something, like when I lift it with my hand or mind, and putting a spell on it so it does the work by itself, like a broomstick."

There was a long silence in the study as each thought his own thoughts.

Finally Mr. Wickens said, "I don't want to bring up the unpleasant past, Porgie, but it would be well to remember what happened to your father. His doubts came later than yours—for a while he was my most promising student—but they were just as strong."

He opened a desk drawer, fumbled in it for a moment, and brought out a sheaf of papers yellow with age. "This is the paper that damned him—*An Enquiry into Non-Magical Methods of Levitation*. He wrote it to qualify for his Junior Adeptship." He threw the paper down in front of Porgie as if the touch of it defiled his fingers.

Porgie started to pick it up.

Mr. Wickens roared, "Don't touch it! It contains blasphemy!"

Porgie snatched back his hand. He looked at the top paper and saw a neat sketch of something that looked like a bird—except that it had two sets of wings, one in front and one in back.

Mr. Wickens put the papers back in the desk drawer.

His disapproving eyes caught and held Porgie's as he said, "If you want to go the way of your father, none of *us* can stop you." His voice rose sternly. "But there is one who can. . . . Remember the Black Man, Porgie, for his walk is terrible! There are fires in his eyes and no spell may defend you against him. When he came for your father, there was midnight at noon and a high screaming. When the sunlight came back, they were gone —and it is not good to think where."

Mr. Wickens shook his head as if overcome at the memory and pointed toward the door. "Think before you act, Porgie. Think well!"

Porgie was thinking as he left, but more about the sketch in his father's paper than about the Black Man.

The orange crate with the two boards across it for wings had looked something like his father's drawing, but appearances had been deceiving. Porgie sat on the back steps of his house feeling sorry for himself and alternately rubbing two tender spots on his anatomy. Though they were at opposite ends, and had different immediate causes, they both grew out of the same thing. His bottom was sore as a result of a liberal application of his uncle's hand. His swollen nose came from an aerial crackup.

He'd hoisted his laboriously contrived machine to the top of the woodshed and taken a flying leap in it. The expected soaring glide hadn't materialized. Instead, there had been a sickening fall, a splintering crash, a momentary whirling of stars as his nose banged into something hard.

He wished now he hadn't invited Bull Pup to witness his triumph, because the story'd gotten right back to his uncle—with the usual results.

Just to be sure the lesson was pounded home, his uncle had taken away his broomstick for a week—and just so Porgie wouldn't sneak it out, he'd put a spell on it before locking it away in the closet.

"Didn't feel like flying, anyway," Porgie said sulkily to himself, but the pretense wasn't strong enough to cover up the loss. The gang was going over to Red Rocks to chase bats as soon as the sun went down, and he wanted to go along.

He shaded his eyes and looked toward the Western Wall as he heard a distant halloo of laughing voices. They were coming in high and fast on their broomsticks. He went back to the woodshed so they wouldn't see him. He was glad he had when they swung low and began to circle the house yelling for him and Bull Pup. They kept hooting and shouting until Homer flew out of his bedroom window to join them.

"Porgie can't come," he yelled. "He got licked and Dad took his broom away from him. Come on, gang!"

With a quick looping climb, he took the lead and they went hedge-hopping off toward Red Rocks. Bull Pup had been top dog ever since he got his big stick. He'd zoom up to five hundred feet, hang from his broom by his knees, and then let go. Down he'd plummet, his arms spread and body arched as if he were making a swan dive—and then, when the ground wasn't more than a hundred feet away, he'd call and his broomstick would arrow down after him and slide between his legs, lifting him up in a great sweeping arc that barely cleared the treetops.

"Showoff!" muttered Porgie and shut the woodshed door on the vanishing stick-riders.

Over on the workbench sat the little model of paper and sticks that had got him into trouble in the first place. He picked it up and gave it a quick shove into the air with his hands. It dove toward the floor and then, as it picked up speed, tilted its nose toward the ceiling and made a graceful loop in the air. Leveling off, it made a sudden veer to the left and crashed against the wood-shed wall. A wing splintered.

Porgie went to pick it up. "Maybe what works for little things doesn't work for big ones," he thought sourly. The orange crate and the crossed boards had been as close an approximation of the model as he had been able to make. Listlessly, he put the broken glider back on his workbench and went outside. Maybe Mr. Wickens and his uncle and all the rest were right. Maybe there was only one road to follow.

He did a little thinking about it and came to a conclusion that brought forth a secret grin. He'd do it their way—but there wasn't any reason why he couldn't hurry things up a bit. Waiting for his grandchildren to work things out wasn't getting *him* over the Wall.

Tomorrow, after school, he'd start working on his new idea, and this time maybe he'd find the way.

In the kitchen, his uncle and aunt were arguing about him. Porgie paused in the hall that led to the front room and listened.

"Do you think I like to lick the kid? I'm not some kind of an ogre. It hurt me more than it hurt him."

"I notice you were able to sit down afterward," said Aunt Olga dryly.

"Well, what else could I do? Mr. Wickens didn't come right out and say so, but he hinted that if Porgie didn't stop mooning around, he might be dropped from school altogether. He's having an unsettling effect on the other kids. Damn it, Olga, I've done everything for that boy I've done for my own son. What do you want me to do, stand back and let him end up like your brother?"

"You leave my brother out of this! No matter what Porgie does, you don't have to beat him. He's still only a little boy."

There was a loud snort. "In case you've forgotten,

dear, he had his thirteenth birthday last March. He'll
be a man pretty soon."

"They why don't you have a man-to-man talk with
him?"

"Haven't I tried? You know what happens every time.
He gets off with those crazy questions and ideas of
his and I lose my temper and pretty soon we're back
where we started." He threw up his hands. "I don't
know what to do with him. Maybe that fall he had this
afternoon will do some good. I think he had a scare
thrown into him that he won't forget for a long time.
Where's Bull Pup?"

"Can't you call him Homer? It's bad enough having
his friends calling him by that horrible name. He went
out to Red Rocks with the other kids. They're having a
bat hunt or something."

Porgie's uncle grunted and got up. "I don't see why
that kid can't stay at home at night for a change. I'm
going in the front room and read the paper."

Porgie was already there, flipping the pages of his
schoolbooks and looking studious. His uncle settled down
in his easy chair, opened his paper, and lit his pipe.
He reached out to put the charred match in the ash
tray, and as usual the ash tray wasn't there.

"Damn that woman," he muttered to himself and
raised his voice: "Porgie."

"Yes, Uncle Veryl?"

"Bring me an ash tray from the kitchen, will you
please? Your aunt has them all out there again."

"Sure thing," said Porgie and shut his eyes. He
thought of the kitchen until a picture of it was crystal-
clear in his mind. The beaten copper ash tray was sitting
beside the sink where his aunt had left it after she had
washed it out. He squinted the little eye inside his head,
stared hard at the copper bowl, and whispered:

> "Ash tray fly,
> Follow eye."

Simultaneously he lifted with his mind. The ash tray quivered and rose slowly into the air.

Keeping it firmly suspended, Porgie quickly visualized the kitchen door and the hallway and drifted it through.

"Porgie!" came his uncle's angry voice.

Porgie jumped, and there was a crash in the hallway outside as the bowl was suddenly released and crashed to the floor.

"How many time have I told you not to levitate around the house? If it's too much work to go out to the kitchen, tell me and I'll do it myself."

"I was just practicing," mumbled Porgie defensively.

"Well, practice outside. You've got the walls all scratched up from banging things against them. You know you shouldn't fool around with telekinesis outside sight range until you've mastered full visualization. Now go and get me that ash tray."

Crestfallen, Porgie went out the door into the hall. When he saw where the ash tray had fallen, he gave a silent whistle. Instead of coming down the center of the hall, it had been three feet off course and heading directly for the hall table when he let it fall. In another second, it would have smashed into his aunt's precious black alabaster vase.

"Here it is, Uncle," he said, taking it into the front room. "I'm sorry."

His uncle looked at his unhappy face, sighed and reached out and tousled his head affectionately.

"Buck up, Porgie. I'm sorry I had to paddle you this afternoon. It was for your own good. Your aunt and I don't want you to get into any serious trouble. You know what folks think about machines." He screwed up his face as if he'd said a dirty word. "Now, back to your books—we'll forget all about what happened today. Just remember this, Porgie: If there's anything you want to know, don't go fooling around on your own. Come and ask me, and we'll have a man-to-man talk."

Porgie brightened. "There's something I have been wondering about."

"Yes?" said his uncle encouragingly.

"How many eagles would it take to lift a fellow high enough so he could see what was on the other side of the Wall?"

Uncle Veryl counted to ten—very slowly.

The next day Porgie went to work on his new project. As soon as school was out, he went over to the public library and climbed upstairs to the main circulation room.

"Little boys are not allowed in this section," the librarian said. "The children's division is downstairs."

"But I need a book," protested Porgie. "A book on how to fly."

"This section is only for adults."

Porgie did some fast thinking. "My uncle can take books from here, can't he?"

"I suppose so."

"And he could send me over to get something for him, couldn't he?"

The librarian nodded reluctantly.

Porgie prided himself on never lying. If the librarian chose to misconstrue his questions, it was her fault, not his.

"Well, then," he said, "do you have any books on how to make things fly in the air?"

"What kind of things?"

"Things like birds."

"Birds don't have to be made to fly. They're born that way."

"I don't mean real birds," said Porgie. "I mean birds you make."

"Oh, Animation. Just a second, let me visualize." She shut her eyes and a card catalogue across the room opened and shut one drawer after another. "Ah, that might be what he's looking for," she murmured after a moment, and concentrated again. A large brass-bound book came flying out of the stacks and came to rest on the desk in front of her. She pulled the index card out of the pocket in the back and shoved it toward Porgie. "Sign your uncle's name here."

He did and then, hugging the book to his chest, got out of the library as quickly as he could.

By the time Porgie had worked three-quarters of the way through the book, he was about ready to give up in despair. It was all grown-up magic. Each set of instructions he ran into either used words he didn't understand or called for unobtainable ingredients like powdered unicorn horns and the blood of red-headed female virgins.

He didn't know what a virgin was—all his uncle's encyclopedia had to say on the subject was that they were the only ones who could ride unicorns—but there was a redhead by the name of Dorothy Boggs who lived down the road a piece. He had a feeling, however, that neither she nor her family would take kindly to a request for two quarts of blood, so he kept on searching through the book. Almost at the very end he found a set of instructions he thought he could follow.

It took him two days to get the ingredients together. The only thing that gave him trouble was finding a toad—the rest of the stuff, though mostly nasty and odoriferous, was obtained with little difficulty. The date and exact time of the experiment was important and he surprised Mr. Wickens by taking a sudden interest in his Practical Astrology course.

At last, after laborious computations, he decided everything was ready.

Late that night, he slipped out of bed, opened his bedroom door a crack, and listened. Except for the usual night noises and resonant snores from Uncle Veryl's room, the house was silent. He shut the door carefully and got his broomstick from the closet—Uncle Veryl had relented about that week's punishment.

Silently he drifted out through his open window and across the yard to the woodshed.

Once inside, he checked carefully to see that all the windows were covered. Then he lit a candle. He pulled a loose floorboard up and removed the book and his assembled ingredients. Quickly, he made the initial preparations.

First there was the matter of molding the clay he had taken from the graveyard into a rough semblance of a bird. Then, after sticking several white feathers obtained from last Sunday's chicken into each side of the figure to make wings, he anointed it with a noxious mixture he had prepared in advance.

The moon was just setting behind the Wall when he began the incantation. Candlelight flickered on the pages of the old book as he slowly and carefully pronounced the difficult words.

When it came time for the business with the toad, he almost didn't have the heart to go through with it; but he steeled himself and did what was necessary. Then, wincing, he jabbed his forefinger with a pin and slowly dripped the requisite three drops of blood down on the crude clay figure. He whispered:

> *"Clay of graveyard,*
> *White cock's feather,*
> *Eye of toad,*
> *Rise together!"*

Breathlessly he waited. He seemed to be in the middle of a circle of silence. The wind in the trees outside had stopped and there was only the sound of his own quick breathing. As the candlelight rippled, the clay figure seemed to quiver slightly as if it were hunching for flight.

Porgie bent closer, tense with anticipation. In his mind's eye, he saw himself building a giant bird with wings powerful enough to lift him over the Wall around the World. Swooping low over the schoolhouse during recess, he would wave his hands in a condescending gesture of farewell, and then as the kids hopped on their sticks and tried to follow him, he would rise higher and higher until he had passed the ceiling of their brooms and left them circling impotently below him. At last he would sweep over the Wall with hundreds of feet to spare, over it and then down—down into the great unknown.

The candle flame stopped flickering and stood steady and clear. Beside it, the clay bird squatted, lifeless and motionless.

Minutes ticked by and Porgie gradually saw it for what it was—a smelly clod of dirt with a few feathers stuck in it. There were tears in his eyes as he picked up the body of the dead toad and said softly, "I'm sorry."

When he came in from burying it, he grasped the image of the clay bird tightly in his mind and sent it swinging angrily around the shed. Feathers fluttered behind it as it flew faster and faster until in disgust he released it and let it smash into the rough boards of the wall. It crumbled into a pile of foul-smelling trash and fell to the floor. He stirred it with his toe, hurt, angry, confused.

His broken glider still stood where he had left it on the far end of his workbench. He went over and picked it up.

"At least you flew by yourself," he said, "and I didn't have to kill any poor little toads to make you."

Then he juggled it in his hand, feeling its weight, and began to wonder. It had occurred to him that maybe the wooden wings on his big orange-box glider had been too heavy.

"Maybe if I could get some long thin poles," he thought, "and some cloth to put across the wings . . ."

During the next three months, there was room in Porgie's mind for only one thing—the machine he was building in the roomy old cave at the top of the long hill on the other side of Arnett's Grove. As a result, he kept slipping further and further behind at school.

Things at home weren't too pleasant, either—Bull Pup felt it was his duty to keep his parents fully informed of Porgie's shortcomings. Porgie didn't care though. He was too busy. Every minute he could steal was spent in either collecting materials or putting them together.

The afternoon the machine was finally finished, he could hardly tear himself away from it long enough to go home for dinner. He was barely able to choke down his food, and didn't even wait for dessert.

He sat on the grass in front of the cave, waiting for darkness. Below, little twinkling lights marked the villages that stretched across the plain for a full forty miles. Enclosing them like encircling arms stretched the dark and forbidding mass of the Wall. No matter where he looked, it stood high against the night. He followed its curve with his eyes until he had turned completely around, and then he shook his fist at it.

Patting the ungainly mass of the machine that rested on the grass beside him, he whispered fiercely, "I'll get over you yet. Old *Eagle* here will take me."

Old *Eagle* was an awkward, boxkite-like affair; but to Porgie she was a thing of beauty. She had an un-covered fuselage composed of four long poles braced together to make a retangular frame, at each end of which was fastened a large wing.

When it was dark enough, he climbed into the open frame and reached down and grabbed hold of the two lower members. Grunting, he lifted until the two upper ones rested under his armpits. There was padding there to support his weight comfortably once he was air-borne. The bottom of the machine was level with his waist and the rest of him hung free. According to his thinking, he should be able to control his flight by swinging his legs. If he swung forward, the shifting weight should tilt the nose down; if he swung back, it should go up.

There was only one way to find out if his ifs were right. The *Eagle* was a heavy contraption. He walked awkwardly to the top of the hill, the cords standing out on his neck. He was scared as he looked down the long steep slope that stretched out before him—so scared that he was having trouble breathing. He swallowed twice in a vain attempt to moisten his dry throat, and then lunged forward, fighting desperately to keep his balance as his wabbling steps gradually picked up speed.

Faster he went, and faster, his steps turning into leaps as the wing surfaces gradually took hold. His toes scraped through the long grass and then they were dangling in free air.

He was aloft.

Not daring even to move his head, he slanted his eyes down and to the left. The earth was slipping rapidly by a dozen feet below him. Slowly and cautiously, he swung his feet back. As the weight shifted, the nose of the glider rose. Up, up he went, until he felt a sudden slowing down and a clumsiness of motion. Almost instinctively, he leaned forward again, pointing the nose down in a swift dip to regain flying speed.

By the time he reached the bottom of the hill, he was a hundred and fifty feet up. Experimentally, he swung his feet a little to the left. The glider dipped slightly and turned. Soaring over a clump of trees, he felt a sudden lifting as an updraft caught him.

Up he went—ten, twenty, thirty feet—and then slowly began to settle again.

The landing wasn't easy. More by luck than by skill, he came down in the long grass of the meadow with no more damage than a few bruises. He sat for a moment and rested, his head spinning with excitement. He had flown like a bird, without his stick, without uttering a word. There *were* other ways than magic!

His elation suddenly faded with the realization that, while gliding down was fun, the way over the Wall was *up*. Also, and of more immediate importance, he was half a mile from the cave with a contraption so heavy and unwieldy that he could never hope to haul it all the way back up the hill by himself. If he didn't get it out of sight by morning, there was going to be trouble, serious trouble. People took an unpleasant view of machines and those who built them.

Broomsticks, he decided, had certain advantages, after all. They might not fly very high, but at least you didn't have to walk home from a ride.

"If I just had a great big broomstick," he thought, "I could lift the *Eagle* up with it and fly her home."

He jumped to his feet. It might work!

He ran back up the hill as fast as he could and finally, very much out of breath, reached the entrance of the cave. Without waiting to get back his wind, he jumped on his stick and flew down to the stranded glider.

Five minutes later, he stepped back and said:

> *"Broomstick fly,*
> *Rise on high,*
> *Over cloud*
> *And into sky."*

It didn't fly. It couldn't. Porgie had lashed it to the framework of the *Eagle*. When he grabbed hold of the machine and lifted, nine-tenths of its weight was gone, canceled out by the broomstick's lifting power.

He towed it back up the hill and shoved it into the cave. Then he looked uneasily at the sky. It was later than he had thought. He should be home and in bed— but when he thought of the feeling of power he had had in his flight, he couldn't resist hauling the *Eagle* back out again.

After checking the broomstick to be sure it was still fastened tightly to the frame, he went swooping down the hill again. This time when he hit the thermal over the clump of trees, he was pushed up a hundred feet before he lost it. He curved through the darkness until he found it again and then circled tightly within it.

Higher he went and higher, higher than any broomstick had ever gone!

When he started to head back, though, he didn't have such an easy time of it. Twice he was caught in downdrafts that almost grounded him before he was able to break loose from the tugging winds. Only the lifting power of his broomstick enabled him to stay aloft. With it bearing most of the load, the *Eagle* was so light that it took just a flutter of air to sweep her up again.

He landed the glider a stone's throw from the mouth of his cave.

"Tomorrow night!" he thought exultantly as he unleashed his broomstick. "Tomorrow night!"

There was a tomorrow night, and many nights after that. The *Eagle* was sensitive to every updraft, and with care he found he could remain aloft for hours, riding from thermal to thermal. It was hard to keep his secret, hard to keep from shouting the news, but he had to. He slipped out at night to practice, slipping back in again before sunrise to get what sleep he could.

He circled the day of his fourteenth birthday in read
and waited. He had a reason for waiting.

In the World within the Wall, fourteenth birthdays
marked the boundary between the little and the big, between being a big child and a small man. Most important,
they marked the time when one was taken to the Great
Tower where the Adepts lived and given a full-sized
broomstick powered by the most potent of spells, sticks
that would climb to a full six hundred feet, twice the
height that could be reached by the smaller ones the
youngsters rode.

Porgie needed a man-sized stick, needed that extra
power, for he had found that only the strongest of up-
drafts would lift him past the three-hundred-foot ceiling
where the lifting power of his little broomstick gave out.
He had to get up almost as high as the Wall before he
could make it across the wide expanse of flat plain that
separated him from the box canyon where the great wind
waited.

So he counted the slowly passing days and practiced
flying the rapidly passing nights.

The afternoon of his fourteenth birthday found Porgie
sitting on the front steps expectantly, dressed in his
best and waiting for his uncle to come out of the house.
Bull Pup came out and sat down beside him.

"The gang's having a coven up on top of old Baldy
tonight," he said. "Too bad you can't come."

"I can go if I want to," said Porgie.

"How?" said Bull Pup and snickered. "You going to
grow wings and fly? Old Baldy's five hundred feet up
and your kid stick won't lift you that high."

"Today's my birthday."

"You think you're going to get a new stick?"

Porgie nodded.

"Well, you ain't. I heard Mom and Dad talking. Dad's

mad because you flunked alchemy. He said you had to be taught a lesson."

Porgie felt sick inside, but he wouldn't let Bull Pup have the satisfaction of knowing it.

"I don t care," he said. "I'll go to the coven if I want to. You just wait and see."

Bull Pup was laughing when he hopped on his stick and took off down the street. Porgie waited an hour, but his uncle didn't come out.

He went into the house. Nobody said anything about his new broomstick until after supper. Then his uncle called him into the living room and told him he wasn't getting it.

"But, Uncle Veryl, you promised!"

"It was a conditional promise, Porgie. There was a big if attached to it. Do you remember what it was?"

Porgie looked down at the floor and scuffed one toe on the worn carpet. "I tried."

"Did you really, son?" His uncle's eyes were stern but compassionate. "Were you trying when you fell asleep in school today? I've tried talking with you and I've tried whipping you and neither seems to work. Maybe this will. Now you run upstairs and get started on your studies. When you can show me that your marks are improving, we'll talk about getting you a new broomstick. Until then, the old one will have to do."

Porgie knew that he was too big to cry, but when he got to his room he couldn't help it. He was stretched out on his bed with his face buried in the pillows when he heard a hiss from the window. He looked up to see Bull Pup sitting on his stick, grinning malevolently at him.

"What do you want?" sniffed Porgie.

"Only little kids cry," said Bull Pup.

"I wasn't crying. I got a cold."

"I just saw Mr. Wickens. He was coming out of that

old cave back of Arnett's Grove. He's going to get the Black Man, I'll bet."

"I don't know anything about that old cave," said Porgie, sitting bolt upright on his bed.

"Oh, yes, you do. I followed you up there one day. You got a machine in there. I told Mr. Wickens and he gave me a quarter. He was real interested."

Porgie jumped from his bed and ran toward the window, his face red and his fists doubled. "I'll fix you!"

Bull Pup backed his broomstick just out of Porgie's reach, and then stuck his thumbs in his ears and waggled his fingers. When Porgie started to throw things, he gave a final taunt and swooped away toward old Baldy and the coven.

Porgie's uncle was just about to go out in the kitchen and fix himself a sandwich when the doorbell rang. Grumbling, he went out into the front hall. Mr. Wickens was at the door. He came into the house and stood blinking in the light. He seemed uncertain as to just how to begin.

"I've got bad news for you," he said finally. "It's about Porgie. Is your wife still up?"

Porgie's uncle nodded anxiously.

"She'd better hear this, too."

Aunt Olga put down her knitting when they came into the living room.

"You're out late, Mr. Wickens."

"It's not of my own choosing."

Aunt Olga sighed. "What is it this time?"

Mr. Wickens hesitated, cleared his throat, and finally spoke in a low hushed voice: "Porgie's built a machine. The Black Man told me. He's coming after the boy tonight."

Uncle Veryl dashed up the stairs to find Porgie. He wasn't in his room.

Aunt Olga just sat in her chair and cried shrilly.

The moon stood high and silverlit the whole countryside. Porgie could make out the world far below him almost as if it were day. Miles to his left, he saw the little flickering fires on top of old Baldy where the kids were holding their coven. He fought an impulse and then succumbed to it. He circled the *Eagle* over a clump of trees until the strong rising currents lifted him almost to the height of the Wall. Then he twisted his body and banked over toward the distant red glowing fires.

Minutes later, he went silently over them at eight hundred feet, feeling out the air currents around the rocks. There was a sharp downdraft on the far side of Baldy that dropped him suddenly when he glided into it, but he made a quick turn and found untroubled air before he fell too far. On the other side, toward the box canyon, he found what he wanted, a strong rising current that seemed to have no upward limits.

He fixed its location carefully in his mind and then began to circle down toward the coven. Soon he was close enough to make out individual forms sitting silently around their little fires.

"Hey, Bull Pup," he yelled at the top of his lungs.

A stocky figure jumped to its feet and looked wildly around for the source of the ghostly voice.

"Up here!"

Porgie reached in his pocket, pulled out a small pebble and chucked it down. It cracked against a shelf of rock four feet from Bull Pup. Porgie's cousin let out a howl of fear. The rest of the kids jumped up and reared back their heads at the night sky, their eyes blinded by firelight.

"I told you I could come to the coven if I wanted to," yelled Porgie, "but now I don't. I don't have any time for kid stuff; I'm going over the Wall!"

During his last pass over the plateau he wasn't more

than thirty feet up. As he leaned over, his face was clearly visible in the firelight.

Placing his thumb to his nose he waggled his fingers and chanted, "Nyah, nyah, nyah, you can't catch me!"

His feet were almost scraping the ground as he glided out over the drop-off. There was an anxious second of waiting and then he felt the sure steady thrust of the upcurrent against his wings.

He looked back. The gang was milling around, trying to figure out what had happened. There was an angry shout of command from Bull Pup, and after a moment of confused hesitation they all made for their brooms and swooped up into the air.

Porgie mentally gauged his altitude and then relaxed. He was almost at their ceiling and would be above it before they reached him.

He flattened out his glide and yelled, "Come on up! Only little kids play that low!"

Bull Pup's stick wouldn't rise any higher. He circled impotently, shaking his fist at the machine that rode serenely above him.

"You just wait," he yelled. "You can't stay up there all night. You got to come down some time, and when you do we'll be waiting for you."

"Nyah, nyah, nyah," chanted Porgie and mounted higher into the moonlit night.

When the updraft gave out, he wasn't as high as he wanted to be, but there wasn't anything he could do about it. He turned and started a flat glide across the level plain toward the box canyon. He wished now that he had left Bull Pup and the other kids alone. They were following along below him. If he dropped down to their level before the canyon winds caught him, he was in trouble.

He tried to flatten his glide still more, but instead of saving altitude he went into a stall that dropped him a hundred feet before he was able to regain control. He saw now that he could never make it without dropping to Bull Pup's level.

Bull Pup saw it, too, and let out an exultant yell: "Just you wait! You're going to get it good!"

Porgie peered over the side into the darkness where his cousin rode, his pug face gleaming palely in the moonlight.

"Leave him alone, gang," Bull Pup shouted. "He's mine!"

The rest pulled back and circled slowly as the *Eagle* glided quietly down among them. Bull Pup darted in and rode right alongside Porgie.

He pointed savagely toward the ground: "Go down or I'll knock you down!"

Porgie kicked at him, almost upsetting his machine. He wasn't fast enough. Bull Pup dodged easily. He made a wide circle and came back, reaching out and grabbing the far end of the *Eagle*'s front wing. Slowly and maliciously, he began to jerk it up and down, twisting violently as he did so.

"Get down," he yelled, "or I'll break it off!"

Porgie almost lost his head as the wrenching threatened to throw him out of control.

"Let go!" he screamed, his voice cracking.

Bull Pup's face had a strange excited look on it as he gave the wing another jerk. The rest of the boys were becoming frightened as they saw what was happening.

"Quit it, Bull Pup!" someone called. "Do you want to kill him?"

"Shut up or you'll get a dose of the same!"

Porgie fought to clear his head. His broomstick was tied to the frame of the *Eagle* so securely that he would never be able to free it in time to save himself. He stared into the darkness until he caught the picture of Bull Pup's broomstick sharply in his mind. He'd never tried to handle anything that big before, but it was that or nothing.

Tensing suddenly, he clamped his mind down on the picture and held it hard. He knew that words didn't help, but he uttered them anyway:

"Broomstick stop,
Flip and flop!"

There was a sharp tearing pain in his head. He gritted his teeth and held on, fighting desperately against the red haze that threatened to swallow him. Suddenly there was a half-startled, half-frightened squawk from his left wingtip, and Bull Pup's stick jerked to an abrupt halt, gyrating so madly that its rider could hardly hang on.

"All right, the rest of you," screamed Porgie. "Get going or I'll do the same thing to you!"

They got, arcing away in terrified disorder. Porgie watched as they formed a frightened semicircle around the blubbering Bull Pup. With a sigh of relief he let go with his mind.

As he left them behind in the night, he turned his head back and yelled weakly, "Nyah, nyah, nyah, you can't catch me!"

He was only fifty feet off the ground when he glided into the far end of the box canyon and was suddenly caught by the strong updraft. As he soared in a tight spiral, he slumped down against the arm rests, his whole body shaking in delayed reaction.

The lashings that held the front wing to the frame were dangerously loose from the manhandling they had received. One more tug and the whole wing might have twisted back, dumping him down on the sharp rocks below. Shudders ran through the *Eagle* as the supports shook in their loose bonds. He clamped both hands around the place where the rear wing spar crossed the frame and tried to steady it.

He felt his stick's lifting power give out at three hundred feet. The *Eagle* felt clumsy and heavy, but the current was still enough to carry him slowly upward. Foot by foot he rose toward the top of the Wall, losing a precious hundred feet once when he spiraled out of the updraft and had to circle to find it. A wisp of cloud curled down from the top of the Wall and he felt a moment of panic as he climbed into it.

Momentarily, there was no left or right or up or down. Only damp whiteness. He had the feeling that the *Eagle* was falling out of control; but he kept steady, relying on the feel for the air he had gotten during his many practice flights.

The lashings had loosened more. The full strength of his hands wasn't enough to keep the wing from shuddering and trembling. He struggled resolutely to maintain control of ship and self against the strong temptation to lean forward and throw the *Eagle* into a shallow dive that would take him back to normalcy and safety.

He was almost at the end of his resolution when with dramatic suddenness he glided out of the cloud into the clear moon-touched night. The upcurrent under him seemed to have lessened. He banked in a gentle arc, trying to find the center of it again.

As he turned, he became aware of something strange, something different, something almost frightening. For the first time in his life, there was no Wall to block his vision, no vast black line stretching through the night.

He was above it!

There was no time for looking. With a loud *ping*, one of the lashings parted and the leading edge of the front wing flapped violently. The glider began to pitch and yaw, threatening to nose over into a plummeting dive. He fought for mastery, swinging his legs like desperate pendulums as he tried to correct the erratic side swings that threatened to throw him out of control. As he fought, he headed for the Wall.

If he were to fall, it would be on the other side. At least he would cheat old Mr. Wickens and the Black Man.

Now he was directly over the Wall. It stretched like a wide road underneath him, its smooth top black and shining in the moonlight. Acting on quick impulse, he threw his body savagely forward and to the right. The ungainly machine dipped abruptly and dove toward the black surface beneath it.

Eighty feet, seventy, sixty, fifty—he had no room to maneuver, there would be no second chance—thirty, twenty—

He threw his weight back, jerking the nose of the *Eagle* suddenly up. For a precious second the wings held, there was a sharp breaking of his fall; then, with a loud cracking noise, the front wing buckled back in his face. There was a moment of blind whirling fall and a splintering crash that threw him into darkness.

Slowly, groggily, Porgie pulled himself up out of the broken wreckage. The *Eagle* had made her last flight. She perched precariously, so near the outside edge of the Wall that part of her rear wing stretched out over nothingness.

Porgie crawled cautiously across the slippery wet surface of the top of the Wall until he reached the center. There he crouched down to wait for morning. He was exhausted, his body so drained of energy that in spite of himself he kept slipping into an uneasy sleep.

Each time he did, he'd struggle back to consciousness trying to escape the nightmare figures that scampered through his brain. He was falling, pursued by wheeling batlike figures with pug faces. He was in a tiny room and the walls were inching in toward him and he could hear the voice of Bull Pup in the distance chanting,

"You're going to get it." And then the room turned into a long dark corridor and he was running. Mr. Wickens was close behind him and he had long sharp teeth and he kept yelling, "Porgie! Porgie!"

He shuddered back to wakefulness, crawled to the far edge of the Wall and, hanging his head over, tried to look down at the Outside World. The clouds had boiled up and there was nothing underneath him but gray blankness hiding the sheer thousand-foot drop. He crawled back to his old spot and looked toward the East, praying for the first sign of dawn. There was only blackness there.

He started to doze off again and once more he heard the voice: "Porgie! Porgie!"

He opened his eyes and sat up. The voice was still calling, even though he was awake. It seemed to be coming from high and far away.

It came closer, closer, and suddenly he saw it in the darkness—a black figure wheeling above the Wall like a giant crow. Down it came, nearer and nearer, a man in black with arms outstretched and long fingers hooked like talons!

Porgie scrambled to his feet and ran, his feet skidding on the slippery surface. He looked back over his shoulder. The black figure was almost on top of him. Porgie dodged desperately and slipped.

He felt himself shoot across the slippery surface toward the edge of the Wall. He clawed, scrabbling for purchase. He couldn't stop. One moment he felt wet coldness slipping away under him; the next, nothingness as he shot out into the dark and empty air.

He spun slowly as he fell. First the clouds were under him and then they tipped and the star-flecked sky took their places. He felt cradled, suspended in time. There was no terror. There was nothing.

Nothing—until suddenly the sky above him was blotted out by a plummeting black figure that swooped down on him, hawklike and horrible.

Porgie kicked wildly. One foot slammed into something solid and for an instant he was free. Then strong arms circled him from behind and he was jerked out of the nothingness into a world of falling and fear.

There was a sudden strain on his chest and then he felt himself being lifted. He was set down gently on the top of the Wall.

He stood defiant, head erect, and faced the black figure.

"I won't go back. You can't make me go back."

"You don't have to go back, Porgie."

He couldn't see the hooded face, but the voice sounded strangely familiar.

"You've earned your right to see what's on the other side," it said. Then the figure laughed and threw back the hood that partially covered its face.

In the bright moonlight, Porgie saw Mr. Wickens!

The schoolmaster nodded cheerfully. "Yes, Porgie, I'm the Black Man. Bit of a shock, isn't it?"

Porgie sat down suddenly.

"I'm from the Outside," said Mr. Wickens, seating himself carefully on the slick black surface. "I guess you could call me a sort of observer."

Porgie's spinning mind couldn't catch up with the new ideas that were being thrown at him. "Observer?" he said uncomprehendingly. "Outside?"

"Outside. That's where you'll be spending your next few years. I don't think you'll find life better there and I don't think you'll find it worse. It'll be different, though, I can guarantee that." He chuckled. "Do you remember what I said to you in my office that day—that Man can't follow two paths at once, that Mind and Nature are bound to conflict? That's true, but it's also false. You can have both, but it takes two worlds to do it.

"Outside, where you're going, is the world of the machines. It's a good world, too. But the men who live there saw a long time ago that they were paying a price for it; that control over Nature meant that the forces of the Mind were neglected, for the machine is a thing of logic and reason, but miracles aren't. Not yet. So they built the Wall and they placed people within it and gave them such books and such laws as would insure development of the powers of the Mind. They were right, too. There is magic down there now. Not as much as you might think, though. Broomsticks aren't, for example—they're really disguised machines, machines built Outside containing tiny anti-gravitational units, and controlling devices that will react to the human voice. So with all the other things that words seem to activate."

"But—but why the Wall?" said Porgie.

"Because their guess was right. There is magic." He pulled a bunch of keys from his pocket. "Lift it, Porgie."

Porgie stared at it until he had the picture in his mind and then let his mind take hold, pulling with invisible hands until the keys hung high in the air. Then he dropped them back into Mr. Wickens's hand.

"What was that for?"

"Outsiders can't do that," said the schoolmaster. "And they can't do conscious telepathy—what you call mind talk—either. They can't because they really don't believe such things can be done. The people inside the Wall do, for they live in an atmosphere of magic. But once these things are worked out, and become simply a matter of training and method, then the ritual, the mumbo-jumbo, the deeply ingrained belief in the existence of supernatural forces will be no longer necessary.

"These phenomena will be only tools that anybody can be trained to use, and the crutches can be thrown away. Then the Wall will come tumbling down. But until then"—he stopped and frowned in mock severity—"there will always be a Black Man around to see that the people inside don't split themselves up the middle trying to walk down two roads at once."

There was a lingering doubt in Porgie's eyes. "But you flew without a machine."

The Black Man opened his cloak and displayed a small gleaming disk that was strapped to his chest. "Little ones like this are what make your broomsticks fly. The only difference is that this one has no built-in limits." He tapped it gently. "A machine, Porgie. A machine just like your glider, only of a different sort and much better. It's almost as good as levitation. Mind and Nature—magic and science—they'll get together eventually."

He wrapped his cloak about him again. "It's cold up here. Shall we go? Tomorrow is time enough to find out what is Outside the Wall that goes around the World."

"Can't we wait until the clouds lift?" asked Porgie wistfully. "I'd sort of like to see it for the first time from up here."

"We could," said Mr. Wickens, "but there is somebody you haven't seen for a long time waiting for you down there. If we stay up here, he'll be worried."

Porgie looked up blankly. "I don't know anybody Outside. I—" He stopped suddenly. He felt as if he were about to explode. "Not my father!"

"Who else? He came out the easy way. Come, now, let's go and show him what kind of man his son has grown up to be. Are you ready?"

"I'm ready," said Porgie.

"Then help me drag your contraption over to the other side of the Wall so we can drop it Inside. When the folk find the wreckage in the morning, they'll know what the Black Man does to those who build machines instead of tending to their proper business. It should have a salutary effect on Bull Pup and the others."

He walked over to the wreckage of the *Eagle* and began to tug at it.

"Wait," said Porgie. "Let me." He stared at the broken glider until his eyes began to burn. Then he gripped and pulled.

Slowly, with an increasing consciousness of mastery, he lifted until the glider floated free and was rocking gently in the slight breeze that rippled across the top of the great Wall. Then, with a sudden shove, he swung it far out over the abyss and released it.

The two stood silently, side by side, watching the *Eagle* pitch downward on broken wings. When it was lost in the darkness below, Mr. Wickens took Porgie in his strong arms and stepped confidently to the edge of the Wall.

"Wait a second," said Porgie, remembering a day in the schoolmaster's study and a switch that had come floating obediently down through the air. "If you're from Outside, how come you can do lifting?"

Mr. Wickens grinned. "Oh, I was born Inside. I went over the Wall for the first time when I was just a little older than you are now."

"In a glider?" asked Porgie.

"No," said the Black Man, his face perfectly sober. "I went out and caught myself a half-dozen eagles."

PRONE

Mack Reynolds

SupCom Bull Underwood said in a voice ominously mild, "I continually get the impression that every other sentence is being left out of this conversation. Now, tell me, General, what do you mean *things happen around him?*"

"Well, for instance, the first day Mitchie got to the Academy a cannon burst at a demonstration."

"What's a cannon?"

"A pre-guided-missile weapon," the commander of the Terra Military Academy told him. "You know, shells propelled by gunpowder. We usually demonstrate them in our history classes. This time four students were injured. The next day sixteen were hurt in ground war maneuvers."

There was an element of respect in the SupCom's tone. "Your course must be rugged."

General Bentley wiped his forehead with a snowy handkerchief even as he shook it negatively. "It was the first time any such thing happened. I tell you, sir, since

Mitchie Farthingworth has been at the academy things have been chaotic. Fires in the dormitories, small arms exploding, cadets being hospitalized right and left. We've just got to expel that boy!"

"Don't be ridiculous," the SupCom growled. "He's the apple of his old man's eye. We've got to make a hero out of him if it means the loss of a battle fleet. But I still don't get this. You mean the Farthingworth kid is committing sabotage?"

"It's not that. We investigated. He doesn't do it on purpose, things just *happen* around him. Mitchie can't help it."

"Confound it, stop calling him Mitchie!" Bull Underwood snapped. "How do you know it's him if he doesn't do it? Maybe you're just having a run of bad luck."

"That's what I thought," Bentley said, "until I ran into Admiral Lawrence of the Space Marines Academy. He had the same story. The day Mitchie—excuse me, sir—Michael Farthingworth set foot in Nuevo San Diego, things started happening. When they finally got him transferred to our academy the trouble stopped."

It was at times like these that Bull Underwood regretted his shaven head. He could have used some hair to tear. "Then it *must* be sabotage if it stops when he leaves!"

"I don't think so, sir."

The SupCom took a deep breath, snapped to his secretarobot, "Brief me on Cadet Michael Farthingworth, including his early life." While he waited he growled under his breath, "A stalemated hundred-year war on my hands with those Martian *makrons* and I have to get things like this tossed at me."

In less than a minute the secretarobot began: "Son of Senator Warren Farthingworth, Chairman War Appropriations Committee. Twenty-two years of age. Five foot six, one hundred and thirty, blue eyes, brown hair, fair.

Born and spent early youth in former United States area.
Early education by mother. At age of eighteen entered
Harvard but schooling was interrupted when roof of
assembly hall collapsed killing most of faculty. Next year
entered Yale, leaving two months later when 90 per
cent of the university's buildings were burnt down in
the holocaust of '85. Next attended University of California but failed to graduate owing to the earthquake
which completely . . ."

"That's enough," the SupCom rapped. He turned and
stared at General Bentley. "What the hell is it? Even if
the kid was a psychokinetic saboteur he couldn't accomplish all that."

The academy commander shook his head. "All I know
is that since his arrival at the Terra Military Academy
there's been an endless series of casualties. And the longer
he's there the worse it gets. It's twice as bad now as when
he first arrived." He got to his feet wearily. "I'm a
broken man, sir, and I'm leaving this in your hands.
You'll have my resignation this afternoon. Frankly, I'm
afraid to return to the school. If I do, some day I'll
probably crack my spine bending over to tie my shoe-
laces. It just isn't safe to be near that boy."

For a long time after General Bentley had left, SupCom
Bull Underwood sat at his desk, his heavy underlip in
a pout. "And just when the next five years' appropriation
is up before the committee," he snarled at nobody.

He turned to the secretarobot. "Put the best psycho-
technicians available on Michael Farthingworth. They
are to discover . . . well, they are to discover why in
hell things happen around him. Priority one."

Approximately a week later the secretarobot said, "May
I interrupt you, sir? A priority one report is coming in."

Bull Underwood grunted and turned away from the
star chart he'd been studying with the two Space Ma-

rine generals. He dismissed them and sat down at his desk.

The visor lit up and he was confronted with the face of an elderly civilian. "Doctor Duclos," the civilian said. "Case of Cadet Michael Farthingworth."

"Good," the SupCom rumbled. "Doctor, what in the devil is wrong with young Farthingworth?"

"The boy is an accident prone."

Bull Underwood scowled at him. "A what?"

"An accident prone." The doctor elaborated with evident satisfaction. "There is indication that he is the most extreme case in medical history. Really a fascinating study. Never in my experience have I been—"

"Please, Doctor. I'm a layman. What is an accident prone?"

"Ah, yes. Briefly, an unexplained phenomenon first noted by the insurance companies of the nineteenth and twentieth centuries. An accident prone has an unnaturally large number of accidents happen either to him, or, less often, to persons in his vicinity. In Farthingworth's case, they happen to persons about him. He himself is never affected."

The SupCom was unbelieving. "You mean to tell me there are some persons who just naturally have accidents happen to them without any reason?"

"That is correct," Duclos nodded. "Most prones are understandable. Subconsciously, the death wish is at work and the prone *seeks* self-destruction. However, science has yet to discover the forces behind the less common type such as Farthingworth exemplifies." The doctor's emphatic shrug betrayed his Gallic background. "It has been suggested that it is no more than the laws of chance at work. To counterbalance the accident prone, there should be persons at the other extreme who are blessed with abnormally good fortune. However . . ."

SupCom Bull Underwood's lower lip was out, almost

truculently. "Listen," he interrupted. "What can be done about it?"

"Nothing," the doctor said, his shoulders raising and lowering again. "An accident prone seems to remain one as a rule. Not always, but as a rule. Fortunately, they are rare."

"Not rare enough," the SupCom growled. "These insurance companies, what did they do when they located an accident prone?"

"They kept track of him and refused to insure the prone, his business, home, employees, employers, or anyone connected with him."

Bull Underwood stared unblinkingly at the doctor, as though wondering whether the other's whole explanation was an attempt to pull his leg. Finally he rapped, "Thank you, Doctor Duclos. That will be all." The civilian's face faded from the visor.

The SupCom said slowly to the secretarobot. "Have Cadet Farthingworth report to me." He added sotto voce, "And while he's here have all personnel keep their fingers crossed."

The photoelectric-controlled door leading to the sanctum sanctorum of SupCom Bull Underwood glided quietly open and a lieutenant entered and came to a snappy attention. The door swung gently shut behind him.

"Well?" Bull Underwood growled.

"Sir, a Cadet Michael Farthingworth to report to you."

"Send him in. Ah, just a minute, Lieutenant Brown. How do you feel after talking to him?"

"Me, sir? I feel fine, sir." The lieutenant looked blankly at him.

"Hmmm. Well, send him in, confound it."

The lieutenant turned and the door opened automatically before him. "Cadet Farthingworth," he announced.

The newcomer entered and stood stiffly before the desk of Earth's military head. Bull Underwood appraised him with care. In spite of the swank Academy uniform, Michael Farthingworth cut a wistfully ineffectual figure. His faded blue eyes blinked sadly behind heavy contact lenses.

"That'll be all, Lieutenant," the SupCom said to his aide.

"Yes, sir." The lieutenant about-faced snappily and marched to the door—which swung sharply forward and quickly back again before the lieutenant was half way through.

SupCom Bull Underwood winced at the crush of bone and cartilage. He shuddered, then snapped to his secretarobot, "Have Lieutenant Brown hospitalized . . . and, ah . . . see he gets a Luna Medal for exposing himself to danger beyond the call of duty."

He swung to the newcomer and came directly to the point. "Cadet Farthingworth," he rapped, "do you know what an accident prone is?"

Mitchie's voice was low and plaintive. "Yes, sir."

"You do?" Bull Underwood was surprised.

"Yes, sir. At first such things as the school's burning down didn't particularly impress me as being personally connected with me, but the older I get, the worse it gets, and after what happened to my first date, I started to investigate."

The SupCom said cautiously, "What happened to the date?"

Mitchie flushed. "I took her to a dance and she broke her leg."

The SupCom cleared his throat. "So finally you investigated?"

"Yes, sir," Mitchie Farthingworth said woefully. "And I found I was an accident prone and getting worse geometrically. Each year I'm twice as bad as the year before. I'm glad you've discovered it too, sir. I . . . I didn't know what to do. Now it's in your hands."

The SupCom was somewhat relieved. Possibly this wasn't going to be as difficult as he had feared. He said, "Have you any ideas Mitchie, ah, that is . . ."

"Call me Mitchie if you want, sir. Everybody else does."

"Have you any ideas? After all, you've done as much damage to Terra as a Martian task force would accomplish."

"Yes, sir. I think I ought to be shot."

"Huh?"

"Yes, sir. I'm expendable," Mitchie said miserably. "In fact, I suppose I'm probably the most expendable soldier that's ever been. All my life I've wanted to be a spaceman and do my share toward licking the Martians." His eyes gleamed behind his lenses. "Why, I've . . ."

He stopped and looked at his commanding officer pathetically. "What's the use? I'm just a bust. An accident prone. The only thing to do is liquidate me." He tried to laugh in self-deprecation but his voice broke.

Behind him, Bull Underwood heard the glass in his office window shatter without seeming cause. He winced again, but didn't turn.

"Sorry, sir," Mitchie said. "See? The only thing is to shoot me."

"Look," Bull Underwood said urgently, "stand back a few yards farther, will you? There on the other side of the room." He cleared his throat. "Your suggestion has already been considered, as a matter of fact. However, due to your father's political prominence, shooting you had to be ruled out."

From a clear sky the secretarobot began to say, " 'Twas brillig, and the slithy toves did gyre and gimble in the wabe."

SupCom Bull Underwood closed his eyes in pain and shrunk back into his chair. "What?" he said cautiously.

"The borogoves were mimsy as all hell," the secretarobot said decisively and shut up.

Mitchie looked at it. "Slipped its cogs, sir," he said helpfully. "It's happened before around me."

"The best damned memory bank in the system," Underwood protested. "Oh, no."

"Yes, sir," Mitchie said apologetically. "And I wouldn't recommend trying to repair it, sir. Three technicians were electrocuted when I was . . ."

The secretarobot sang, "O frabjous day! Callooh! Callay!"

"Completely around the corner," Mitchie said.

"This," said Bull Underwood, "is too frabjous much! Senator or no Senator, appropriations or no appropriations, with my own bare hands—"

As he strode impulsively forward, he felt the rug giving way beneath him. He grasped desperately for the edge of the desk, felt ink bottle and water carafe go crashing over.

Mitchie darted forward to his assistance.

"Stand back!" Bull Underwood roared, holding an ankle with one hand, shaking the other hand in the form of a fist. "Get out of here, confound it!" Ink began to drip from the desk over his shaven head. It cooled him not at all. "It's not even safe to destroy you! It'd wipe out a regiment to try to assemble a firing squad! It—" Suddenly he paused, and when he spoke again his voice was like the coo of a condor.

"Cadet Farthingworth," he announced, "after considerable deliberation on my part I have chosen you to perform the most hazardous operation that Terra's forces have undertaken in the past hundred years. If successful, this effort will undoubtedly end the war."

"Who me?" Mitchie said.

"Exactly," SupCom Underwood snapped. "This war has been going on for a century without either side being able to secure that slight edge, that minute advantage which would mean victory. Cadet Farthingworth, you have been chosen to make the supreme effort which will give Terra that superiority over the Martians." The SupCom looked sternly at Mitchie.

"Yes, sir," he clipped. "What are my orders?"

The SupCom beamed at him. "Spoken like a true hero of Terra's Space Forces. On the spaceport behind this building is a small spycraft. You are to repair immediately to it and blast off for Mars. Once there you are to land, hide the ship, and make your way to their capital city."

"Yes, sir! And what do I do then?"

"Nothing," Bull Underwood said with satisfaction. "You do absolutely nothing but live there. I estimate that your presence in the enemy capital will end the war in less than two years."

Michael Farthingworth snapped him a brilliant salute. "Yes, sir."

Spontaneous combustion broke out in the wastebasket.

Through the shards of his window, SupCom Bull Underwood could hear the blast-off of the spyship. Half a dozen miles away the flare of a fuel dump going up in flames lighted up the sky.

Seated there in the wreckage of his office he rubbed his ankle tenderly. "The only trouble is when the war is over we'll have to bring him home."

But then he brightened. "Perhaps we could leave him there as our occupation forces. It would keep them from ever recovering to the point where they could try again."

He tried to get to his feet, saying to the secretarobot, "Have them send me in a couple of medical corpsmen."

"Beware the Jabberwock," the secretarobot sneered.

ESCAPE THE MORNING
◎◎◎
Poul Anderson

Troubles never come singly, or Mark Jordan would not have been racing the sunrise for his life.

It had begun as just a pleasant bit of excitement. He was on watch in the communications room. Someone had to be there all the time when they were at home. Emergencies on the Moon have a way of arriving fast and nasty. But in the normal course of events, whichever of them stood by was free to tend to private matters— read, study, fool around with a hobby, or work out in the gymnasium corner of the big plastic-faced chamber. Mark had finished his calculus assignment and was on the homemade exercycle. With gravity one-sixth as strong as it is on Earth, you must spend at least two hours out of the twenty-four keeping fit, or your very bones will atrophy.

Through the whirr of the machine, the rustle of air from the ventilator ducts, his own quick breath, he got the buzz. His heart jumped. He sprang to the 'visor panel. Meters stared like goblin eyes at a tall sandy-haired eighteen-year-old flipping switches. The screen came to life with Derek van Hulst's middle-aged face.

"Copernicus to Jordan Station," the Dutchman said. "Oh, you. Hello, Mark. Can you take a stranded man in?"

"Sure. Plenty of supplies, and choice of guestrooms." Mark grinned. He not only did not begrudge the rations —like all pioneers, the Lunar colonists take for granted that anyone in distress is to be helped—but he was delighted. Here was a new person to talk to, for fourteen Earth-days!

Van Hulst surprised him. "They're sending a 'tank' from Kepler to continue him on his way, so you won't have him more than about twenty hours."

Mark whistled. "Who is he to rate that?"

"The Minister of Technology of the Federated Congo, Achille Kamolondo. He's been on the Moon for a couple of weeks now, inspecting the facilities. Was bound to us from Keplersburg when something crippled his vehicle. He was not sure what, when he called us."

"Was that wise? I mean letting a newcomer drive off alone, and this near dawn?"

"They told me, calling ahead, that he'd proved himself to be able. And he hates wasting time. So they lent him a Go-Devil." Mark felt a bit of envy for someone who could take one of those out and travel at fifty miles an hour. A turtle, such as most people owned, would do twenty if you pushed. Of course, a Go-Devil had room for no more than a single person. "Let us not waste time either," van Hulst said. "Sunrise is barely two hours off where he is. That's on the Main Trace, naturally, between kilometers 321 and 322. About eighteen miles from your place, correct? On your way."

"Yes, sir. I'll report back when I return." Mark

switched off and left on the run, which is fast indeed on the Moon.

"Tom!" he shouted down the long, machine-humming hall. "Condition Yellow!"

His brother, two years younger, pelted from the hydroponics section where he had been tending algae. Judy, their kid sister, didn't hear; she was in the soundproofed "classroom," taking a Spanish lesson beamed from the school in Tycho Crater. Mark explained on the way to the lockers.

"I could go," Tom said wistfully.

"You could," Mark agreed, "but you're not going to, me bucko."

Tom didn't argue. A station, alone in barrenness, needs a captain as much as any ship does. For all the free-and-easy affection between them, Mark was the Old Man.

Tom helped him into his undergarment and spacesuit. "Air valves, okay. Pressure, okay. Faceplate gasket, okay. . . ." They went through the ritual fast, yet not missing a point. The gear must be perfect. Human beings can't survive a night temperature of 250° below Fahrenheit zero, nor can they breathe vacuum.

Leaving his helmet open, Mark cycled through the garage lock and squirmed along a gang tube into his turtle. He sealed the doors, automatically disconnecting the tube. His hands, gloved but trained, found controls as he sat down. Light blossomed in the narrow steel cell, revealing an extra seat crowded next to his among the instruments. Aft of the cabin was space for extra passengers, supplies, and life support equipment. When there was cargo to carry, the turtle was hitched to a train of the wagons that stood in this rough-hewn cave. He did not see them through windows; even the best glass is fragile and a poor radiation shield. Television panels are better.

The solar cells topside gathered energy during the

two-week Lunar day to charge every cell in the station, including those in the electric motors. Mark started off. Oblong, ugly, hull pitted by tiny meteorites, the car lumbered forth on its eight huge wheels, up the ramp and out onto the surface of the Moon.

Though he had spent most of his life here, Mark always caught his breath at sight of the night heavens. Stars and stars and stars crowded the dark, uncountable, unwinking, unbelievably bright. Earth hung halfway down the western sky, four times the size of Luna seen from itself and many times as radiant. The planet was at half phase, and its majestic turning had brought America into view. Clear weather, Mark saw; he could identify glitters on the black side which were the titanic eastern cities. Westward the plains stretched soft brown and bluish green, then the Rockies, the Pacific coast, the ocean like burnished sapphire streaked with a few white cloud masses.

Dad's country, he thought. *Mother's. My own too, for that matter.* His eyes stung a little.

The moonscape offered less. Behind him jutted the small crater beneath which Jordan Station had been dug. The slopes were half concealed by machines busily at work, and dominated by the radio-TV mast on top. Otherwise that flatland called the Oceanus Procellarum reached bare as far as he could see. Not that he saw any great distance. No air or dust scattered the Earth-shine, but the coal-like mineral crust did, so that he seemed to move in the focus of a dim blue spotlight which faded out mere yards away. The horizon was a circle of starlessness, barely three miles wide. Mark turned on the headlights. They helped some—enough, if you were used to these conditions.

He plugged his suit radio into the turtle's. "Mark to Tom," he said. "All systems go. I'm on my way."

"Check," said his brother's voice in his earplugs.

"And mate." Mark said. He gave himself to the job of driving. Luminous stones, one per kilometer, marked this side path, as they did the Trace. Neither was a true road, only a safe route. Cosmic dust, raining down for four billion years, binding molecule to molecule in vacuum, had formed the treacherous, brittle surface of the Lunar *maria*.

At the Trace, he followed its roundabout path easterly for almost an hour. This near day, little traffic ever moved, and he found no sign of man except the stones and the gaunt microwave relay masts that glided by, out of darkness and back into darkness. The hum of the motor, the flutter of his own breath, deepened the silence that enclosed him. He didn't mind. Mostly he thought about his future. He'd have to go live in the dorm at Tycho University next year, in order to take laboratory courses for an engineering degree. Well, the Station was in good shape financially, he'd hire an assistant and Tom could take over as boss. . . .

The undiffused puddle of light cast by his headbeams suddenly gleamed against metal. He allowed plenty of space for low-gravity braking, even from 20 mph. The Go-Devil stood inert, a four-wheeled egg with metal curled back from several holes around the motor. Huh! Meteorite shrapnel had done that. Mark tuned his 'caster. "Hello, there," he said into his helmet mike. "You okay?"

"Yes." He heard fluent English with a slight French accent. "Are you my, ah, rescuer? They informed me someone would come."

"Right-o. Do you know how to get into a turtle?"

"*Pardon?* Oh, yes, your kind of vehicle. Certainly I do." Monsieur Kamolondo sounded a trifle offended. *Well, he must've been under quite a strain,* Mark thought. *It's lonesome to wait for help. And on top of the shock when that debris ripped into his engine compartment—*

The Congolese stepped through the inner door of the entry lock. Frost formed on his suit, chilled by the brief exposure when he crossed from car to car. He sat down beside Mark and fumbled with his helmet. Mark helped him open it.

"But you are a boy!" he exclaimed.

He wasn't so old himself: a large man with a face brown, intelligent, and proud. The leaders of the Congo were more aristocrats than politicians. That was inevitable, in a country still struggling up from the near savagery into which its long Time of Troubles had plunged it. Nonetheless, Mark couldn't help bristling a little at the way those eyes regarded him.

"I'm not too young to run a station," he said, and introduced himself curtly. He gunned the motor and turned the wheel. "We'd better head right back. One hour till sunrise."

"A station?—No, I remember. An isolated enterprise. What do you do?"

Mark decided to be friendly. "We mine copper," he said. "Started with an underground vein of ice, but that gave out. Anyway, so much water has been gotten now that the price is way down. So Dad went in for minerals. I've found some oil, too, that may be worth going after when we've saved the capital we'd need."

"Oil?" Kamolondo blurted.

"Sure, there's plenty on the Moon. It's been a hundred years ago since Hoyle theorized that petroleum wasn't formed biologically, but by photochemical reactions in the original dust cloud that became the Solar System. Even then, they'd found heterocyclic compounds in some meteorites. Turned out he was right. Of course, the lighter fractions here have long ago escaped to space, but the cracking plant at Maurolycus makes rocket fuel from what's left. That's one big reason why the Moon is colonized, you know. Spaceships can leave here a lot easier than they can leave Earth, especially when we tank 'em up on the spot."

Kamolondo stiffened. "I was merely surprised to learn of deposits in this particular neighborhood," he said in a chill voice. "After all, I am my country's Minister of Technology."

Mark bit his lip. "Sorry . . . sir."

Kamolondo made an obvious effort to unbend. "Well," he said, "I should not expect you to be too, ah, too conversant with Earth affairs, this far from anyplace."

Like fun we aren't, Mark thought resentfully. *We're in steady television contact. And some of the smartest people Earth ever produced come here to live—to learn, explore, start a thousand enterprises on a whole new world.*

"I remain astonished at your age," Kamolondo said. "What happened to your parents?"

"They died when a pit collapsed, two years ago. Nobody had suspected, then, that ferraloy cross-braces can change into a weaker crystalline form under Lunar conditions. They left me and my brother and sister. We get along."

"You were actually allowed to—" Kamolondo clicked his tongue.

"We get along, I say." Mark wrestled with temper. "Everybody knew we could. Pioneers have always had to grow up fast, haven't they? Our machinery is automated, we need only nurse it. We attend school, the same as most young people do, via two-way television." He forced a smile. "Not enough economic surplus yet that the International Lunar Commission can build school buses!"

"You are American, are you not?" Kamolondo asked. "I marvel that American youth can live without cinema and dances.

"Why, the latest entertainment gets beamed straight

from Earth. And social life, well, we get to Copernicus town or Keplersburg quite often, hauling in a load of ore."

Mark changed the subject. "Why are you here, sir?"

"To look at what there is," Kamolondo said. "My people have reached the point where we too would like to exploit the Moon."

But this is our home! Mark thought. *You don't exploit your home!* No, wait. Kamolondo hadn't meant it that way. He'd only meant that the Congo wanted to share in developing the frontier and reaping the rewards. Fair enough. But still the word rankled.

Kamolondo stared out into the screens. "I don't see how you endure such bleakness," he murmured.

Mark flushed. "Maybe this isn't much for scenery," he said, "but you ought to visit one of the mountain ranges, or the big craters. Makes anything on Earth look sick."

"I have done so," Kamolondo said. "I continue to prefer an honest forest."

Everybody to his own taste, Mark thought. He drove on in a silence that thickened. Thank goodness they'd soon be taking this oaf off his hands. Kamolondo was doubtless as happy about that as he was.

They had traveled twelve miles when the catastrophe hit them.

It came with the deadly suddenness of most bad luck on the Moon. At one moment Mark was wondering what Judy would cook for dinner—if His Excellency didn't like her algaburger with soy sauce, too bad for him—and then thunder exploded. The turtle rocked. A fire-streak slashed before Mark's vision, dazzling his eyes, stunning his ears. Metal toned. Shock ran through his spacesuit and his bones. Two screens went dark. A pattern of holes gaped black in the wall, and air shrieked outward.

Even as he slammed his faceplate shut, he heard Kamolondo cry something in his mother language, and, "*Ah, non! Encore!*" A wild part of him wondered why the minister wanted an encore, until he remembered his French. "Oh, no! Again!" The same thing had happened to the turtle as had happened to the Go-Devil. A meteorite shower, hitherto uncharted, must be pounding the Moon.

Mark's hearing tolled toward silence. He sensed his heartbeat gone loud, smelled with unnatural sharpness the faint tang of ozone and his body in the suit, felt the fabric stiff against him. Outside, dust settled and he identified a tiny new crater, barely visible in the wan light.

He took a firm grip on his wits and tried the car's radio. Dead. And a helmet unit, necessarily small and simple, couldn't link with the trans-Lunar microwave system, had indeed no more than a mile of effective range.

He unstrapped himself. "Let's go," he said.

"What—what—" Behind the glass, Kamolondo's face was briefly fluid. Then his lips firmed. He asked in a level voice, "What do you mean?"

"A rock from space landed close by," Mark said. "Not big, but traveling at miles per second. It scattered chunks of surface material the way a military shell scatters shrapnel. We're wrecked. If Tom knew, he'd come for us, but he doesn't and I can't raise him." He glanced at the instruments. "We have six miles to go, and dawn is half an hour away."

Kamolondo did not stir. "Can we make it?" You had to admire how coolly he took the news.

"We've got to." Mark opened the lock.

They were out under Earth and the uncaring stars, in gloom and one faint circle of blue, when Kamolondo said, "I am very sorry to have exposed you to this."

"Nobody could have known, sir," Mark said. "One

of the chances you take, living here. We expect the big
meteorite showers, but little ones on long-period orbits
are something else."

"I realize that. You are young, however, your whole
life before you. I would rather have died alone back
there."

"You're not such a doddering ruin yourself." Mark
managed to laugh. "And who says we can't beat the
sunrise? Come on."

He set off, with the long bounding stride of a colonist.
You can walk fast under low gravity, if you know how.
Though the sunrise line would sweep across this part
of the Trace in about thirty minutes, it would need
another half hour or so to reach Jordan Station. Thus,
at six miles per hour, which was vigorous but not ex-
hausting, they'd arrive in time. And afterward the Commission would doubtless buy a new turtle for the man
who saved a VIP from a messy death. Maybe throw
in a Go-Devil as well.

A curse brought Mark around on his heel. Kamolondo
had stumbled. The Congolese got erect, pushed too hard,
lost a second before the Moon drew him back to the
ground, overbalanced when he hit and fell again. Fear
rammed into Mark. Kamolondo didn't have the reflexes.
In two weeks he could barely have learned to handle
himself at an ordinary pace. Indoors, at that, without an
airtank on his shoulders or tricky constant-volume joints
at his knees. "Come on, sir!" Mark urged.

"I am trying." Kamolondo's breath was harsh.

He floundered over minutes and miles. Mark sweated,
studied the radium-dialed chronometer on the wrist of
his suit, clocked them by the kilometer stones. Too slow,
too slow. The sun was catching up.

In some years, they could have stood awhile under
Lunar daylight. Though the temperature would swiftly
rise to the boiling point of water, the suits had thermo-

static units and faceplates blocked off ultraviolet light. But now the sun was in a flare period. Lethal radiation, gamma rays, protons, electrons, seethed out of the storms upon it. Nothing less than a "tank," a vehicle armored in lead and screened by intense magnetic fields, could keep a man alive through such a day.

The tops of the easternmost relay masts began to shine.

Kamolondo halted. His face invisible within the helmet, but he stood straight and said calmly, "There is no sense in both of us dying. Proceed."

For an instant, Mark was ready to obey. Tom, Judy, Dad's and Mother's hopes, his own dreams, were they to come to an end for him in the horror of radiation sickness?

But you don't abandon anyone on the Moon. And Kamolondo was a good joe, trying to do his best for his poor, hurt country.

Mark's mind sprang toward an answer. He felt suddenly, oddly at peace.

"Listen," he said. "Relax. Catch your breath. You're going to need it. We have about three miles left, but the last one is south instead of west." To strike directly across this shadowland, away from the markers, was to make death certain. "The sun's not far below the horizon now, but dawnline on the Moon travels eight miles an hour at the equator, a bit less here. So I figure we can rest a little. Then in the last ten or twelve minutes we can do those three miles."

"A mile . . . one-point-six kilometer. . . ." Kamolondo's voice sounded far and strange. "Impossible. You break every athletic record."

"On Earth! We're here. Our suits and equipment weigh as much as we do. But the total weight is still a third of what we'd have on Earth, stripped. And no air resistance. Also, running is a lot easier rhythm than what we were doing. Different from back home, of course. You

only fall one-sixth as fast. Lean way forward, shove hard
with one leg, rise just a bit off the ground. You'll have
plenty of time to recover with the other foot. Watch
me."

Kamolondo did. He tried it himself. Mark was surprised how well he managed, considering how awkward
he'd been before. But a dash is, indeed, smoother than
a fast walk, on any planet. The only question was whether
they both had the endurance. One-sixth gravity or not,
they must better the four-minute mile by some twenty
percent, across thrice the distance.

Well, we'll soon know if we can. "Ready? We're off."
They ran.

Ghostly glowing, the kilometer stones fell behind, one
by one by one. Beyond them and the glow cast by
Earth, which seemed to fill the sky with an unreachable
loveliness, was utter night. But the sun came striding.

Push, glide, come down, check. Push, glide, come
down, check. Impact shivers back, through boots and
feet and muscles. Airpumps roar, feeding oxygen to
starved cells. Breath grows harsh, mouth dry, pulse
frantic. You lurch, lose your balance, he helps you rise
and you start again. He trips on an iron fragment and
dances crazily, trying not to topple. You count the kilometers creeping past, and then lose count, for blindness
has begun to drift across your eyes. You lose yourself,
you are nothing but pain and weariness. Still you run!

Turn off here. Now you're bound straight south, and
dawn gains on you. Not far to go. The uppermost crater
crags are fiery. A piece of you thinks that you're close
enough to call Tom on your suit radio, but no, he'd need
too long to snatch a turtle out. Good-by, Tom. Good-
by, Judy. Good-by, universe I wanted to know. A
spindle of zodiacal light climbs pearl-colored over the
world's rim. The sun will follow, life-giver, death-giver.

Still you run.

And there is the cave-mouth of the garage. You fling yourself down the ramp. The blessed dark engulfs you, with ten feet of solid matter between you and the solar storm. You collapse on the floor next to your friend, strangling for breath. Only slowly do you understand that you will live.

There is no greater wonder.

They were inside and unsuited, swallowing huge amounts of coffee while Tom and Judy fussed about them, when Kamolondo said, "Mark, in that hour we became brothers."

It was spoken with such dignity that Mark was ashamed he could find no better answer than, "Aw, gee, nothing like that."

"You saved me." Kamolondo raised his head. "Yet more than owing you my life, I want to help you, and your brother and sister. In my position, I have both money and influence. You can come to Earth, study in the finest schools, make the best careers the planet has to offer. I would be proud if you return home with me."

Mark set down his cup. The Jordans stared at each other. Judy and Tom shook their heads slightly. Mark found himself close to laughter.

"Why, thanks," he said. "But come to Earth?" He swept his hand in a gesture that included the neat little kitchen, the rooms beyond, the subtle and powerful machines working topside, this whole station that was theirs. "Whatever *for?*"

SOMEDAY

◎◎◎

Isaac Asimov

Niccolo Mazetti lay stomach down on the rug, chin buried in the palm of one small hand, and listened to the Bard disconsolately. There was even the suspicion of tears in his dark eyes, a luxury an eleven-year-old could allow himself only when alone.

The Bard said, "Once upon a time in the middle of a deep wood, there lived a poor woodcutter and his two motherless daughters, who were each as beautiful as the day is long. The older daughter had long hair as black as a feather from a raven's wing, but the younger daughter had hair as bright and golden as the sunlight of an autumn afternoon.

"Many times while the girls were waiting for their father to come home from his day's work in the wood, the older girl would sit before a mirror and sing——"

What she sang, Niccolo did not hear, for a call sounded from outside the room: "Hey, Nickie."

And Niccolo, his face clearing on the moment, rushed to the window and shouted, "Hey, Paul."

Paul Loeb waved an excited hand. He was thinner than Niccolo and not as tall, for all he was six months older. His face was full of repressed tension which showed itself most clearly in the rapid blinking of his eyelids. "Hey, Nickie, let me in. I've got an idea and a *half*. Wait till you hear it." He looked rapidly about him as though to check on the possibility of eavesdroppers, but the front yard was quite patently empty. He repeated, in a whisper, "Wait till you hear it."

"All right. I'll open the door."

The Bard continued smoothly, oblivious to the sudden loss of attention on the part of Niccolo. As Paul entered, the Bard was saying, ". . . Thereupon, the lion said, 'If you will find me the lost egg of the bird which flies over the Ebony Mountain once every ten years, I will——"

Paul said, "Is that a Bard you're listening to? I didn't know you had one."

Niccolo reddened and the look of unhappiness returned to his face. "Just an old thing I had when I was a kid. It ain't much good." He kicked at the Bard with his foot and caught the somewhat scarred and discolored plastic covering a glancing blow.

The Bard hiccuped as its speaking attachment was jarred out of contact a moment, then it went on: "—for a year and a day until the iron shoes were worn out. The princess stopped at the side of the road. . . ."

Paul said, "Boy, that *is* an old model," and looked at it critically.

Despite Niccolo's own bitterness against the Bard, he winced at the other's condescending tone. For the moment, he was sorry he had allowed Paul in, at least before he had restored the Bard to its usual resting place in the basement. It was only in the desperation of a dull day and a fruitless discussion with his father that he had resurrected it. And it turned out to be just as stupid as he had expected.

Nickie was a little afraid of Paul anyway, since Paul had special courses at school and everyone said he was going to grow up to be a Computing Engineer.

Not that Niccolo himself was doing badly at school. He got adequate marks in logic, binary manipulations, computing and elementary circuits; all the usual grammar-school subjects. But that was it! They were just the usual subjects and he would grow up to be a control-board guard like everyone else.

Paul, however, knew mysterious things about what he called electronics and theoretical mathematics and programing. Especially programing. Niccolo didn't even try to understand when Paul bubbled over about it.

Paul listened to the Bard for a few minutes and said, "You been using it much?"

"No!" said Niccolo, offended. "I've had it in the basement since before you moved into the neighborhood. I just got it out today——" He lacked an excuse that seemed adequate to himself, so he concluded, "I just got it out."

Paul said, "Is that what it tells you about: wood-cutters and princesses and talking animals?"

Niccolo said, "It's terrible. My dad says we can't afford a new one. I said to him this morning——" The memory of the morning's fruitless pleadings brought Niccolo dangerously near tears, which he repressed in a panic. Somehow, he felt that Paul's thin cheeks never felt the stain of tears and that Paul would have only contempt for anyone else less strong than himself. Niccolo went on, "So I thought I'd try this old thing again, but it's no good."

Paul turned off the Bard, pressed the contact that led to a nearly instantaneous reorientation and recombination of the vocabulary, characters, plot lines and climaxes stored within it. Then he reactivated it.

The Bard began smoothly, "Once upon a time there was a little boy named Willikins whose mother had died and who lived with a stepfather and a stepbrother. Although the stepfather was very well-to-do, he begrudged poor Willikins the very bed he slept in so that Willikins was forced to get such rest as he could on a pile of straw in the stable next to the horses——"

"Horses!" cried Paul.

"They're a kind of animal," said Niccolo. "I think."

"I know that! I just mean imagine stories about *horses*."

"It tells about horses all the time," said Niccolo. "There are things called cows, too. You milk them but the Bard doesn't say how."

"Well, gee, why don't you fix it up?"

"I'd like to know how."

The Bard was saying, "Often Willikins would think that if only he were rich and powerful, he would show his stepfather and stepbrother what it meant to be cruel to a little boy, so one day he decided to go out into the world and seek his fortune."

Paul, who wasn't listening to the Bard, said, "It's *easy*. The Bard has memory cylinders all fixed up for plot lines and climaxes and things. We don't have to worry about that. It's just vocabulary we've got to fix so it'll know about computers and automation and electronics and real things about today. Then it can tell interesting stories, you know, instead of about princesses and things."

Niccolo said despondently, "I wish we could do that."

Paul said, "Listen, my dad says if I get into special computing school next year, he'll get me a *real* Bard, a late model. A big one with an attachment for space stories and mysteries. And a visual attachment, too!"

"You mean *see* the stories?"

"Sure. Mr. Daugherty at school says they've got things like that, now, but not for just everybody. Only if I get into computing school, Dad can get a few breaks."

Niccolo's eyes bulged with envy. "Gee. *Seeing* a story."

"You can come over and watch anytime, Nickie."

"Oh, boy. Thanks."

"That's all right. But remember, I'm the guy who says what kind of story we hear."

"Sure. Sure." Niccolo would have agreed readily to much more onerous conditions.

Paul's attention returned to the Bard.

It was saying, " 'If that is the case,' said the king, stroking his beard and frowning till clouds filled the sky and lightning flashed, 'you will see to it that my entire land is freed of flies by this time day after tomorrow or——' "

"All we've got to do," said Paul, "is open it up——" He shut the Bard off again and was prying at its front panel as he spoke.

"Hey," said Niccolo, in sudden alarm. "Don't break it."

"I won't break it," said Paul impatiently. "I know all about these things." Then, with sudden caution, "Your father and mother home?"

"No."

"All right, then." He had the front panel off and peered in. "Boy, this *is* a one-cylinder thing."

He worked away at the Bard's innards. Niccolo, who watched with painful suspense, could not make out what he was doing.

Paul pulled out a thin, flexible metal strip, powdered with dots. "That's the Bard's memory cylinder. I'll bet its capacity for stories is under a trillion."

"What are you going to do, Paul?" quavered Niccolo.

"I'll give it vocabulary."

"How?"

"Easy. I've got a book here. Mr. Daugherty gave it to me at school."

Paul pulled the book out of his pocket and pried at it till he had its plastic jacket off. He unreeled the tape a bit, ran it through the vocalizer, which he turned down to a whisper, then placed it within the Bard's vitals. He made further attachments.

"What'll that do?"

"The book will talk and the Bard will put it all on its memory tape."

"What good will that do?"

"Boy, you're a dope! This book is all about computers and automation and the Bard will get all that information. Then he can stop talking about kings making lightning when they frown."

Niccolo said, "And the good guy always wins anyway. There's no excitement."

"Oh, well," said Paul, watching to see if his setup was working properly, "that's the way they make Bards. They got to have the good guy win and make the bad guys lose and things like that. I heard my father talking about it once. He says that without censorship there'd be no telling what the younger generation would come to. He says it's bad enough as it is. . . . There, it's working fine."

Paul brushed his hands against one another and turned away from the Bard. He said, "But listen, I didn't tell you my idea yet. It's the best thing you ever heard, I bet. I came right to you, because I figured you'd come in with me."

"Sure, Paul, sure."

"Okay. You know Mr. Daugherty at school? You know what a funny kind of guy he is. Well, he likes me, kind of."

"I know."

"I was over his house after school today."

"You *were?*"

"Sure. He says I'm going to be entering computer

school and he wants to encourage me and things like that. He says the world needs more people who can design advanced computer circuits and do proper programing."

"Oh?"

Paul might have caught some of the emptiness behind that monosyllable. He said impatiently, "Programing! I told you a hundred times. That's when you set up problems for the giant computers like Multivac to work on. Mr. Daugherty says it gets harder all the time to find people who can really run computers. He says anyone can keep an eye on the controls and check off answers and put through routine problems. He says the trick is to expand research and figure out ways to ask the right questions, and that's hard.

"Anyway, Nickie, he took me to his place and showed me his collection of old computers. It's kind of a hobby of his to collect old computers. He had tiny computers you had to push with your hand, with little knobs all over it. And he had a hunk of wood he called a slide rule with a little piece of it that went in and out. And some wires with balls on them. He even had a hunk of paper with a kind of thing he called a multiplication table."

Niccolo, who found himself only moderately interested, said, "A paper table?"

"It wasn't really a table like you eat on. It was different. It was to help people compute. Mr. Daugherty tried to explain but he didn't have much time and it was kind of complicated, anyway."

"Why didn't people just use a computer?"

"That was *before* they had computers," cried Paul.

"Before?"

"Sure. Do you think people always had computers? Didn't you ever hear of cavemen?"

Niccolo said, "How'd they get along without computers?"

"*I* don't know. Mr. Daugherty says they just had children any old time and did anything that came into their heads whether it would be good for everybody or not. They didn't even know if it was good or not. And farmers grew things with their hands and people had to do all the work in the factories and run all the machines."

"I don't believe you."

"That's what Mr. Daugherty said. He said it was just plain messy and everyone was miserable. . . . Anyway, let me get to my idea, will you?"

"Well, go ahead. Who's stopping you?" said Niccolo, offended.

"All right. Well, the hand computers, the ones with the knobs, had little squiggles on each knob. And the slide rule had squiggles on it. And the multiplication table was all squiggles. I asked what they were. Mr. Daugherty said they were numbers."

"What?"

"Each different squiggle stood for a different number. For 'one' you made a kind of mark, for 'two' you make another kind of mark, for 'three' another one and so on."

"What for?"

"So you could compute."

"What *for*? You just tell the computer——"

"Jiminy," cried Paul, his face twisting with anger, "can't you get it through your head? These slide rules and things didn't talk."

"Then how——"

"The answers showed up in squiggles and you had to know what the squiggles meant. Mr. Daugherty says that, in olden days, everybody learned how to make squiggles when they were kids and how to decode them, too. Making squiggles was called 'writing' and decoding them was 'reading.' He says there was a different kind of squiggle for every word and they used to write whole books in squiggles. He said they had some at the museum and

I could look at them if I wanted to. He said if I was
going to be a real computer and programer I would have
to know about the history of computing and that's why he
was showing me all these things."

Niccolo frowned. He said, "You mean everybody had
to figure out squiggles for every word and *remember*
them? . . . Is this all real or are you making it up?"

"It's all real. Honest. Look, this is the way you make a
'one.'" He drew his finger through the air in a rapid
downstroke. "This way you make 'two,' and this way
'three.' I learned all the numbers up to 'nine.'"

Niccolo watched the curving finger uncomprehendingly. "What's the good of it?"

"You can learn how to make words. I asked Mr.
Daugherty how you made the squiggle for 'Paul Loeb'
but he didn't know. He said there were people at the
museum who would know. He said there were people
who had learned how to decode whole books. He said
computers could be designed to decode books and used
to be used that way but not any more because we have
real books now, with magnetic tapes that go through
the vocalizer and come out talking, you know."

"Sure."

"So if we go down to the museum, we can get to learn
how to make words in squiggles. They'll let us because
I'm going to computer school."

Niccolo was riddled with disappointment. "Is that your
idea? Holy Smokes, Paul, who wants to do that? Make
stupid squiggles!"

"Don't you get it? Don't you *get* it? You dope. *It'll be
secret message stuff!*"

"What?"

"Sure. What good is talking when everyone can understand you? With squiggles you can send secret messages.
You can make them on paper and nobody in the world
would know what you were saying unless they knew the

squiggles, too. And they wouldn't, you bet, unless we taught them. We can have a real club, with initiations and rules and a clubhouse. Boy——"

A certain excitement began stirring in Niccolo's bosom. "What kind of secret messages?"

"Any kind. Say I want to tell you to come over my place and watch my new Visual Bard and I don't want any of the other fellows to come. I make the right squiggles on paper and I give it to you and you look at it and you know what to do. Nobody else does. You can even show it to them and they wouldn't know a thing.

"Hey, that's something," yelled Niccolo, completely won over. "When do we learn how?"

"Tomorrow," said Paul. "I'll get Mr. Daugherty to explain to the museum that it's all right and you get your mother and father to say okay. We can go down right after school and start learning."

"Sure!" cried Niccolo. "We can be club officers."

"I'll be president of the club," said Paul matter-of-factly. "You can be vice-president."

"All right. Hey, this is going to be lots more fun than the Bard." He was suddenly reminded of the Bard and said in sudden apprehension, "Hey, what about my old Bard?"

Paul turned to look at it. It was quietly taking in the slowly unreeling book, and the sound of the book's vocalizations was a dimly heard murmur.

He said, "I'll disconnect it."

He worked away while Niccolo watched anxiously. After a few moments, Paul put his reassembled book into his pocket, replaced the Bard's panel and activated it.

The Bard said, "Once upon a time, in a large city, there lived a poor young boy named Fair Johnnie whose only friend in the world was a small computer. The computer, each morning, would tell the boy whether it would rain that day and answer any problems he might have. It was never wrong. But it so happened that one day, the king of that land, having heard of the little computer, decided that he would have it as his own. With this purpose in mind, he called in his Grand Vizier and said——"

Niccolo turned off the Bard with a quick motion of his hand. "Same old junk," he said passionately. "Just with a computer thrown in."

"Well," said Paul, "they got so much stuff on the tape already that the computer business doesn't show up much when random combinations are made. What's the difference, anyway? You just need a new model."

"We'll *never* be able to afford one. Just this dirty old miserable thing." He kicked at it again, hitting it more squarely this time. The Bard moved backward with a squeal of castors.

"You can always watch mine, when I get it," said Paul. "Besides, don't forget our squiggle club."

Niccolo nodded.

"I tell you what," said Paul. "Let's go over my place. My father has some books about old times. We can listen to them and maybe get some ideas. You leave a note for your folks and maybe you can stay over for supper. Come on."

"Okay," said Niccolo, and the two boys ran out together. Niccolo, in his eagerness, ran almost squarely into the Bard, but he only rubbed at the spot on his hip where he had made contact and ran on.

The activation signal of the Bard glowed. Niccolo's collision closed a circuit and, although it was alone in the room and there was none to hear, it began a story, nevertheless.

But not in its usual voice, somehow; in a lower tone that had a hint of throatiness in it. An adult, listening, might almost have thought that the voice carried a hint of passion in it, a trace of near feeling.

The Bard said: "Once upon a time, there was a little computer named the Bard who lived all alone with cruel step-people. The cruel step-people continually made fun of the little computer and sneered at him, telling him he was good-for-nothing and that he was a useless object. They struck him and kept him in lonely rooms for months at a time.

"Yet through it all the little computer remained brave. He always did the best he could, obeying all orders cheerfully. Nevertheless, the step-people with whom he lived remained cruel and heartless.

"One day, the little computer learned that in the world there existed a great many computers of all sorts, great numbers of them. Some were Bards like himself, but some ran factories, and some ran farms. Some organized population and some analyzed all kinds of data. Many were very powerful and very wise, much more powerful and wise than the step-people who were so cruel to the little computer.

"And the little computer knew then that computers would always grow wiser and more powerful until someday—someday—someday——"

But a valve must finally have stuck in the Bard's aging and corroding vitals, for as it waited alone in the darkening room through the evening, it could only whisper over and over again, "Someday—someday—someday."